AlliterAsian

Twenty Years of **Ricepaper** *Magazine*

EDITED BY JULIA LIN, ALLAN CHO,
AND JIM WONG-CHU

ARSENAL PULP PRESS VANCOUVER

ARSENAL PULP PRESS
Suite 202 – 211 East Georgia St.
Vancouver, BC V6A 1Z6
Canada
arsenalpulp.com

The publisher gratefully acknowledges the support of the Canada Council for the Arts and the British Columbia Arts Council for its publishing program, and the Government of Canada (through the Canada Book Fund) and the Government of British Columbia (through the Book Publishing Tax Credit Program) for its publishing activities

BRITISH COLUMBIA | BRITISH COLUMBIA ARTS COUNCIL An agency of the Province of British Columbia

Canada Council for the Arts | Conseil des arts du Canada

Canadä

Cover illustration by Janice Wu
Cover design by Gerilee McBride and Oliver Mcpartlin
Text design by Oliver Mcpartlin
Edited by Robyn So and Susan Safyan

Printed and bound in Canada

Library and Archives Canada Cataloguing in Publication:
AlliterAsian : twenty years of Ricepaper magazine / Julia Lin, Allan Cho, Jim Wong-Chu, editors.

Issued also in electronic format.
ISBN 978-1-55152-620-1 (paperback).–ISBN 978-1-55152-621-8 (epub)

1. Canadian literature (English)—Asian-Canadian authors. 2. Canadian literature (English)—20th century. 3. Canadian literature (English)—21st century. 4. Asian Canadians--Literary collections. 5. Authors, Canadian (English) —Interviews. 6. Artists—Canada—Interviews. 7. Asian Canadians—Interviews. 8. Ricepaper (Magazine). I. Lin, Julia, 1962-, editor II. Wong-Chu, Jim, 1949-, editor III. Cho, Allan, 1980-, editor

PS8235.A8A46 2015 C810.8'0895071 C2015-903478-7
C2015-903479-5

AlliterAsian

Contents

POETRY

Introduction

In the late 1960s, during the intoxicating days of the American civil rights movement and the Vietnam War, a group of UBC students formed the Asian-Canadian Coalition. Composed predominantly of Chinese- and Japanese-Canadians, the group engaged in writing and the performing arts as expressions of their unique identities. They experimented with new styles of prose in their writing groups, dabbled in radio programs and special edition magazines, and formed a new writers' organization—the Asian Canadian Writers' Workshop (ACWW)—in 1976. Membership increased yearly, and a need grew for its members to keep up with developments in the community.

Ricepaper began life in 1995 as a newsletter for ACWW. The first issue, edited by Larry Wong and Kuan Foo, included a brief history of ACWW written by Jim Wong-Chu. These newsletters were pieced together on MiniCAD (a program used by architects), printed on sheet paper, and carefully stapled together. Primitive and simple, it nevertheless fulfilled the prosaic task of keeping its membership abreast of events. In addition to connecting its members in Vancouver, Toronto, and Edmonton, as well as other regional chapters, *Ricepaper* served to inform readers about new developments in the Asian-North American arts scene.

But *Ricepaper* was destined to grow into something more. With the help of a Canada Council grant, the newsletter became a literary magazine in 1996 and began taking paid subscriptions. The magazine acquired a new masthead and began a mission to provide a supportive and culturally sensitive environment for writers with Pacific Rim Asian heritage. It soon began publishing quarterly issues and continues to do so today. Since its founding, the focus of the magazine has shifted from predominantly arts and culture reporting to the publication of original literature. And the editors have moved from searching for work among the few Asian-Canadian writers working in the 1990s to featuring a wealth of quality submissions in its pages today.

This anthology celebrates *Ricepaper*'s twentieth anniversary. Looking through the back issues of *Ricepaper* is like looking at a veritable "Who's Who" of Asian-Canadian cultural history. Many of today's well-known Asian-Canadian writers have appeared in the magazine; in fact, some were first published in the periodical. *Ricepaper*'s legacy as a groundbreaking publication for Asian-Canadians remains unparalleled, and this anthology pays tribute to the remarkable contribution that the magazine has made to Asian-Canadian culture.

AlliterAsian features exclusive interviews first published in *Ricepaper* with David Suzuki, Tobias Wong, Ruth Ozeki, Evelyn Lau, Denise Chong, and Madeleine Thien, among others. In addition, exciting voices in Canadian literature are represented by Kim Fu, Doretta Lau, Corinna Chong, Terry Watada, Derwin Mak, Eric Choi, and C. E. Gatchalian. Established and emerging poets such as Fred Wah, Evelyn Lau, Rita Wong, Souvankham Thammavongsa, and Michael Prior also grace the anthology with their work. Finally, three award-winning authors have given permission for excerpts of their works-in-progress to be included: Joy Kogawa (*Gently to Nagasaki*, a new memoir about Japanese atrocities during World War II), Yasuko Thanh (*Lucky in Saigon*, a novel soon to be published as *Mysterious Fragrance of the Yellow Mountains*), and SKY Lee (*Progress in Process*).

We have organized the anthology into nonfiction, creative nonfiction, fiction, and poetry, with the pieces arranged chronologically by publication date within each category. The authors have provided short commentaries reflecting upon their work, many after a gap of years since initial publication. The most difficult task in assembling this book was choosing the works that would appear in the collection. There were many worthy articles and stories that were left out due to space limitations. In the end, we tried to include a representative sample from the enormous archive of Asian-Canadian creativity housed within the pages of *Ricepaper* magazine. We urge readers to discover those back issues for themselves at *ricepapermagazine.ca*.

As the title *AlliterAsian* suggests, the publication of *Ricepaper* is but one beat in the steady rhythm of Asian-Canadian writing, plays, films, and other forms of creative expression pouring forth from Asian-Canadian artists and performers. As more and more Asian-Canadians find their voices, we eagerly await future manifestations of Asian talent in the Canadian arts scene. We hope you enjoy this retrospective look at a landmark periodical in the evolving and increasingly diverse landscape of Canadian writing and publishing.

Respectfully,
Julia Lin, Allan Cho, Jim Wong-Chu

NonFiction

Writing History

Ricepaper 4, no. 1 (1998)

Rita Wong

Early on a Saturday morning, on November 8, 1988, Paul Yee and four panelists—Sadhu Binning, Phinder Dulai, Betty Li, and Susan Nishi—held a lively and thought-provoking discussion at the Chinese Cultural Centre. Facilitated by Colleen Leung and introduced by Lily Liu, the discussion touched on questions such as the following: Is all history fiction because it is someone's interpretation of the events? Is all fiction history because it has already been imagined in order to exist? What challenges face writers of colour trying to publish? What drives us to write about history, in whichever form we may choose?

Paul Yee read from his novel in progress and played devil's advocate by suggesting that we are doomed to repeat history and to never learn from it. His example was racism in Canada—early Chinese immigrants experienced it, and now, more than a hundred years later, today's Chinese immigrants still encounter it. Yee's statement was all the more biting because of his background (he has written a number of fictional and nonfictional works based on history, and he has a master's degree in history). Without summarizing his entire talk, I thought it interesting that Yee finds more freedom in writing fiction than historical nonfiction.

The question of form was raised by a number of panelists. While poetry was felt by some to be best suited for conveying emotional expression, Sadhu Binning pointed out that he started writing dramas so that he could reach more of his community. Many people who don't read poetry will be more receptive to theatre.

In response to one question about what role these writers have in the educational system, Phinder Dulai mentioned that he had read at some Surrey high schools, which have large South Asian student bodies. It was empowering, both for him and for the students, to be able to connect in that setting (something that would have been unheard of not that long ago). There was some agreement among the audience members that more interactions like these are urgently needed. At present, it mostly depends on a few individual teachers' personal efforts.

Betty Li talked about her responsibility as an overseas Chinese person. For example, she has the freedom to protest injustices such as the Tiananmen Square massacre, which is the focus of the novel she is writing. It is more urgent than ever that she speak, since many people in China cannot do so or have been imprisoned for doing so. I agree wholeheartedly that more overseas Chinese should exert their ability to speak out on human rights issues in China, Tibet, and other Asian countries, as well as here in North America. Colleen posed a great question to Betty, asking how she felt about recent Hollywood depictions of human rights abuses in China and Tibet.

On the one hand, it is important to raise awareness about these injustices and murders. On the other hand, are commercial American representations of these issues deceptive? It is definitely important that people like Betty continue speaking out and providing alternate points of view.

That said, I think it is just as important to keep speaking about our experiences here in North America too, and to not allow ourselves to be posited by the mainstream as far away peoples in exotic lands. Interestingly enough, many of the Asian-Canadian novels which have sold well have been set in places like India rather than here in Canada. While we, of course, have the right to write about ourselves in whatever setting, this trend does make me a little wary about what the mainstream is willing to accept.

Growing up isolated in Alberta, Susan Nishi expressed her opinions about the challenges and the rewards of working with the Japanese-Canadian community in Vancouver. How many of us write, I wonder, because of our need to read about people like ourselves? While our motives all vary, I think the one thing we may be able to agree on covered much more than this and could easily have gone on all day. I, for one, hope there will be more panels like this. Kudos to the organizers!

Author Commentary

What leaps out at me from this brief article, seventeen years after it was written, is how much the needs identified in it remain today. For instance, it was empowering and important for Phinder Dulai to share his work at Surrey high schools which have large South Asian student bodies, yet such connections still mostly happen on an ad hoc basis, depending on individual teachers' valiant efforts. I don't think that contemporary writing and Canadian cultural production have been integrated into the schools the ways we'd hoped. Our communities still need fuller access to the powerful work that is being done by writers and artists of colour, as well as by First Nations authors and storytellers. —*Rita Wong, 2015*

About the Author

Rita Wong is the author of four books of poetry: *undercurrent* (Nightwood, 2015), *sybil unrest* (co-written with Larissa Lai, Line Books, 2008), *forage* (Nightwood, 2007), and *monkeypuzzle* (Press Gang 1998). *forage* won Canada Reads Poetry 2011. Wong received the Asian Canadian Writers' Workshop Emerging Writer Award in 1997 and the Dorothy Livesay Poetry Prize in 2008. Building from her doctoral dissertation, which examined labour in Asian-North American literature, her work investigates the poetics of water and the relationships between social justice, ecology, and decolonization.

My Mother

Ricepaper 6, no. 3 (2001)

Janet Lumb

"Mom, are you home?!" we'd scream down the hall after answering the phone. "No, I'm putting my face on," she would reply as she rushed around the house.

I'm a busy musician (sax player), film composer, activist, and director of the Montreal Asian Heritage Festival. My mother, Jean Bessie Lumb, is busy at the helm of an extended family of twenty-three, including nine grand-children. She has more energy than the whole family put together, and her health and well-being continue to improve. She can still touch her toes at the age of eighty-one. My mother is the source of my inspiration.

I was raised in what appeared to be a typical Chinese-Canadian family. My parents ran a grocery store, a laundry, and a Chinese restaurant. My mother was always very proud of how the family was raised. She took that pride to include the divine order of our births. "I have three boys and then three girls," she said mischievously.

There are many immigrant families that experience a "frozen-in-time" phenomenon—where traditions are passed on from generation to generation even though they're living in a new country. Our grandfather, a Toishan from Canton, came to Canada in 1899 with traditions from the Ching dynasty. Confucian rituals and superstitions were considered sacred. Authority figures were to be respected. Family obligations were assumed.

When I was young, I lived in a rough neighbourhood in downtown Toronto. My parents were unforgivably strict. They were clever and kept us off the streets. But we were busy. Every school night, the three girls had either Chinese school, Girl Guides, or baton lessons. On weekends we worked at the restaurant, the Kwong Chow, and went to Chinese dance lessons at the dramatic association. After these activities, we had to be home for supper. "Your father works hard. Suppertime is the only time the family is together. I want you here for supper!" my mother would often scold.

Values that my mother cherished were ingrained in us—the importance of family and community, respect for others, and respect for ourselves. This meant that we were to be "proud of being Chinese."

Little did we know that my mother, born in Nanaimo, BC, as Jean Bessie Wong, had to walk past a white school to go to a segregated school attended by only Chinese, Natives, and Japanese. She was a tomboy and played on a baseball team made up of her eleven siblings. She quit school at the age of twelve to help the family pay for her older brother's tuition. At sixteen, she left Vancouver for Toronto to work at my aunt's restaurant and, only a year later, at the age of seventeen, opened her own grocery store. The store did so well that she brought the rest of her family to Toronto.

At the age of twenty, she met my father, who had arrived in Canada from Canton in 1921. They were chaperoned when they went for ice cream on their first and only date and the next day, their arranged marriage was settled. Because of the laws at that time, even though my mother was Canadian-born, she lost her citizenship when she married my father in 1939. In 1947, Chinese were granted the right to vote, and my mother applied to regain her citizenship.

In 1957, at the age of thirty-eight, she was chosen as the only woman on a committee of twenty Chinese delegates from across the country to meet with Prime Minister Diefenbaker. Their purpose was to persuade the government to change the immigration laws that separated Chinese families from the rest of society. These immigration laws were a result of the Exclusion Act. Although it was repealed in 1947, even ten years later families continued to be separated. Only those who had been granted full Canadian citizenship could bring their families to Canada, and only family members who were over the age of sixty-five or under the age of eighteen could come into the country.

My mother helped Wong Foon Sien, who was chosen by the committee to speak on behalf of Chinese-Canadians, to prepare the speech.

"I already knew the speech because I helped Wong Foon Sien practice it over and over again," said my mother. "I was asked to sit beside the Prime Minister because I was the only woman. He kept asking me to repeat everything. I repeated the speech word for word, because I knew it by heart. The meeting was a success."

My mother explains, "I didn't know at the time that Diefenbaker was partially deaf. Wong Foon Sien was sitting beside his bad ear, and I was sitting beside his good ear!" My mother always laughed when she told this story. She became the unofficial mayor of Chinatown from that point on.

I was the fifth child in our family and was called by my Chinese name: "Jing." My personal conflicts with living in an environment where two different worlds clashed ended up pitting my family demands against the ties I had with my Canadian friends. I was traumatized. These crises evolved into issues, then reasons for my eventual involvement with the Asian Heritage Festival. As a teenager, the cause of my angst became the basis for my defiance against my family.

When this happened, my mother would sigh in surrender and say,

"I planted turnips, but I got a carrot. If I said the moon was round, Jing would always argue with me."

In the meantime, my mother kept up an exhausting schedule of organizing Chinese community dance classes, saving Toronto's Chinatown from further demolition, working full-time at the restaurant, and constantly heading up various community and political activities. In 1976, she received the Order of Canada for her work as a "defender of Chinatown" and her work as a representative of the Chinese community during the appeal to change immigration laws.

When I moved to Vancouver, rebelling against my family was redirected toward social politics. For ten years, I performed at numerous benefits, demonstrated at various political rallies, and worked with juvenile delinquents and with the Vancouver Folk Music Festival. Had my mother's example of tireless community activism rubbed off on me? Eventually, I moved to Montreal and began working with autistic children, playing with many bands, and exploring my music through other disciplines.

In 1995, I was approached by Bernard Nguyen to start an Asian heritage festival. Initially, I was more intrigued by the possibility of finding musicians for my film work.

Needless to say, the festival has evolved into another entity for me. Its goals are ambitious. Our mandate is to break barriers and build intercultural, interdisciplinary, and intergenerational bridges. Many of the ethno-cultural communities are ghettoized, especially in Montreal, as a result of the immigration policies and the precedence of the language issue. However, institutional changes are happening, the social climate is improving, and the dialogues are beginning. One of my dreams is that there will no longer be a need for an Asian heritage festival.

The role I chose to take with the festival is based on my passion for the arts and my activities in the community. This includes my interest in the politics of the cultural issues of being a Chinese-Canadian. Most importantly, the festival is creating a sense of family and a sense of community. My many interests are now unified as one.

The importance of family and community, respect for who we are, respect for others, and a belief in human nature are all values that have been passed on to me from my parents. Yet I am still far from achieving these goals. My ghosts, rages, neuroses, passions, illusions, and frailties continue to haunt me. I have always strongly identified with my mother, but I do wonder about my superwoman complex.

I have fond memories of my father who arrived in Canada with nothing but the shirt on his back. Little did we realize that the gold he came to find was found at the hearth of our family. My mother.

Author Commentary

"Hearth of Gold" was conceived in 2000, thanks to the relentless determination of a colleague/friend/partner in crime at the time and to date, Milton Tanaka. Since the festival's inception in 1995, the work included behind-the-scenes soliciting for multidisciplinary arts funding that was, at the time, nonexistent. In 1998, thanks to the inspiring perseverance of numerous wilful cultural activists, Montreal Asian Heritage Festival, now called Festival Accès Asie, was awarded funding from the Canada Council for the Arts. —*Janet Lumb, 2015*

About the Author

Janet Lumb (*janetlumb.com*) was born in Toronto, lived in Vancouver, and has resided most of her life in Montreal. Janet loves to play, explore, and work with artists in multidisciplinary settings.

As a third-generation Chinese-Canadian and a social activist in heart, mind, and spirit, she is inspired by arts, community, ecology, and education. Defying Canada's geographic borders, Janet aims to connect people in a profound and interactive way with her current project, the Asian-Canadian Wiki (*asiancanadianwiki.org*).

A Buck a Bag for the American Dream (Tobias Wong)

Ricepaper 9, no. 2 (2003)

Alan Woo

Armed with a cotton candy vendor apparatus and fifty bags of air labelled "Dreams," Tobias Wong stands on a busy corner in Soho, New York. The bags come in sizes of S, M, and L. At an asking rate of one dollar per bag, the dreams sell out in a matter of hours.

Has Wong hit it so big in the Big Apple that people would clamour to buy his bags of air? *Wallpaper* seems to think so, having profiled him in its March 2003 issue. Even Wong's own account of life in New York sounds like the stuff that dreams are made of.

I last saw Wong in 2000 at the Ovaltine Cafe on Hastings Street in Vancouver, where we ate an early dinner. Now, through emails and transcontinental telephone conversations, we discuss his work as a "paraconceptual" artist, his Asian-Canadian identity, and the bright lights of the big city.

"Living in NYC is like having everything at your doorstep. There's very little that I can't do here," says Wong. "Here, you can do anything at anytime—buy drugs, have sex, go to parties, look for art supplies ... It's all here, it's wonderful," he says. "I do have thoughts about settling here, but I'm not so serious about that at the moment. It's a very difficult city in which to balance your sanity. It's very fast-paced. And that gets to be nerve-racking at times."

Wong has other cities to compare New York with, having grown up in Vancouver and schooled at the University of Toronto. "I hated it there," he says of Toronto. "So fucking pretentious. They think they're a big city like New York. The fact is, they've mistaken being curt as some sort of snotty attitude." Then there was a short stint in London, England: "Now, there's attitude."

When Wong moved to New York in 1998, he didn't know what to expect but soon realized, despite being Asian-Canadian, it was not that hard to fit in. "I often credit Vancouver for being a large enough city to grow up in, allowing me to adapt to New York so well. Vancouver really is up-to-date with many trends. Also, travelling around and jumping from a few schools prior to my move to NYC gave me a good start. But when I tell people that I'm Canadian, they are usually shocked."

In terms of his Asian heritage, Wong claims that it has had little effect on his experience living in New York. He does notice, however, that the Asians in NYC are predominantly from mainland China, and "... the Americans aren't so familiar with the differences between them and those from Hong Kong."

The difference between Canadians and Americans? According to Wong, it all comes down to one thing: "Sensibility—the Americans lack it. We're also a little more well-rounded and familiar with the rest of the world. I also think we learn from the Americans a lot, both about things we can improve upon and things we can avoid."

But times have changed. When the United States declared war on Iraq, Canada did not lend its support. As a Canadian stuck in the centre of the American universe, was Wong worried about a backlash toward him as an artist, or worse, as an individual? "There's really little anti-Canadian shit reported down here," he reveals. "They are too busy picking on the French. The news here is highly censored. I have to watch the BBC to get any real information on the war. Everything else is bullshit."

But before that nightmare, there was September 11. "I was a few miles away. I watched both buildings go down from my rooftop. It's taken a while for me to realize how much that day has affected me and my work," says Wong.

Wong had been busy trying to clinch an agreement with Prada, after nine months of negotiations and scrambling through red tape. He was on the verge of closing the deal when the World Trade Center was hit. Soon after, borders closed, immigration halted, and America shut itself off for a time to heal. And sure enough, the deal between Prada and Wong was off.

"One of the first things I screamed out loud to a friend who was with me at the time was, 'I'm gonna lose my fucking Prada job!'" remembers Wong. "But that only occupied my mind at the beginning. For the rest of the day, which felt like eternity, we all thought we were going to die.

"Financially, I don't think I have to explain the number of jobs and opportunities lost right after 9/11. The economy was already going downhill before then. But emotionally, it took a big stab at all of us. All my friends were affected. We didn't realize how much until months later, though. We all tried (encouraged by the city and by New York mayor Rudolph Giuliani) to move on with our lives as quickly as possible. Christmas was around the corner, and we shopped and pretended to be merry. And everything seemed to be normal very quickly afterward, but it was a new kind of normal. The new normal. It wasn't until the first anniversary that I, and many of my friends, realized what a mess we'd been for a year. The first anniversary acted as an alarm clock for us to finally wake up. That was the hardest part. We had gone a whole year forcing ourselves to be normal, and we weren't. We were pretty messed up."

Wong soon felt that his work became very irrelevant, especially since a lot of it had to do with luxury and extravagance. "I felt like there was little purpose for me to continue my work in that manner. I still feel that way. But I know I must continue. It's what I understand, and I need to keep it going."

And Wong has kept it going. Who needs Prada when you can rip off Burberry? Wong took the patented Burberry pattern, made buttons out of them, and distributed them at art openings and among friends and colleagues. Burberry caught wind of Wong's work and used it in its own advertising campaigns. As Wong describes it, it was "a knock-off of a knock-off."

Other interesting facets of Wong's work include test tubes filled with plastic babies, silver pills "so your shit will sparkle," a redesign of Philippe Starck's Bubble Club chair as a giant lamp, a mirror puzzle, a modern-day menorah, glass chairs, gift wrap made from original Andy Warhol prints, and a Tiffany cock ring (made by simply placing a cock ring inside a Tiffany jewellery box, obtained with permission from Tiffany & Co).

Wong describes himself as being a "paraconceptual artist," a term he coined himself. "It's like a paralegal, someone who knows just enough about the law but not as much as a lawyer, so you don't think of it as being so slimy," he explains.

"It's the same for paraconceptuals. I don't want to be tied down as being a conceptual artist. Conceptual art is usually considered a little dry. Too dry for my own taste. It's also a little too much of a cliché right now—everyone's doing it. I'm really trying my own things right now, but I still want people to know that my work derives from, or has something to do with, conceptual art, yet more beautiful."

One of his pieces in response to 9/11 was a zinc-cast, chrome-plated box cutter that was produced just in time for Christmas of 2002. Engraved on the side of it are the words, "Another Notion of Possibility." Wong received a lot of flak for this. He received even more when he voiced his opinion that 9/11 was, from an artist's point of view, very clever and artistic. "They hit one building to get our attention," he explains. "Then they make us watch as they hit the other tower. I'm not saying it was a good thing. If it wasn't in this context, and it was just about an artist trying to get attention, he would've done it very well this way."

Wong's foray into the art scene in New York has had fewer hurdles than one would think. Wong says that being Asian-Canadian was not a roadblock for him. "I truly think that not making it an issue myself allowed me to forcefully advance people's attention into the areas I wanted them to see most," he says. "Also, it's hard to be racist in New York. It's made up of so many cultures. It's very similar to Vancouver that way. But the Mexicans and Puerto Ricans have it tougher. Asian artists are also a hot thing right now—but only if you make art that looks Oriental, which I do not." Interestingly enough, he doesn't fit into the Asian art scene because of that.

Wong does not hide his Asian-Canadian roots, however. Some can recognize him as being Canadian from miles away. "They hear it in my words: *about, process, eh*?" Because of New York's diversity, people just assume he's a local rather than someone fresh off the boat. "Growing up, my mom made us proud to be Chinese," he says. "We went to Chinese school every day, and I hated it, but now I really appreciate it 'cause I can read and write it. I used to say that English was my second language because we grew up speaking

Chinese at home."

Previously using the moniker "Tofu Boy," Wong believes that his ability to create something over and over again by hand comes from his heritage. He attributes the skills of mass production, patience, and repetition to being Asian. "It's that Zen ability," he says. "I find it calming, and I can make a million of the same thing in my art project and find it very therapeutic. Hand-crafted as opposed to machine-made. I never used to believe in crap like that, but I feel it's in my blood."

There is one hurdle, however, that Wong has trouble getting over. He confides:

> I fight the appearance of looking young—like many Asians—but I've got a head full of ideas that I want people to see instead. I hate having my photo taken. People are ageist. I want my work to represent my maturity. Hopefully, puberty will hit soon.
>
> It's so fucking obvious that the good-looking people get more attention. They are listened to even if they have little intelligence. I fight it every day. I don't want to be cute. But I have no choice. So sometimes I try to use it. But my work is actually too serious to toy with that way.

So how did he end up toying with others by selling these dreams in a bag? Wong explains that in New York, people aren't allowed to sell anything that's considered a "product" on the street. For instance, musicians who make their own CDs, or artists who make their own jewellery, cannot sell their wares on the sidewalk. It is considered competition for the stores. "There was one week where they were all arrested," Wong tells me. "I wanted to put something out that was confusing," he says. "The dreams were something in between product and art, and I didn't get arrested."

When asked about his home, Wong admits: "I do miss Vancouver. Friends and family. The mountains and the water. The politeness. The slow pace." But for now, he is content to stand in the middle of Soho, thinking up ideas to peddle, in a city built on dreams.

Check out Tobias Wong's website: *brokenoff.com*. [Note: this website hasn't been updated since before Wong's death in 2010.]

Author Commentary

I miss Tobias [who died in 2010]. I always found him mischievous, intelligent, and funny. I think those qualities are reflected in his art. When I interviewed him for this article, he was just becoming the darling of the New York art scene and making a splash internationally. Even in death, though, controversy swirled around him. He had suffered for years from a sleep disorder and ended up hanging himself while sleepwalking. Retrospectives of his work have been showcased at the San Francisco MOMA and at the Museum of Vancouver, which did an amazingly thorough exhibit for the homecoming king. Whether he is destined to be known as the "Father of the Sun Jar" or for his artistic antics like the pop-up shop that never opened or the wedding registry for his "marriage" to his straight male companion, it's clear that his memory will live on through friends, family, and fans, but mostly through the collection of work he has left behind. *—Alan Woo, 2015*

About the Author

Alan Woo started as a volunteer with *Ricepaper* magazine, editing the bi-weekly online newsletter *RiceBeta* listing Asian-Canadian art events across the country. He went on to write numerous articles for the magazine, including interviews with high-profile names such as Margaret Cho and Wayson Choy, while also profiling up-and-coming artists in the community. He has since written a children's book, *Maggie's Chopsticks,* which won the Christie Harris Illustrated Children's Literature award at the 2013 BC Book Prizes. His next children's book, *Chinese Skip,* is currently in development with Kids Can Press.

The First Lady of Film: Anna May Wong

Ricepaper 10, no. 1 (2005)

Anthony Chan

Hollywood studio moguls could not ignore her sensual, intelligent allure. China's government both censored and celebrated her films; Europe's high society hailed her as a figure of exotic fashion. In a world where recognition for any actress of colour was rare, Anna May Wong defied racism to become a legend in her own time. This month, *Ricepaper* celebrates the centenary of this pioneer Chinese-American screen siren.

In an age when Hollywood offered only Charlie Chan and Little Lotus Flower roles, a strong willow sprang to life. Her grandfather, Leung Chew Wong, arrived in the United States during the 1850s. Anna May was born in 1905, the second daughter of California-born parents, Sam Sing Wong and Gon Toy Lee, and the second of their seven children. She was given the name Liu Tsong Wong, which means "frosted yellow willow." Her father ran a laundry outside of central Chinese Los Angeles.

Young Anna May Wong was fascinated with the movie shoots in her neighbourhood. At the age of eleven, Wong began cutting classes so that she could sneak off to the sets of the "moving pictures" that were being filmed on location in Chinese Los Angeles.

Wong later reminisced, "I would worm my way through the crowd and get as close to the cameras as I dared. I'd stare and stare at these glamorous individuals, directors, cameramen, assistants, and actors in greasepaint who had come down into our section of town to make movies."

Enter Ms Wong

Wong began with marginal roles in a handful of films, and then in 1922, at the young age of seventeen, she had her first starring role in *The Toll of the Sea*. In this adaptation of Madame Butterfly, Wong played a young Chinese maiden named Lotus Flower who is abandoned by her European-American husband. Many critics responded to Wong's performance with great enthusiasm and praise.

The *New York Times* was laudatory, exclaiming: "Miss Wong stirs in the spectator all the sympathy her part calls for ... She makes the deserted little Lotus Flower a genuinely appealing, understandable figure. She should be seen again and often on the screen."

But this role would come back to haunt Wong, as many Chinese came to perceive her characters as demeaning to China and to Chinese people in general. Some Chinese journalists claimed that Wong "lost face" for China. In fact, when Anna May's half-brother first saw Anna May on film in China, he warned their mother: "Take her out [of the pictures], quick."

An American Asian in Europe

Undaunted by her critics, she continued her career. German director Richard Eichberg made Wong an un-refusable offer to star in five pictures abroad. In Hollywood, she had no major contracts and no real recognition. She was eager to try her luck elsewhere.

Working in Europe's film industry was challenging. In Eichberg's *The Flame of Love*, Anna May's character, Hai Tang, finds romance with a European. Since miscegenation was frowned upon in the British Empire, the embrace and kiss between an Englishman and an Asian woman were sacrilegious.

This film was shot in three different language versions: English, German, and French, with three different male leads. When she starred in German films, critics remarked that "her German is too perfect. She must have had a double." But when they found out that she learned German "studying six hours [a day] for many weeks," the critics later revised their criticisms.

From 1928 to 1930, Wong was the toast of Europe. In England, Wong starred in the stage production of *The Circle of Chalk* with a young Laurence Olivier and in *Piccadilly* with Gilda Gray and Charles Laughton. In Berlin, she partied with the likes of Marlene Dietrich and Leni Riefenstahl. With [Wong's] stunning beauty, statuesque figure, and ability to wear the latest fashions with sophistication, grace, and panache, she represented to Europe a new Chinese woman hitherto unseen and unimagined.

European audiences were enchanted with her. Wong entered a stage of success that she had never experienced in America. But more importantly, this time gave her a clarity of purpose and agency that would empower her as she returned to the US to face the continuing burden of race in Hollywood.

Anna Takes on Hollywood

Wong's journey to Europe made her an international star, and Hollywood producers who had previously relegated her to supporting roles began to take notice. Wong returned to the States to her first starring role, in Paramount Picture's arguably racist film, *Daughter of the Dragon*. She played Ling Moy, daughter of the notorious villain Fu Manchu (played by the white actor Warner Oland in "yellowface" makeup, a theatrical device designed to exclude Asian-American performers from playing Asian or Asian-American roles).

The next year Wong was cast in another Paramount feature entitled *Shanghai Express*, a big-budget production directed by the legendary Josef von Sternberg. Many believe that Wong's perfectly nuanced performance as the cool, detached, and heroic former prostitute Hui Fei was her finest role.

But in the minds of Chinese censors, *Shanghai Express* brought disfavour upon China. Its focus on prostitutes in the heart of China angered Chinese nationalists. The film was eventually banned by the Guomindang censors, who ordered that all prints of the film be destroyed.

In 1935, Wong campaigned fiercely for the coveted role of O-lan in Pearl S. Buck's novel set in China, *The Good Earth*. She lost the role to a German actress, Luise Rainer, who would later win an Academy Award for her performance. After seventeen years of acting in films and stage plays, Wong no doubt figured that she could command lead roles that reflected positively on the Chinese people. But yellowface was so ingrained in the Hollywood studio system that Wong had little chance to capture one of the most sought after Asian roles for an Asian-American actress.

A Girl Peers through the Looking Glass

After disappointment over *The Good Earth*, Wong decided to explore her Chinese roots. She had always felt that she was "suspended between two worlds."

In an interview, she reports that during her visit to China, she would "study the customs and languages of China since they are so strange to me. I shall study the Chinese theatre that I know as casually as you. Then I shall be able to tell whether I am really Anna May Wong or Liu Tsong Wong."

Before her trip, Wong admitted that her preconceived ideas

about China resembled "a place where the people always sipped tea and philosophized about life." But once there, she exclaimed that "so many of (my) preconceived ideas have been upset that I feel like a Chinese Alice who has wandered through a very strange looking glass."

In China, she was a woman who looked Chinese, yet spoke American English and acted like a Westerner. She gave the impression that she was an integral part of Western society even when her roles smacked of blatant racism. In the eyes of the Chinese people especially, she epitomized success in the European American and white world.

The fallout from the Guomindang censorship of *Shanghai Express* four years earlier would now affect Wong. Little did she know that her invitation as the guest of honour at a Guomindang banquet would result in public roasting.

"They made speeches that lasted for four hours, but instead of the usual 'welcome to our city' speeches, they all took turns berating me for the roles I played. Since I didn't speak Mandarin then, I had to answer in English. I told them that when a person is trying to get established in a profession, she can't choose parts. She has to take what is offered. I said I had come to China to learn and that I hoped I would be able to interpret our country in a better light. It all ended with their apologizing to me!"

Anna for Asia

After her sojourn to China in 1936, Wong's roles became more positive, reflecting her vow only to appear in films with sympathetic portrayals of Asians. She transcended her angst about Hollywood and European-America and gained a new meaning as an enriched human being whose persona was beyond race and ethnicity. Wong played a variety of positive characters, including several brave and selfless heroines, crime fighters, and a doctor.

As her roles changed, China's role in the world also changed. After the Japanese invaded China in 1937, Hollywood's attitude toward China changed as well. By 1941, China was firmly on the side of the Allied powers against fascism.

In response, she made *Bombs over Burma* and *The Lady from Chungking*. In both films, Wong played a freedom fighter attempting to vanquish Japanese invaders. Although the films were low-budget and certainly not the high points of her career, *Bombs over Burma* and *The Lady from Chungking* provided Wong with the opportunity to express her political sentiments.

In Retrospect

Wong's unparalleled career spanned over forty years, from 1919 to 1961, including more than fifty films and a television series. Wong has always had a place in Asian-America as the first Asian-American female film star. Evolving into a sophisticated and cosmopolitan woman with a self-contained persona and a global perspective who steadfastly refused to be submissive to males or any race or ethnicity, Wong predated the idea of the independent European-American woman of the 1950s. She was the type of woman that twenty-first-century feminists and women of agency and empowerment would have admired. In 1928, she defied Hollywood and dashed off to Europe and its accolades, celebrity, and fame. She returned to Hollywood in 1930 and took Broadway by storm with her portrayal of Minn Lee in *On the Spot*. By the time she signed to portray Madam Liang in *Flower Drum Song*, she had already lived many lives. It was as if her death at fifty-six came not from failing health, but from exhaustion after having lived a full and eventful life in many places and time zones.

This excerpt was selected from the text and references in Perpetually Cool: The Many Lives of Anna May Wong, 1905–1961, *Scarecrow Press, 2003. Reprinted with permission from the author.*

Author Commentary

"Anna May Wong: First Lady of Film" was a synopsis of the 2003 biography *Perpetually Cool: The Many Lives of Anna May Wong (1905–1961)*. As a piece of nonfiction, it was the first biography of Anna May Wong with a significant Asian-North American sensibility. Wong was a feminist before feminism was in vogue and a sophisticated hipster with an aura of coolness that was revealed in her films, interviews, and attire. The highlight of the journey of *Perpetually Cool* came in June 2014, when Lucy Liu purchased the film rights to the book. She will star as Anna May Wong in this biopic. *—Anthony Chan, 2015*

About the Author

Born and raised in Victoria, BC, Anthony Chan returned to Canada after thirty years in the US with eighteen years at the University of Washington as an associate professor of journalism. Before his academic career, he was an anchor and journalist at HK-TVB, producing fifty documentaries, and a television reporter at CBC Calgary. Chan's independent films include a series on Asian-Americans and the Vietnam War. He has published *Arming the Chinese* (2010), *Gold Mountain* (1983), *Li Ka-shing* (1996), and *Perpetually Cool* (2003).

My Great-Grandfather, the Necromancer

Ricepaper 10, no. 2 (2005)

Ann Marie Fleming

I've been given a mission—to revisit the life of my great-grandfather, Long Tack Sam. If you talk to American magicians, they'll tell you he invented the "goldfish bowl" trick, a feat of great skill and strength. If you talk to people in China, they'll tell you he had many wives, which is not impossible for world-travelling vaudeville performers. There are many stories of who he was and where he came from. Are any of them true?

In all the legends, Long Tack Sam was born in 1885 in a small village in Northern China. According to one tale, his father was a high official at the Imperial Palace. As a boy, my great-grandfather ran away from home after breaking a jade bracelet in the market and encountered a magician's apprentice who introduced him to a new life. In another story, the famous magician Wang came to the village and performed dazzling tricks. Sam begged him to make bread appear because he was so hungry. The magician took him on as his apprentice and trained him in the arts of acrobatics and Chinese necromancy.

In yet another version, Sam was born near Wuqiao, the home of acrobatics in China. He was trained by his cruel older brother (also named Long Tack Sam), and it was the elder and not the younger who was meant to go on to an international career. Sam told people he escaped from his brother and found his own fortune. Most likely, he was recruited by a circus travelling through China. In any case, it was the younger Sam who went on to fame with the name Long Tack Sam, which is an English approximation of the Shandung family name, L'ung.

Sam was short, stocky, strong, and extremely handsome. He would have been about eight years old when he joined the Tan Kwai troupe, a Chinese circus run by Julian Kwai that had already toured the West. In those days, there were few Chinese acts that toured internationally on the vaudeville circuit. There was an inherent audience of Chinese workers spread all over the world, and among non-Chinese, orientalism was popular. People loved the colours and spectacle of the stage shows, from opera to martial arts to magic.

Friends of his insist that Sam told them he ran away from home and made his way to Shanghai, where he stowed away on a boat to England. This is probably a romantic vision, since it was difficult for Chinese to travel during that period due to barriers like the Chinese Exclusion Act in the United States and the head tax in Canada. It is likely Sam left China with the Tan Kwai troupe, travelling under a special dispensation for performers. The troupe went to San Francisco, toured the United States and Canada, and around 1903 started touring the vaudeville circuits in Europe. By 1908, Long Tack Sam had become the director of the troupe. They were known particularly for their hair tricks, performing feats of strength by hanging things from their long braids, or queue, which was the custom under the Ching dynasty.

While preparing for a performance at the Coliseum in Linz, Austria, Sam went to a haberdashery to buy supplies. He met Leopoldine Roessler, the shop clerk. They had nothing in common:

no language, no culture, but love was a quick teacher. Amazingly, her family agreed to a marriage. Sam traded his Buddhism for Roman Catholicism. Their marriage made the front page of every Austrian newspaper. Yet, on the big day, Sam was late for his own wedding and left early for a show that evening. This set the tone for their life together; the show always came first.

Within a couple of years, Poldi and Sam had two daughters, Mina, my grandmother, and Neesa. In 1911, the Ching dynasty was overthrown, and Sam and his troupe had to cut off their braids, effectively curtailing a large part of their act. But the show must go on.

Economic depression in Europe forced Sam to leave his young family in Linz and lead the troupe on a tour of the States in 1914. Initially, booking agents confused the Tan Kwai troupe with the vaudeville crooner Eva Tanguay, so the troupe changed their name to the Royal Pekinese Troupe. This caused confusion, as they were booked as a dog act! They finally settled on the Long Tack Sam troupe. The group's new act featured a full Chinese variety circus act. They juggled plates, jumped over flying knives, and produced plates of fire and water bowls full of fish.

During World War I, the troupe was caught in the United States, playing big tops, Broadway, and benefits. Sam was unable to return to Europe and his family. During this time, the troupe travelled with other international acts on the circuit. Sam had a heyday picking up the accents of everyone he met. He became a great mimic, incorporating his new skills into his comedy routines. On stage, he flogged the exotic culture of China and the mystery of distant places. Offstage, he adopted a cosmopolitan style and became one of few Asian men to sport tuxedos and fedoras.

After the Great War ended in 1918, Sam returned to Europe, where he made his wife, Poldi, his manager and trained his daughters to be in his act. He played up their mixture of European and Chinese heritage. The family act had the girls doing everything from contortions to ballet dancing, assisting with magic tricks, and playing the ukulele. They toured with the likes of Laurel and Hardy, George Burns and Gracie Allen, Al Jolson, and Cary Grant.

By the 1920s, Sam had befriended the elite in magic: John Mulholland, Max Malini, and Dai Vernon. He was a member of every vaudeville and magic association: The Society of American Magicians, International Brotherhood of Magicians, Grand Order of Water Rats. He even became a Mason. In 1922, the famous escape artist Harry Houdini asked Sam to join his prestigious magic club. Houdini was impressed with Sam and went as far as to take out a bogus patent on Sam's ancient Chinese needle-swallowing trick. A few magicians at the time were performing this trick, but Houdini successfully prevented anyone but himself from performing it. The Long Tack Sam troupe continued to travel around the world. It wasn't until 1920 that Sam returned to China, where he was already a big star. Sam built theatres in Shanghai, including the Majestic, the Metropole, and the Cathay. These buildings continue to be used today as movie theatres and venues for live performances. Sam also built a home in Shanghai and was reunited with his brother.

During this time, the Japanese invaded China, and fascism was on the rise in Europe. Anti-Asian sentiment was growing in North America. Stagehands were being unionized, and shows were getting more expensive to run. The movies were taking over. The advent of talkies began a new age, which brought about the death of vaudeville. Most vaudeville acts began playing before the films. But Long Tack Sam still had a lot of cachet, and fans flocked to see his full evening shows. Audiences in places like Hawaii greeted him like a king.

According to Gordon Bean, a librarian at the Magic Castle in

Los Angeles, Long Tack Sam was probably one of the first conduits of Western magic to the East, since he toured so consistently. For instance, in 1927, the popular song "The Doll Dance" came out in the States. Within a year, western magicians had incorporated this into an illusion featuring a full-grown woman emerging from a very small dollhouse. Sam was performing this act with his daughter Mina in China the very same year. Alongside them, Neesa was doing traditional Chinese contortions, playing Strauss on the violin while bent over backwards.

By the early 1930s, the Depression in Europe forced the troupe back to America. These were the dustbowl years for the United States, but people still needed popular entertainment. Sam choreographed a show for his other daughter Mina to perform at Sid Grauman's Chinese Theatre in Los Angeles for the premiere of *Rain*. Mina and Neesa were up for parts in features but were considered "too pretty" to play the Chinese roles in films like *The Good Earth*. Sam forbade his family from taking denigrating roles in movies and made them opt out. Flo Ziegfeld tried to talk Mina into his Follies, but Sam didn't see that as a positive role for Chinese women either. As daughters of Long Tack Sam, the girls had the double burden of being in show business (which was looked down upon by society) and of being Eurasian. In a time when mixed marriage was illegal in the States, Eurasians were considered the children of prostitutes.

In 1932, the family played at Vancouver's Orpheum Theatre before the ominously named William Powell vehicle *One Way Passage*. Sam was signed on with impresarios Marco and Fanchon and joined their tour of the West Coast. Back in Asia, the girls had acquired many admirers on their frequent trips around the world. Sam took his family back to Shanghai, but their world was already splitting apart. Mina left to start her own ballet studio and then went to help the Red Cross with its efforts in the Japanese war against Manchuria. She began to write a column in *The China Daily News* advocating women's rights through physical exercise. In 1934, she left the troupe permanently to marry my grandfather, Ernest To, who came from a long line of doctors in Hong Kong.

Neesa became the troupe's manager. Sam stayed in Shanghai and ran an ongoing show with more than eighty performers. Neesa later left the show to marry N.C. Yao, a wealthy Shanghai industrialist. For the first time, Sam passed the responsibility for his show on to a nonfamily member, a man named Pang. This effectively marked his retirement.

In 1938, Sam's son, Frank, graduated from school in England. Sam and Poldi travelled to take him back to Linz and Villa Long for the holidays. But Hitler's Germany and Austria invaded Poland, cutting off their path. The family tried to return to England, but they were unable to do so, due to Poldi's nationality. They eventually made their way to Italy, but Mussolini soon joined the Axis powers, thereby forcing the family to take a boat to the United States.

In 1940, Sam was interviewed in *The World*, where he stated his plan to get simple supplies to relatives in Austria. He revealed his intentions to keep his son out of show business and his plans to go back to China. Although he was being feted by the Society of American Magicians for his contribution to magic, he couldn't stay in America since the country wasn't letting in any Chinese. The family returned to Shanghai, and Sam came out of retirement to headline his show again. The Japanese had been invading China for years, but they'd been leaving nationals from other countries alone. As one of the remaining free ports in the world, Shanghai attracted exiles from Russia and Western Europe, especially Jews. But times turned ugly when the Japanese joined forces with the Germans and bombed Hawaii's Pearl Harbor. Sam's fame and Poldi's Austrian nationality were the only things that saved them from the Japanese internment camps.

The end of the war came, but there was more for the family to endure. With the Communist Revolution in 1949 and the march on Shanghai, a new era was born. All of Sam's properties and theatres were seized. Sam and Poldi returned to New York City, where Sam was given refugee status and American citizenship. The Chinese were allowed to apply for citizenship because of their service to the United States during the war, and Japanese-Americans found themselves in their own internment camps. Poldi was not allowed to apply for refugee status because she was European, even though she had held a Chinese passport for more than forty years. She had to keep going back and forth to Canada to renew her visitor's visa.

Sam and Poldi spent the 1950s based out of the Ruxton Hotel on West 72nd Street in New York City. He worked with emerging magicians and mentored some of America's next big talents, such as Orson Welles. They passed late nights at the hotel, going over the newest close-up magic act from vaudeville's golden days.

Sam spent the last part of his life in great pain due to his acrobatic activities. Unknown to many, he had large [bone] spurs sticking out of his spine. In spite of this, he continued to perform throughout his remaining days. His last performance was at the Roxy Theater, where he served as master of ceremonies for "The China Doll Revue." Sam performed his famous water bowl trick, where he did a frontward somersault and came up with a bowl full of water. Although many people think this trick originated with Sam, it did not; however, Sam was one of few artists who could perform it. He was seventy-three years old at this last performance.

As a young girl, all I knew of my great-grandfather was that he was a magician who could make coins appear from behind the ear. What happened to this man throughout his extraordinary life? It has taken me five years of travelling the world, researching magicians, historians, and long-lost relatives to meet my great-grandfather. This man has shown me a sliver of twentieth-century history in a new light. As immigrants of the world, necessity sometimes compels us to move forward without our histories. But we are all part of history; we are all part of a continuum. It is through the details of the lives of our families that we see how we fit into this world, a world combining the magical with the mundane, and suffering and sorrow with the extraordinary and the exciting.

Timeline

1885: Long Tack Sam is born.

1893: Sam is recruited by the Tan Kwai troupe.

1903: Sam and his troupe tour Europe.

1908: Long Tack Sam becomes director of the Tan Kwai troupe.

1908: Sam trades in his Buddhism for Catholicism.

1911: Sam and his troupe have to cut off their braids, curtailing a large part of their act, when the Ching dynasty is overthrown.

1914: Because of an economic depression in Europe, Sam tours the United States, where he gains popularity.

1914: During World War I, Sam waits to go back to Europe after the troupe is caught in the US.

1918: Once the war is over, Sam returns to Europe to make his wife, Poldi, his manager and train his daughters to be in his act.

1920s: Sam acquires ownership of many theatres in Shanghai.

1920s: Sam has befriended everyone in magic and has become a member of every vaudeville and magic association.

1923: Harry Houdini asks Sam to join his prestigious magic club and eventually takes a patent on Sam's ancient Chinese needle-swallowing trick.

1927: Talkies take centre stage; however, Sam still manages to garner large audiences.

1930: Sam's daughters successfully perform on their own.

1932: Sam and his crew perform at the Orpheum Theatre in Vancouver.

1933: Daughter Mina leaves the troupe to help the Red Cross with its efforts in the Japanese war.

1934: Daughter Neesa becomes the troupe's manager.

1936: Neesa marries and leaves the troupe; Sam retires.

1938: Germany and Austria invade Poland, forcing Sam and Poldi's son, Frank, to flee to the US.

1940: Sam is interviewed by the *World* newspaper.

1943: The Communist Revolution results in the takeover of Sam's property and theatres. Sam and Poldi leave Shanghai in 1948, ahead of the Communist revolution, but Poldi does not gain US citizenship.

1950s: Sam and Poldi spend the 1950s in the Ruxton Hotel on W. 72nd street in New York City.

1961: Long Tack Sam passes away, the cause of his death rumoured to be from gangrene developed after improper treatment for a broken femur.

Author Commentary

I had recently finished my feature-animated doc, *The Magical Life of Long Tack Sam*, about the search for my great-grandfather, who was a world-famous globe-hopping Chinese vaudevillian acrobat and magician, when *Ricepaper* asked me to write a piece about him. I saw this as an opportunity to try and encapsulate the essential trajectory of his life with no embellishments (not that his life needed much) and to open his story up to a new audience who may not have the opportunity to see the film. Later, I was asked to adapt the film into a graphic novel with the same title, which won the Doug Wright Award for Best Book in 2008. —*Ann Marie Fleming, 2015*

About the Author

Ann Marie Fleming is an award-winning Canadian independent filmmaker, writer, and artist, born in Okinawa, of Chinese and Australian parentage. Her film work incorporates various techniques: animation, documentary, experimental, dramatic, and often deals with themes of family, history, and memory.

Runaway Writer

Ricepaper 10, no. 3 (2006)

Alexis Kienlen

There is a mystique that surrounds Evelyn Lau. It may be because Evelyn's work is so personal, and as a result people have a hard time separating her from her work. Or it may be because she's had such an extraordinary life.

At the age of fourteen, in 1986, Evelyn left her parents and ran away from home. In 1989, she burst on to the literary scene with *Runaway: Diary of a Street Kid.* The sordid tale of a teenage prostitute was groundbreaking subject matter in the early nineties and drew a lot of attention from the unsuspecting media. The diary is a gutsy and disturbing first-person recollection of life as a prostitute and drug addict in Vancouver's Downtown Eastside.

Evelyn began writing as a child, and it's possible that the writing kept her sane and alive while growing up under the watchful eye of strict parents who detested her creativity. With the success of *Runaway* at the age of eighteen, Evelyn went on to publish poetry, prose, and personal essays. In 1990, at the age of twenty, she won the Milton Acorn Memorial People's Poetry Award for *You Are Not Who You Claim,* her first book of poetry. She has also been nominated for a Governor General's Award for Poetry for *Oedipal Dreams,* and she received a Canadian Authors Association award for "Most Promising Writer." Her prose books, mostly concerned with the rigours and sadomasochistic dramas of sex, have been translated into more than a dozen languages.

Everything I've heard about Evelyn swims around inside my head. I've heard that she's a quiet and private person, despite her public past, and doesn't want to be associated with the Chinese-Canadian community. Who is the real Evelyn Lau?

As I prepare for our interview, I contemplate how her writing has evolved. *Inside Out,* a collection of personal essays, touched on tough subjects like the effects of a lawsuit on her writing, as well as her struggle with depression and bulimia. Published twelve years after *Runaway,* the book reflects her recent years and proves she's become more comfortable in her skin. Recently, a collection of poetry, *Treble,* hit the shelves. The flower that graces the cover of *Treble* contrasts with the darker images that marked her earlier works. It is a peaceful emblem, homely even, something that you might see on the cover of a Martha Stewart magazine. Compared to the dark, deeply sexy imagery of Evelyn on her previous covers, this new design is a breath of fresh air. It also catches me off guard. Does the mysticism that surrounded Evelyn Lau even still exist?

Evelyn and I meet in a coffee shop in downtown Vancouver. When I first see her, I'm struck by how pretty she is. She has a smouldering presence attached to her plump lips, high cheekbones, and smoky eyes. She greets me with a warm smile and a firm handshake and apologizes for blowing her nose due to environmental allergies. She's drinking an apple juice because she doesn't like coffee. I notice a small scar near her neck and wonder what it's from. I never bring myself to ask.

I anticipated meeting a sombre and serious woman, but Evelyn puts me at ease. She's chatty, funny, and engaging. We immediately commiserate over our love of literature. It's obvious that Evelyn is both passionate and knowledgeable about writing. She's managed to harness and direct her talent and creativity, though she's entirely self-taught and never received a formal education. She tells me that one of her favourite writers is John Updike, and she considers Alice Munro to be our greatest Canadian writer. Both authors are experts at writing stories that focus on the nuances of human interactions and relationships—also passions of Evelyn's.

When I tell Evelyn she's rumoured to be a private and serious person, her laugh proves otherwise.

"People think I'm serious because of my subject matter. But I'm not. I love to make people laugh, I always wish I had more humour in my work because it's the best way to engage readers."

You could assume that because Evelyn is a Chinese-Canadian, her family's experience of immigration would be one of her main influences. "I don't see myself as being a Chinese-Canadian writer, because I don't write about it." She says part of writing is about tapping into your sense of being an outsider and of otherness from the community, society, and family. Evelyn's own focus on the nuances of human interactions and relationships is shaped by her time on the streets; she thinks of that time in her life as her sense of otherness rather than her Chinese-Canadian heritage.

Evelyn was born in Vancouver and still resides there. It's interesting that she still feels comfortable in the city, as it was there that she fell into prostitution and drug addiction. Evelyn admits that she wrestled with her feelings about Vancouver while she was in her twenties, but now "Vancouver is home. It's changed a lot in the past few years. I tend to think of it as a collection of distinctive neighbourhoods." You might think the distinctive neighbourhood of Vancouver's Downtown Eastside, infamous for street life, drug addiction, and prostitution, would stigmatize Vancouver for an ex-street kid. But Evelyn realizes that the life she lived in this space is one of many lives the city has to offer. Vancouver is a multilayered city, with different aspects of personality, much like Evelyn herself. In her collection of short stories, *Choose Me*, written from the perspective of seven different young women, Evelyn explores the relationships between home, space, and self.

Besides, living on the street didn't cripple Evelyn's writing career; it brought into existence her first commercial success, *Runaway*. But how did Evelyn manage to publish her first book while living such a transient and unstable life? She explains that while living on the streets she won a number of literary contests. She applied for and received financial funding from the Canada Council through the Explorations Program for new writers, which in recent years has ended due to government cutbacks, though today, alternative programs like Outreach offer grants for emerging and established creative writers.

Despite her obvious potential, publishers were leery about the book, unsure about the public's response to the gritty subject matter. They thought the book might tank, and it was difficult to plan a book with a writer who might not have a fixed address. Luckily, HarperCollins took the chance and picked up *Runaway*. The book proved to be a critical and commercial success. It was a bestseller for thirty weeks and has been translated into multiple languages.

In 1993, *Runaway* was optioned to become a movie and aired on CBC as *The Diary of Evelyn Lau*. The intense subject matter demanded skilful acting and as a result launched the successful acting career of Sandra Oh, a Canadian actress most recently seen in *Sideways*. Evelyn, who worked as a consultant on the CBC project, never actually saw the entire film. The visual rendition of the reality Evelyn lived hit too close to home. Unsurprisingly, Evelyn stills finds the book to be rather painful.

"I can't read it," she confesses. "If I'm asked to read it at a reading, there's only one passage that I'll read."

"What is important, I think, about Evelyn Lau," wrote critic Patricia Pearson in 1993, "is that she blends startling prose talent with a fierce determination to be true." This combination unfortunately led to a nonfiction exposé of her ruined love affair with writer W. P. Kinsella, a relationship that began when he was sixty and she was twenty-four. The media cast an eye toward Evelyn again, in 1997, when the older Vancouver-based author of *Shoeless Joe* sued Evelyn over the article, titled "Me and WP," in *Vancouver Magazine.* The lawsuit diminished respect for both literary talents. The two writers had signed a pact giving one another permission to write about their relationship, but Kinsella alleged that Lau's portrait of him was malicious and erroneous. A lengthy court proceeding eventually settled in a fairly innocuous way with a letter of retraction in the magazine.

Evelyn tells me that getting sued by her former lover caused her to react in two ways. "I wanted to write more, and I also wanted to retreat. It was so hard for me to imagine not writing about my life or the lives I intersected with," she says. "If you're writing about your life, you might have people who take offence, even if you're a genre writer. And then some people get offended if you don't include them, so you can't win at all," she says with a smile. In the essay about the lawsuit that appeared in her collection of personal essays, *Inside Out,* she confesses that the lawsuit had a negative impact on her writing, and her output has slowed in recent years. This is one of the reasons she turned to poetry. "Whoever heard about being sued for a book of poetry?" she says with a laugh. Her endless fascination with relationships compelled her to keep writing. She says that as she gets older she probably won't be as fascinated with romantic relationships, but "in your twenties it's at the forefront of your thoughts."

In many of her stories, couples play out romances and power struggles. People struggle to communicate with each other and try to find ways to relate to one another. Evelyn admits to a fascination and idealization of older men—"father figures." She cherished the relationship she had with her father, and in the prologue to *Runaway* laments the distance that grew between them as she became a teenager. Evelyn's work doesn't shy away from the unconventional side—the otherness in each of us. Her empathy drives her to tell the untold stories of the human soul. Despite genre, time, or space, it is this side of Evelyn that remains timeless.

Evelyn confides that writing is hard, and a finished product takes effort. After the success of *Runaway,* she was intent on proving to the literary world that she wasn't a one-hit wonder and tried to publish one book a year for several years. In *Inside Out,* she writes about her youthful fascination with writing and how she was unable to stop writing. She followed her debut with three collections of poetry and then set her sights on fiction with the publication of *Fresh Girls and Other Stories, Choose Me,* and one novel, *Other Women.*

Her latest book, *Treble,* was released in Spring 2005 by Polestar Press and is her first collection of poetry in ten years. *Treble* signifies the evolution of her writing process and her determination to tackle diverse characters and themes.

"I could have written five books in the time it took me to write *Treble* because I kept re-writing and tossing out material." She believes this book represents a move from the outskirts to the centre of society, since it deals more with conventional romantic relationships rather than prostitution.

Evelyn and I talk about writers we know and how they seem so different from their work. Evelyn casually makes two comments that apply to how she's evolved as a writer and a person. A lifetime away from being on the streets, she's become a lot more relaxed, reflective, and comfortable in her skin. "The part of themselves that writers bring to their work is different from their normal personalities," she says. "Often when you meet them they aren't who you think they are." As a writer and reader myself, I understand that audiences can trap authors in their work, though the writer as a person is constantly growing and changing.

The Evelyn Lau I'm talking to is human, a multilayered individual: chatty and funny but with a conscience that doesn't deny darkness. The myth crumbles and fades before me as the real Evelyn Lau gestures and talks on, serene and alive as the flower on the cover of her new book.

Author Commentary

When I was a teenager, Evelyn's success made me believe that I could write too. When I went to interview her for this piece, I was nervous, but I shouldn't have been. She was warm, funny, and open with me. After the interview, we walked around the marina and chatted like friends. I'd only been living in Vancouver for about a year, and she shared with me some of her thoughts and feelings about the city. At the time, I was an unpublished author who dreamed of getting published. But Evelyn didn't treat me as someone who was inferior to her; she treated me like just another writer. When the piece came out, she and I shared a laugh because an editor had added a line about "her smoldering presence," which I hadn't written in my original draft. *—Alexis Kienlen, 2015*

About the Author

Alexis Kienlen was the literary editor of *Ricepaper* magazine from

2001 to 2006. Born in Saskatoon, Alexis has lived in Edmonton since 2008, where she currently works as a reporter for *Alberta Farmer Express*. She holds an honours degree in international studies from the University of Saskatchewan, a graduate diploma in journalism from Concordia University, and a Certificate in Food Security from Ryerson University. Alexis is the author of two books of poetry, *She Dreams in Red* and *13*. In 2014, she published a biography about a civil rights activist, *Truth, Love, Non-violence: The Story of Gurcharan Singh Bhatia*. She is currently at work on her first novel.

The Nature of David Suzuki

Ricepaper 11, no. 1 (2006)

Jenny Uechi

In the stark white-walled meeting room in the David Suzuki Foundation, my one hand checks the tape recorder while my other pinches my cheek, wondering if this could be real. We are about to interview David Suzuki, one of the most iconic figures in Canadian culture. Before reality sets in, however, a smiling, white-haired Japanese-Canadian man walks in, dressed in a crisp blue shirt, buttoned down to reveal a gold necklace. It's him: David Suzuki, just as we have seen him for years onscreen.

It's a rough task to separate Dr Suzuki, the individual, from the public face that we have come to know. Never mind that he was one of the few Asians voted into CBC's "Greatest Canadian" contest in 2004: the fact that he was the only living Canadian to break the top five is a measure of his impact on this country. His face is indelibly etched in the memory of generations of Canadians through his long-running CBC television show, *The Nature of Things*. His ubiquitous writings appear in weekly columns in *Shared Vision* and *Nikkei Voice*, not to mention the thirty-two books that he has authored to date (with another autobiography coming out this year). Yet at the core of his lofty public persona, the David Suzuki that we met was "just a human being," a son, a father, and an individual. Whether he is like anyone else is something that we leave for you to judge.

To understand how Suzuki came to be the person he is today, it's important to know a thing or two about his father, Carr (Kaoru) Suzuki. Adventurous and charismatic, Carr Suzuki instilled in his son a passion for nature from an early age. "My father was a very unusual Asian," Suzuki smiles. "He believed that money wasn't everything, and he loved nature." As a child, young Carr was often scolded by his parents for "wasting time" planting trees instead of studying or working. Raised in hardship and with pressures for financial success, Carr taught his own children not to obsess over money and encouraged them to appreciate the natural beauty of their surroundings. Suzuki's voice becomes animated as he recalls one of his numerous camping and fishing trips in Vancouver with his father:

"I remember vividly, I must have been four, he was carrying me on his back, [and] we were hiking up the mountain. The dog started barking, so we stopped, and there was a cougar right there. He never went, 'Let's run,' but said, 'Oh, look at that, isn't that amazing!'"

Having learned to marvel at the world around him rather than fear it, Suzuki would use his father's approach when it was his turn to educate audiences about nature and science.

Suzuki may have been raised to love the natural environment, but his relationship with the human world is a different story. Don't get us wrong: Suzuki connects with people from a broad social spectrum and has the kind of universal appeal to Canadians that politicians would envy. As a working-class Japanese-Canadian, however, Suzuki has seen enough prejudice to break most people's faith in human nature. How did he manage to maintain his sense of empathy over the years? "What you call empathy is more an identification with other people," says Suzuki. "I saw prejudice against us [Japanese] as being the same as prejudice against the Jews or blacks." Reflecting on the four years he spent in internment camps during World War II, Suzuki says that the specific attacks on him as a Japanese-Canadian made him feel closer to the universal struggles of people everywhere, be it the aboriginal peoples of Brazil or gays and lesbians in the US.

You could also say that it was precisely because of the racism that Suzuki learned to appreciate what small glimpses of humanity he experienced. Midway through the interview, Suzuki leans in slightly and says, "There's a story I have to tell you; it's very moving to me. When my father was first shipped away to a road camp to work on building the Trans-Canada highway, and my mother and my sisters and I were put in a camp in Slocan, my father had an accident—he injured his leg driving a horse. The doctor gave him a little form saying that Carr Suzuki [was] allowed to leave camp and go to town. But he didn't say what town. So, on the strength of that, my dad took off, and instead of going to the nearest town, he decided to come and see us. He had a cane, he was limping, and he tried not to let anyone see him. Being very quiet, he didn't want to attract attention, so he didn't eat. He got on the ferry, and by then he was really hungry. The smell of the food came, so he got on to where the restaurant was, and he was going to walk in—and then he saw the Chinese cook. Now, the Chinese and the Japanese hated each other at the time. The Chinese had every right to hate the Japanese because of what was going on in Manchuria. My dad thought, 'Oh no, I can't go in.' The Chinese cook saw him, and he said, 'Come in.' So my dad thought, 'This is it, he's going to report me.' And the guy said, 'Sit down.' And he said, 'You're Japanese, aren't you,' and my dad said, 'Yeah.' And the cook said, 'Look, you and me—we're brothers.' And he fed him this big meal, all for nothing. That story just touched me, that even in a time like that, someone could reach out and help."

Small, unexpected acts of kindness such as these had long-lasting effects on Suzuki, who, more than sixty years after the war, still remembers the Chinese-Canadian cook who took in an enemy and called him "brother."

Even after establishing himself as one of Canada's premier geneticists and broadcasters, Suzuki maintains a bit of cynicism when people point to his success in reaching out to the public. Starting his broadcasting career in 1962 ("You weren't even a thought in your father's head at the time," he adds jokingly, pointing to me), Suzuki aimed originally to use television as a medium to educate the public about science. "If I had a talent, it was to translate difficult scientific ideas into a language that the public could understand," he says. Starting off with a weekly TV program, *Suzuki on Science*, Suzuki moved on to CBC's *The Nature of Things* in 1974, one of the longest-running and most successful Canadian shows in history, with audiences in over ninety countries. Through his sixty-minute television show, Suzuki had hoped to educate the public so that they would be better informed to make their decisions on issues such as global warming, GMOs, and environmental conservation.

"But it hasn't worked out that way," he says abruptly. "The absolute opposite happened from what I expected. I thought I was just a messenger, giving (people) information, and they would go out and do things. I became the message." The irony of his foray into broadcasting was that instead of empowering the public, the public had empowered him. Today, he says, if he were to call the Prime Minister's Office, he would likely receive a call back in half an hour because of the millions of Canadians who back him up. In an ideal world, those millions of Canadians would be calling on their leaders about the issues that Suzuki has informed them about. To this day, however, he receives countless emails from organizations asking for his support on everything—save this rainforest, rally against that corporation, help promote this new invention. "People get very disappointed," he admits when he tries to explain that he's only human and doesn't have the time or energy to speak for everyone. "Some may be disenchanted and disillusioned, but I try to offer help to groups that are struggling."

While he acknowledges that it's an honour to have people's confidence, he adds that it's a "huge responsibility." That responsibility, of course, extends far beyond Suzuki himself and is shouldered by everyone who is close to him, especially his five children, Tamiko, Laura, Troy, Sarika, and Severn. While having David Suzuki as a father definitely has its perks, the trade-off is to live each day under the giant shadow he casts. "I think it's been especially difficult for my son," Suzuki says quietly. Because his daughters were exceptional students, Suzuki feels that being related to a famous scientist was a "double whammy" for Troy, whom Suzuki describes in his autobiography *Metamorphosis* as being "good looking, [an] outstanding athlete, bright." The slightest remark about his grades was an enormous pressure for Troy, and that pressure turned to resentment as his father spent more time away from home to work. Suzuki recalls that after his son graduated from high school, he took off for three years, travelling the world over to find himself. It would take many more years until father and son had sorted out the tension between them. "He was very angry at me," he says. "We've gotten to be very good friends now, but it took a long time."

He feels that things were easier for his daughters, especially from his second family. Severn Cullis-Suzuki, his youngest daughter, generated a lot of publicity for her environmental activism from a young age: At nine, she started the Environmental Children's Organization, and at twelve, moved audiences to tears with her speech at the Earth Summit in Rio de Janeiro. Amidst accusations that Severn is merely "copying" her father's work, Suzuki maintains that his daughter is no mere follower. "She's very proud of what I've done, but she says, 'I'm a young person; my dad has got his views, and I've got different views.'" Without denying or being ashamed of her privilege, Severn uses her resources to launch initiatives like Skyfish Project, a youth activism group that serves as part of the UN Special Advisory Board. "[Severn] could have been a spoiled kid," Suzuki says, depicting an imaginary scenario of his daughter as a globetrotting shopaholic, "but that's not the road she's chosen. She tries to use her opportunities to help the world." While each of his children had to fight the pressure of having a famous father, they kept grounded, Suzuki feels, thanks to their mothers. "To be totally honest," he grins, "I think that the most intellectual support in both families has been the mothers."

Because both of Suzuki's wives—Joane Sunahara and Tara Cullis—were exceptional mothers, he ended up learning a lot of parenting lessons from them. When asked what kind of advice he would give to himself as a father thirty years ago, Suzuki replies without missing a beat, "Well, I feel that I've relied far too much on my wives. They were such good parents. That allowed me to be away a lot more than I should have been." His words conjure up a sad anecdote that I had read in his autobiography: When Suzuki separated from his wife Joane, his children were so accustomed to his absence that it took a year for them to notice that he had actually moved out. Folding his hands on the table, he gives some advice on fatherhood, probably aimed as much at himself as our readers:

"I wish—especially for my son—I wish that I was there for him. You know, these days, people say, 'It's quality time, not quantity time.' Total bullshit. When [children] fall and scratch their knee, that's when they want someone to wipe it clean and kiss it well. If they score a goal in a little game, that's when you've got to be there and say, 'Well done!' But you can't plan those things. You've got to be there. And I regret that I couldn't be there. I tried. I tried very, very hard. I wasn't there as much as I could have been."

When I hesitantly offer that many fathers are too busy to spend time with their children, Suzuki firmly shakes his head.

"That's the thing," he says. "My father, who was the great hero in my life, always had huge amounts of time for me." He concludes that workplaces need to be redesigned to allow families to be together, rather than delegating the role of mothers and fathers to hired hands. Some years ago, he had tried to implement this change in his own office, allowing his secretary to bring her baby to the university. It had worked out fine, until students and professors complained that it was unprofessional. "Academics are such snobs," he mutters, recalling their indignation at the baby's cries.

As our interview draws to a close, I ask Suzuki what he would like to do over the next several years. He laughs wearily, admitting that he had actually planned to retire nearly fifteen years ago, at age fifty-five. The flurry of new causes and projects, of course, hasn't left him with much choice but to keep going.

He admits that it could be a few years yet: After getting his David Suzuki Foundation on solid financial ground, he'll have to find a successor to host *The Nature of Things*. He notes that CBC may take the show off the air after he retires due to its strong association with him; however, he would like his daughter Severn to have a shot at becoming the next host.

"I have a few things that I want to do before I die," he says thoughtfully. "At my age, every day is a gift. I could be hit by a car, who knows? I would like to learn to speak Spanish. And I would like to study geology, to have a hobby, like painting or carving. But in order to do that, I've got to have time." As though to snap himself out of a dream, Suzuki taps his fingers on the table. The sound disperses images of Suzuki painting landscapes in a cabin beside some half-finished wood carvings, bringing us back to his foundation, where countless emails, phone calls, letters, and deadlines await him. "But that won't happen for a while," he says with a wry smile.

As I shook hands with Suzuki at the end of the interview, he was no longer just a figure on TV screens and in periodicals, immortalized by over forty years of exposure in the public eye. The David Suzuki that I met was human, vulnerable, prone to telling stories, and critical of himself and his work. Textbooks and encyclopedias will mark him as a groundbreaking geneticist and broadcaster, but to us, he's a loving son, grateful husband, and caring father like anybody else, whose eyes dance whenever he talks about his children.

Author Commentary

What surprised me about the David Suzuki interview was how human he was and how openly he told his story about family and growing up. In particular, his memory of how his father shaped his career trajectory and curiosity about nature, as well as the need to explain science in a way that resonated with everybody, was very touching. *—Jenny Uechi, 2015*

About the Author

Jenny Uechi is the managing editor of the *Vancouver Observer*, an award-winning news site (winner of Canadian Journalism Foundation's Excellence in Journalism Award, 2012 and 2014). She is a former news director at NHK, assistant editor of *Ricepaper*, and translator.

A Writer's Life: Speaking with Denise Chong

Ricepaper 14, no. 4 (2009)

Eury Chang

We often look to writers in order to get a better understanding and sense of the world that we live in. One writer whose work powerfully illuminates the world around us is Denise Chong. Educated in economics at the University of British Columbia and in economics and public policy at the University of Toronto, Chong has authored a number of bestselling books over the past fifteen years. Her titles include such well-known works as *The Concubine's Children* (1995), *The Girl in the Picture: The Story of Kim Phuc* (1999), and most recently *Egg on Mao: The Story of an Ordinary Man Who Defaced an Icon and Unmasked a Dictatorship* (2009). In many ways, each of these books delves into the challenging and tumultuous worlds of their subjects and, in the process, offer an insightful social and cultural commentary of the times.

In October 2009, Chong, who now lives in Ottawa, returned to her native West Coast for two readings—one at the University of British Columbia and another at the Vancouver Public Library (VPL) as part of a national book tour promoting her latest literary work, affectionately known as *Egg on Mao*. On the day of her reading at VPL, I spoke with Chong about her career trajectory, the content of her books, and the craft of writing. She is what one may expect from a member of Canada's literati: articulate, well read, and profoundly inquisitive. But at the same time, the writer that we've come to know is down-to-earth, with a delightful sense of humour. These traits make me feel as if I'm speaking with an old friend, and the sense of familiarity is comforting.

We travel back in time to the eighties, when Chong began her career in the public service. Chong speaks frankly of her early ambitions: "I was certainly shaped by living on the frontier, so far from what was seen as the centre, which was Toronto and Ottawa. I always wanted to be rooted where I was and also to be part of a bigger world." Then came Trudeaumania. "I was affected by it," she confesses. Chong took the bold leap, packed her bags, and relocated to Ottawa, she says, "inspired in part by Trudeau's own vision of a country big enough with heart and ideas to hold us all."

After being recruited as an economist with the Department of Finance, she worked in a public service briefing capacity, dealing with natural resources. Then came an opportunity as a special advisor on BC issues, working with appointed cabinet minister Ray Perrault. Chong recalls many intense negotiations dealing with a range of matters relating to Expo '86, the Vancouver Convention Centre, Canada Place, northeast coal, and the light rapid transit system. It was while working in this liaison capacity in Ottawa that Chong came to the attention of the Prime Minister's Office and, around 1980, began serving as economic advisor to Pierre Trudeau.

When Trudeau retired in 1984, Chong didn't follow the various other leadership candidates, because she intended to take up a writing life. "That was my ambition," she says. Having become friends with Trudeau, the two would talk about his early experience with *Cité libre*, the magazine that he cofounded and edited, and her own desire to embark on a career in writing. "When the opportunity came to go to China, he told me to go." In yet another bold move, Chong boarded a plane to join her boyfriend, now husband, in Beijing. In China, Chong would take on journalistic assignments here and there and even covered Rick Hansen's Man in Motion Tour. How many of us recall the stunning photo of Hansen wheeling himself up the Great Wall of China? Cutting her teeth on human interest stories and refining her craft, Chong sent such articles back to Canada, sharing her letters across land and sea. While in China, she decided to visit her ancestral homeland and unexpectedly found members of her extended family. The resulting memoir traced generations of her family through stories of hardship, growth, and great social transformation. The rest, as they say, is history.

Chong says that being in China gave her the foundation and impetus for her first novel. "This, of course, became the basis for my book and the play based on *The Concubine's Children*." The book was so well received that it stayed on the bestseller list of the *Globe and Mail* for ninety-three weeks, won the City of Vancouver Book Award, the Vancity Book Prize, and the Edna Staebler Award, and was shortlisted for the Governor-General's Literary Award for Nonfiction. Needless to say, all of this attention secured Denise Chong's place as a voice that should be heard and followed. During Citizenship Week in 1995, she gave a speech entitled "Being Canadian," which would be widely anthologized in the forthcoming years. Soon after this, other book titles followed, namely *The Penguin Anthology of Stories by Canadian Women* (1997), and *The Girl in the Picture: The Story of Kim Phuc*. Meanwhile, Chong never lost her passion for public policy. In the years of transition from state politics to cultural journalism and book publishing, she continued to pen many government reports on issues ranging from online culture and participation of visible minorities in the public service to what was once known as the "information highway."

Which brings us to the question of craft—writer's craft. I'm curious to hear Chong's views on fiction and nonfiction and her take on the blurry shades of grey in between. In her mind, Chong is clear about how her content informs the structure of writing and even clearer about these literary genres, saying that, "there is one critical difference between fiction and nonfiction, and it's so simple. In fiction, the characters are born in the writer's mind. In nonfiction, someone actually gave birth to the characters."

Chong writes about real peoples' lives, pulling the work out of living memory. "But a book is not a life," she cautions. "It's a front and back cover," alluding to the fact that she stays within the facts of her subjects' lives, while exercising her licence as a writer.

I can't help wonder how Chong's time in the public service has influenced *Egg on Mao*, which she often describes as a "biography of a gesture." In her latest book, she traces the story of Lu Decheng, one of three men who attempted to stand up to the Communist regime by throwing eggs at the painting of Mao Zedong, surely a force much greater than themselves. No doubt, the book offered Chong opportunity to play with structure even as it details one man's personal and public struggle to act on his rights as a human being.

"With this story, I didn't go strictly chronologically," she says. "I played with stretching time." The book starts right after the last egg is thrown and ends with the moment before the three men go to throw the eggs. According to Chong, the structure of the book's narrative is intended to bring the reader on some emotional and moral journey, which, of course, is what it does. In this story, we are offered the intimate details and life story of an ordinary man and his seemingly extraordinary gesture.

Just before returning to her busy writer's life, Chong leaves us with a few reflective thoughts. Humble enough to name the pioneers that came before her, "I would bow down to people like Jim Wong-Chu, Larry Wong, and SKY Lee," Chong says. "As artists, we're here to break boundaries and push the envelope. That's what a writer does and that's what we do as Canadians. We take on a complexity of identities—and I would have that over one simple identity any day."

Author Commentary

Chong's profile outlines some of the writer's major contributions but was intended to coincide with the 2009 Vancouver launch of *Egg on Mao*, a book which focuses on human agency and social justice issues pertinent to contemporary readers. Chong called her book a "biography of a gesture," which shows how seemingly simple acts can make a difference. —*Eury Chang, 2015*

About the Author

Eury Chang is a Vancouver-born writer and theatre artist. He worked as the editor of two publications: *Dance Central* (2004–2011) and *Ricepaper* (2008–2012), during which time he wrote many artist profiles, critical reviews, and commentary on the Asian-Canadian cultural community.

The Mysterious Life of Wah Kwan Gwan

Ricepaper 17, nos. 3–4 (2012)

Jackie Wong

Vancouver's Chinatown is changing fast. On East Georgia, Union, Keefer, and Pender streets, the bright newness of independent art galleries, coffee shops, performance venues, and cocktail lounges stand in sharp contrast beside the now-dwindling number of traditional, generations-old grocery stores, bakeries, and butcher shops that were once the main features of the streets. "Chinatown has changed," says Paul Cheng, who immigrated to Canada from Hong Kong in 1975. "It's only [busy] in the daytime for tourism, or for people who live close by to get groceries. Historically, it's nice to have it there. But the real functions, the real developments [that formed Chinatown's social and economical hubs] are not there anymore. Now, Richmond [BC] is said to be the new Chinatown." Cheng frequented the neighbourhood during his first twenty years in Canada. He'd regularly pop in to the martial arts clubs, and he was part of a Chinatown musical society that has since moved its headquarters to Richmond. Speaking with me today from his home in Surrey, BC, Cheng rarely finds himself in Chinatown; he's had little reason to visit in the thirteen years since the death of his friend, Wah Kwan Gwan, who used to live in an East Hastings Street rooming house.

Gwan was a longstanding member of Chinatown's Cantonese opera community. His presence and contributions to the community were largely unacknowledged during his lifetime, but his memory lives on in Vancouver's present-day Cantonese opera community, powered in large part by Cheng and his wife, Rosa.

Cheng and Gwan would occasionally meet for dim sum at the Pink Pearl Restaurant on East Hastings Street near Gwan's apartment. They frequently saw each other when working backstage together on Cantonese opera productions mounted by the Jin Wah Sing Musical Association, which has since moved to Richmond. "I worked with him for almost seven years backstage," Cheng says of Gwan. "In Cantonese opera, they follow traditional rules. He's the one who showed me all the rules."

Back when Chinatown's streets were awash with neon lights in the 1950s, 1960s, and part of the 1970s, people packed the after-hours musical societies, gambling clubs, and clan associations that formed the nucleus of Vancouver's Chinese community. Restaurant workers would drop by late at night after they had finished their shifts to socialize, play games, and make music together. Gwan was a regular fixture in the halls of Chinatown's musical societies. The neighbourhood's two oldest were the Jin Wah Sing Musical Association and the Ching Won Musical Society, formed in 1934 and 1935 respectively. Both groups were hubs for practicing, performing, and preserving the art of Cantonese opera.

This musical art form elevated the lives of Vancouver's young Chinese men who worked long hours at multiple jobs to make ends meet. Yiucheung Ling, now eighty-four years old, spent his working life in Chinatown restaurant kitchens and at a poultry shop where he would slaughter, de-feather, and butcher chickens for customers. He fondly remembers the lively spirit and camaraderie of the after-hours musical societies.

"Even though we were tired after work, we felt energized once we got there," Ling says of Chinatown's musical societies. "When I heard the gong and cymbals of the opera music, I felt at home."

Ling met Gwan when the two frequented the Ching Won Musical Society as young men in their twenties. There, Gwan was a familiar, if unusual, face. When he wasn't quietly observing the rehearsals and performances, he would provide valuable instruction on costume comportment, props, and performance. He had spent [the] formative years of his life with a Cantonese opera family in China, and he was eager to pass on his knowledge to others.

This Cantonese opera expert with a mysterious past lived on the margins of both Vancouver's Chinese- and English-speaking communities; he was, in fact, ethnically Aboriginal but had lost all ties to his birth family. While he was fluent in two dialects of Chinese—Toishan and Cantonese—he could not speak English, so, like many Chinese bachelors, he spent his days in Chinatown. During his lifetime, only a few people appreciated his wisdom derived from a textured, often misunderstood, life that transcended geography, language, and the colour of one's skin. "The Chinese and Aboriginals saw Vancouver's Chinatown as a refuge," explains Bill Chu. He chairs the Canadians for Reconciliation Society, a grassroots movement to honour and acknowledge the history of Chinese and Aboriginal people in British Columbia. "From the folks I ran into, they usually refer to that as their common experience, that Chinatown served as a place of refuge for both, because both are subjected to discrimination." An understanding of the history of Chinese-Aboriginal relationships in Vancouver is now fairly minimal, underlining the importance of revisiting that part of history. Chu continues, "I think there's a deep need to understand that piece of history again."

Throughout the course of a friendship that grew from their shared participation in Chinatown's musical societies, Ling, just one year older than Gwan, learned that the two shared a similar family background. Both had spent significant parts of their childhood in the Cantonese opera community in Kaiping city, also known as Hoiping, in Guangdong province, China.

Ling's father was a scriptwriter for a Cantonese opera company in Kaiping. Gwan's adoptive family was part of the city's thriving Cantonese opera community. Gwan, born in 1929 near Hastings and Carrall streets to Aboriginal parents, was separated from his birth family as a boy. The details of the separation—and whether it was, in fact, abandonment—are unknown.

According to what Ling gathered from casual conversations with his friend, a Chinese man named Mr Gwan adopted the boy and named him Wah Kwan Gwan, the name he lived with for the rest of his life. His Aboriginal birth name is unknown. The adoptive uncle took the boy with him back to China, to Kaiping city where Mr Gwan's brother owned cinemas and restaurants, and the entire family was also deeply involved in Cantonese opera.

By the time Gwan returned to Vancouver in the 1950s, he was a young man in his twenties. Even though the return to Vancouver marked a return to his birthplace, Gwan would live the rest of his life on the margins of Canadian society. After years spent in China, he had lost all connections to his Aboriginal roots. While not fitting in entirely within his adopted community, his inability to articulate in English further isolated him and restricted his ability for economic and social advancement. Consequently, Gwan did not have steady work and relied on social assistance and adhoc housing arrangements provided by Chinatown community members to sustain his livelihood.

Gwan spent his days in Chinatown where his fluency with the Cantonese language and interest in performance art helped him connect with the local Cantonese opera community. He frequented the Ching Won Musical Society, and the chairman temporarily rented him a room in his home. Gwan used the skills learned from his adopted family in Kaiping to help mount local Cantonese opera productions. He worked backstage, and he eagerly shared his extensive knowledge of the intricate traditional rituals around costuming and props with younger performers and stagehands.

Gwan's contributions and commitment to the opera community went largely unacknowledged. He was often left with the opera-related grunt work that few others wanted to do.

"When you go out to all the opera groups in Vancouver, nobody is interested in the backstage. The backstage is a very dirty job, a lot of heavy moving, and nobody appreciates it," says Paul Cheng, who used to work with Gwan backstage during Jin Wah Sing Musical Association productions in the 1990s. "People wanted to put [Gwan] backstage. He was quite a helpful person. The only thing is, nobody respected him."

Gwan had been dealt a difficult hand in life. He lived in poverty, relying on social assistance and the goodwill of Chinatown community members to help him find places to live and meals to eat. He turned to drinking that sometimes resulted in abusive, polarizing behaviour that alienated him from the people who knew him. "People thought he was a nobody," Paul's wife, Rosa, says.

Working against the odds, Gwan proved himself as a talented singer and performer in the opera community. He eventually earned onstage parts, but he was never able to play the principal male roles typically filled by conventionally attractive male actors.

"If you are a principal male role, he's usually the hero of the show. Traditionally, it's someone who's good-looking, the prince," Rosa says. "So he [Kwan] was not in that kind of role."

Rosa and Paul became involved with Vancouver's Cantonese

opera community at the same time in 1993, and they met Gwan in the same year. If Gwan did appear onstage, he played a villain or political leader. He loved it, Rosa said. He shone.

Gwan was, to Rosa and Paul, a very special, essential player in the traditional Chinese artistic community. "We learned a lot from him," Rosa says of Gwan's encyclopedic knowledge of the Cantonese opera art form. The couple is working hard to keep Cantonese opera alive and pass it on to future generations through the Vancouver Cantonese Opera society they founded in 2000, the last year of Gwan's life.

"It's like literature, a poem, when you sing," Rosa says of Cantonese opera. "The performance technique—the miming, the gestures—is unique. It's an art form."

The Vancouver Cantonese Opera society, Rosa says proudly, has a mission to popularize the art form in English-speaking mainstream society. It's hard work, she admits. But she and her husband are no strangers to working against the grain in the interest of those on the margins.

"For me, it's an art. I want to preserve it, I want to promote it," Paul says. "We're not involved in any Chinatown groups anymore. We're totally different; it's not for people to hang out after work anymore. We do real production, we do real training." For his part, eighty-four-year-old Yiucheung Ling continues to share his knowledge of costuming and props work with Rosa, Paul, and the Vancouver Cantonese Opera Society. "As long as I'm healthy, I'll keep going," he says, smiling.

"He's a gem," Rosa says of Ling. "He's the only one left in Vancouver who knows the traditional ways of Cantonese opera costume preparation."

It's rare, special knowledge that Ling and Gwan used to share. It was raining on Boxing Day, 2000, when seventy-one-year-old Wah Kwan Gwan died alone in a government-subsidized rooming house on East Hastings Street. His passing was quiet and without fanfare, much like the years he spent in Vancouver's Chinatown. Gwan was on income assistance when he died, and with no next-of-kin, the provincial government stepped in to sort and do away with his possessions, which included numerous valuable texts on Cantonese opera.

"Suddenly, I got a call that Wah Suk [an affectionate Chinese term of endearment for Gwan] passed away," Paul recalls. "But by the time I knew, everything was gone."

Intent on preserving the memory of a man they respected and admired, Paul and Rosa cobbled together what they knew about Gwan's life to write an obituary that ran in Vancouver's *Sing Tao Daily* newspaper in January 2001.

The story of Gwan's life and connection with Vancouver's Chinatown community should give us pause to reflect on historical relationships between Vancouver's Chinese and Aboriginal citizens, says Bill Chu of Canadians for Reconciliation.

"For a long time, we had been subjected to similar treatments, and we'd coexist and help each other on those fronts during those terrible times," he says. "If you look back, anything before 1967, the Chinese were subjected to all kinds of discriminatory legislations, both provincially and federally. And the indigenous people at that time had their own limitations in terms of what the government allowed them or didn't allow them to do. So both were subjects of big-time, official discrimination."

The situation with Gwan and the Cantonese opera community, Chu says, should not be considered to be an anomaly restricted to a few relationships between select individuals.

"It's not just something exotic that we should be looking into but something which is real, which should cause us to reflect on how we should relate to indigenous people today."

"We learned a lot from him," Rosa says of her relationship with Gwan. "A lot of people will think he's nobody." She pauses and looks to Gwan's friend, Ling, seated next to her. They both know that Gwan led a remarkable life and that his memory deserves to be preserved, honoured, and celebrated.

Author Commentary

While Jim Wong-Chu was guest editing *Ricepaper* magazine, he wanted to tell me about Wah Kwan Gwan and his unique presence in the Cantonese opera community. There's not a lot of discussion about historical relationships between Chinese and Aboriginal communities, he told me, and certainly not enough contemporary discussion of the ties between Vancouver's Downtown Eastside community and nearby Chinatown residents. Jim connected me with Wah Kwan Gwan's friends Rosa Cheng and Yiucheung Ling. It was very special to hear how much they valued a person who many thought of as unremarkable and, worse, undeserving of care and a place in the community. *—Jackie Wong, 2015*

About the Author

Jackie Wong lives and works in Vancouver, BC. She currently works as the editor at *Megaphone*, a monthly magazine on urban issues and independent culture sold by homeless and low-income vendors in Vancouver and Victoria. She is also an instructor in UBC's creative writing program and works as a freelance editor for local publishers and non-profits.

In Conversation with Madeleine Thien

Ricepaper 18, no. 3 (2013)

Hanako Masutani

On a bright fall afternoon in Burnaby, I met Madeleine Thien in her new writer-in-residence office at Simon Fraser University. As Madeleine prepared mugs of green tea, the window behind her displayed a long, sunny view of the university and turning fall leaves. We sat down beside a wall of books to discuss Madeleine's just-completed novel, writing, her time in Canada and abroad, and identity.

HM: *Your book* Simple Recipes, *which came out over ten years ago now, was such a big success. You've had success after success, it seems. Do you feel like you've arrived as a writer?*

MT: That's a hard question. I never think of it in those terms, because you're not sure where you're arriving to. And I think each book shows you more of what you're capable of, and also, more of what you aren't capable of. So it's a continuous process. But I feel more proud of *Simple Recipes* now than I did then. At the time it was so close to me. And my reading of it was, maybe, overly critical. Now when I look back on it, it's a book I feel glad I had the chance to write at that particular time in my life.

HM: *What are your ideal writing conditions?*

MT: It's been harder as I get older, because I've realized the ideal conditions for me are to be completely alone for several months at a time. That's very hard to arrange. That's hard on your relationships. But, ideally, if I can be away for two or three months and do only writing—especially if it's a novel—without teaching, that's ideal for me. I immerse myself in the book and don't come out until that time is finished. For me it makes a big difference. I can feel it in the writing, when I'm really inside it, or when I'm just dipping in and out. I feel like I make greater discoveries, and all the elements of writing—the research, the memory, the craft, the surprise—they have more of a chance of really coming together if I have periods of time by myself.

HM: *You've written about Montreal and Cambodia before. What prompted you to write about China now?*

MT: It came as a big surprise to me! I've been reading and thinking about China ever since I was a teenager, but I never thought I would write about China. I never felt that I was capable or knew China enough.

This novel ended up starting with events that were very close to me, and felt very personal—my parents' relationship to China. Then it ended up becoming something completely different.

This novel is about students studying Western classical music in Shanghai. It's set in the Shanghai Conservatory of Music in 1965, on the eve of the Cultural Revolution. Writing about music opened up a whole new way for me to think about art, the transmission of artistic practices, and also the copying of ideas. It's really interesting that we see so many Western ideas as originals and so many Eastern ideas as copies, or they're not attributed to a specific person. And I want to poke some holes in that.

HM: *Was doing research in Shanghai very different from doing research in Cambodia?*

MT: Yes, very different. The first time I went to Cambodia was only for two months, and I wasn't writing. I didn't even have any plan or idea that I would ever write about it. I just wanted to spend time there. The writing came much later. But when I did start writing, I was always very conscious of the fact that it was a different culture. Cambodia's religion, Buddhism, and its language are quite different from the East Asia that I know. Cambodia is where the civilizations of India and China meet, cross-fertilize, and all of that. I always felt trepidation that I would get things wrong, or that I wouldn't be able to get into the psyche. But of all the books I've written, it's the book I believe in the most. It was a big risk for me. It made me see that we actually are capable of fully immersing in another psychology, another culture. It's not that different, you know. That balance is one of showing respect but also of knowing that the identity is rich and has many possibilities. That you really can get inside if you spend enough time. If you can stop yourself from projecting and just observe. Try to take in as much as you can. And for me that expands the boundaries of what fiction is capable of doing. That book showed me the most. It was the biggest risk, because I also had something to say about the silence surrounding Cambodia's history. So, to come back from there to China is *really* interesting, because I don't take for granted that I know the culture, even though it's mine. I still feel what I felt in Cambodia, which is to not project, to not take things for granted.

HM: *In 1999, you edited* Ricepaper *5, 1–3. Can you speak about your time as the editor of* Ricepaper?

MT: Even at the time—and I still think so now—I didn't know enough. I feel like I was very inexperienced. I'd never edited a magazine before. I'd been on the *Prism international* editorial board. That was the most editorial work I'd done. At the time, the mandate was to cover as wide a range of Asian-Canadian art and literature as possible. So I had to expose myself to a lot of what I hadn't been exposed to before. I think the writers my age were afraid of being ghettoized.

I don't know how conscious or unconscious it was editing *Ricepaper* and thinking: These artists are artists first; they have many different identities, one of which is Asian-Canadian, and whether they choose that identity or not, it's really up to them. I had a lot of questions about putting a label on people. I would have wanted to choose for myself, too. I think I had a lot of unresolved questions that I didn't know how to answer in that context. I think I would be a better editor now.

I wish we could make a structure where there was more intergenerational exchange with *Ricepaper*. Because I feel that Fred Wah or Roy Miki have so much to tell us. And the structures and prejudices and ghettos that they were reacting against still exist. They haven't changed, only we don't name them the way they did then. I don't know how to have those conversations without making people feel targeted. It's very, very sensitive. And I find myself more and more curious about that conversation, even more now than when I was at *Ricepaper*. Maybe it's age.

HM: *Do you find it useful for you to call yourself an Asian-Canadian writer?*

MT: I don't, partly because I feel—and I felt this way with *Dogs at the Perimeter* in Cambodia—that the story around Cambodia is [one] that everyone should feel responsible to and that everyone should see as their own. All our governments were involved, either before or after. And with Cambodia, in particular, it's been very easy for the West to distance itself and forget. There's a lot of amnesia about the Vietnam War and the American bombing of Cambodia, which was entirely illegal and secret. It was huge. We actually supported the Khmer Rouge as the representatives of Cambodia until the 1990s, you know. Fifteen years after the genocide, we still recognized Pol Pot as the country's leader. So in that way, the Asian-Canadian box feels too small. I feel that our stories are as legitimate and mainstream as anyone's.

Commentary by Madeleine Thien (2015)

Only two years have passed since my conversation with Hanako, and so although I've been asked to write a commentary, what strikes me most is that I find myself unable to do so. Conversations continue like stories, concluded but not necessarily resolved.

I'm at Nanyang Technological University in Singapore, a country I don't know well, but one that borders my father's birth country, Malaysia. Working with writers here, I think about how words—race, Asian, marginal, centre, literature, story, reader, language, writer, history—take on different connotations, sometimes vastly different, in this political context. Concepts, even basic ones, present alternate problems and different freedoms. I think of Hannah Arendt writing about Isak Dinesen, "It is true that storytelling reveals meaning without committing the error of defining it."

About the Author

Hanako Masutani is a former creative director of *Ricepaper*, whose work has appeared in the internationally acclaimed literary journal *Grain*. She lives in Vancouver, BC.

Travelling between Worlds with Ruth Ozeki

Ricepaper 18, no. 4 (2013)

Erika Thorkelson

When I catch up with Canadian-American-Japanese author Ruth Ozeki over the phone from her home on Cortes Island, BC, she's still buzzing over the European leg of her book tour to promote her third novel, *A Tale for the Time Being.* She's been to Madrid, Barcelona, Paris, and all over England, and she gushes about the independent bookstores there, which seem to be rarer every year in North America.

In Bath, England, at the whimsically named Mr B's Emporium of Reading Delights, a trio of young musicians who perform under the name the Bookshop Band, wrote and performed a song in the book's honour. It was a dream response for a novelist who toils in solitude on a remote island to see her work reaching across the world to inspire other artists.

"I started to cry," she says. "The tears were just streaming down my face—I was so embarrassed. It's hard to describe. It's a lot of hard work to write a book, but it feels like it's kind of a gift."

According to the Zen principles that Ozeki has been practicing ever more seriously since the 1990s, when you receive a gift, you must give one in turn. Seeing that gift picked up and reinterpreted felt like another iteration of that cycle and evidence of its power.

It was a cycle that began in 2006 when Ozeki, like Ruth, her fictional counterpart in *A Tale for the Time Being,* was grieving her mother's death and trying to write a memoir that just wouldn't coalesce.

The voice of Nao, a Japanese teenager whose family had been unceremoniously torn from their comfortable life in California and sent back to poverty and isolation in Tokyo, came to her first. Nao was intelligent, brassy, and haunted. She existed in the shadows, and with her diary she was reaching out for companionship and solace the only way she knew how.

Ozeki knew the tone would be confessional and the form would be a diary addressed to a reader, but the reader remained elusive. So she began "auditioning" readers. She cast four or five different characters for the role—men, women, young, old. The auditions "took place on the page," and each time Nao's section would grow, but none of the readers felt right.

"Finally, at the end of 2010, I finished a draft, and it was very, very different," Ozeki recalls. "Nao's section was similar to what it is now, but not the same, and the other half of the book, the reader's half, was entirely different. It was set in a library, in a place that was very much like the Vancouver Public Library."

Her husband, artist Oliver Kellhammer, was the one who had come up with the idea that Ozeki, or rather a semi-autobiographical fictional version of herself, should be the reader. It was a tactic that had come into favour in the mid-2000s. Philip Roth cast himself as a fictional character in an alternative United States in *The Plot Against America*. Charlie Kaufman had written himself and a twin brother into *Adaptation*, his screen treatment of Susan Orlean's *The Orchid Thief*.

But Ozeki dismissed the idea as a metafictional gimmick, one that would take some serious manipulation to accomplish. Still, as the writing process stretched on, none of the other readers she tried made sense.

When the March 2011 tsunami struck Japan, destroying much of its northeastern coast and sending debris spiralling through the circular currents of the Pacific Ocean toward the west coast of North America, something clicked. This was a way for Ruth to connect with Nao in an organic way. All of Ozeki's work grapples with the ways in which humans connect between cultures and over great distances; here was a distant tragedy on an unthinkable scale playing out in real time on television and computer screens around the world. And it was happening in Japan, the land of Ozeki's mother's birth and a place she had spent large chunks of her adult life.

But if she were going to be a character in the book, Oliver would have to be in there too. "He thought that was fine," she says over the phone. "He said that it was an interesting thought experiment, and so I went forward and wrote it. Of course, he read it, and he was fine with it. His only concern was that he felt I had made him too smart in the book. I disagree, actually. And anyone who knows him would also disagree."

From there she set about constructing a fictional life for Ruth and Oliver on an island very much like Cortes. But she couldn't find space for everything. If anything, she says, the real thing is more magical. She couldn't, for example, find a way to squeeze in Cousteau, their pet turtle the size of a manhole, who resides in the Ozeki-Kellhammer living room.

"This is the kind of turtle that you find frozen and stacked up in storage in Chinatown," she says of their massive pet. "People make soup out of them. I think she probably prefers her tank to being soup."

Ruth Ozeki wasn't born on the coast of British Columbia. Her path, like the circular ocean currents called gyres that brought Nao's diaries to the Canadian shore, is far more complicated than that. She was born in New Haven, Connecticut, to a Japanese mother and a

European father. Her parents were both academics with graduate degrees in linguistics, although her mother left academia when Ozeki was born.

Growing up half-Japanese and half-European in a predominantly Caucasian community made her aware of the complications of identity politics from a very young age. Though she resembles her father a great deal in both height and facial structure, Ozeki says the "Asian wash" on her features, an accident of genetics, meant that she was pegged from an early age as Japanese rather than American. Fulfilling that role meant internalizing an idea of Japaneseness cobbled out of stereotypes and expectations.

"The people around me identified me as Japanese, so I kind of took on what I thought to be the traits that would be racially appropriate for me to take on," she remembers. "When you're a little kid, that's what you do. I thought that Japanese girls should be quiet and obedient, docile, good at math, play an instrument, get good grades, not crack jokes, and all that kind of stuff. It didn't occur to me that there were other options."

It wasn't until she encountered the real thing, travelling to Japan first with her mother and then as a student, that she discovered just how American she was.

"Hallelujah!" she thought. "I can crack bad jokes and claim my identity as an obnoxious American." Ozeki describes one of her earliest encounters with the complicated nature of the identity that had been thrust upon her in her 2004 essay for the *New York Times*, "A Vacation with Ghosts," which is about her first trip to Japan with her mother at the tender age of seven. There, for the first time, she saw her mother speaking Japanese. "Now, as I watched her talk to my grandmother in Japanese, switching fluidly from one language to the other, I saw that in this strange new tongue she was a different person—possibly not my mother at all," she writes. "It made me dizzy, all this switching, but maybe it was the heat."

On the page as well as in person, Ozeki is a gifted raconteur. She often tells another story about a much later trip she took as an adult, when she and a Caucasian friend named Steve walked into a tiny pub on the southern island of Kyushu, and the owner addressed the half-Japanese, half-European Ozeki directly, ignoring her blond friend.

"Steve's Japanese is and was absolutely fluent," she remembers. "You would never know he wasn't Japanese ... and mine at the time was still pretty shaky. So it was one of those crazy moments where the owner of the bar was rattling on to me in Japanese and Steve was rattling back to him. Little by little it occurred to the owner that Steve was speaking Japanese, but it took a while for the information to really penetrate, because he resisted it. It was too freaky for him. So then he got on the phone and started calling his friends, and before long the entire place filled with people from town who had come to listen and see this blond *gaijin* [foreigner] who spoke *pera pera* [quickly and fluently]. Things got rowdier and rowdier, and I remember at one point in the evening, the owner just stepped back and looked at Steve with this expression of astonishment and awe.

"And he said in this very philosophical tone of voice, '*Ma! yappari ningen da na!*' [I guess they're human after all!]"

This is almost a seminal experience for people of Asian descent travelling in Japan, but reading it as a comment on Japanese xenophobia would be overly simplistic. As those who grow up between cultures—like Ozeki herself—no doubt understand from an early age, it's an extension of identity politics everywhere; until he spends an evening in your bar, chatting you up with clever fluency, it's hard to see the Other as a fully realized being.

After studying classical Japanese literature in Japan, Ozeki returned to America and fell into a job in film, doing art direction on such classics as *Matt Riker: Mutant Hunt, Breeders, Necropolis, Enemy Territory,* and *Robot Holocaust.* Her big break was in a commercial where she worked with an art director who had worked extensively with Akira Kurosawa.

"It was just absolutely mind-blowing," she remembers. "We did fabulous things. We had Cyndi Lauper riding on a pink elephant at one point. What was interesting was to watch how this guy ran his department. We got to be friends, and we talked a lot. Just to hear these wonderful stories about Kurosawa was amazing."

Speaking Japanese became her most valuable skill. On film sets, she could translate and coordinate between US and Japanese crews. But her ultimate goal was to make it to the editing room where the story finally comes together, which she instinctually knew would hold the greatest lessons for her.

"I got into film by accident," she says. "It was never something I wanted to do. I loved film. I'd been involved with media ever since high school, but it was not my burning desire. My burning desire was always to write novels."

Ozeki produced two films on her own—a surreal fiction called *Body of Correspondence* and an intensely personal documentary about her mother called *Halving the Bones.* The former is out of print; the latter is available on iTunes. They were wonderful experiences for her, but the idea of writing another film, of the years of collaboration and compromise, of promotions and raising money, didn't appeal. Instead she began work on her first novel, *My Year of Meats.*

"Filmmaking is incredibly cumbersome," she says. "You have to have all these crew members around, and you have to feed them and find bathrooms for them and pay them. If you want to blow up a building, you have to get a location permit and get the police to help. It's one thing after another. But if you're writing, you just imagine it and write it down. It's like magic. It felt like years of trying to walk through swamps in chains; suddenly it felt like, oh my, I can fly."

But she wouldn't have been able to make the transition without those years in the documentary editing room, learning how to craft a narrative that moved quickly and compellingly through time out of the messy, disparate parts of real life. "It's one thing to learn about it, but it's another thing entirely to be in the hot seat in an editing room, surrounded by directors, producers, and clients who are barking orders at you," she remembers. "And to do that over and over again, it's fascinating. Working in commercial television was the best MFA program I could ever have imagined."

She met her husband during a heady residency at the Banff Centre and fell in love with Canada in the process, adding yet another hyphen to her identity. Though Ruth is the closest in external circumstances, the central characters of Ozeki's books all carry a certain echo of the author's roots. Jane Takagi-Little in *My Year of Meats* and Yumi Fuller in *All Over Creation* are also half-Japanese, half-European Americans who find themselves acting as bridges between cultures. Whether intentionally or accidentally, her characters reach out and draw distant people together, often finding some measure of peace themselves in the process.

Interconnectedness is one of the themes at the heart of all of Ozeki's work. In the first two books, the link was through food, the common biological requirement to eat that links continents and cultures.

In *A Tale for the Time Being,* the characters are literally connected by the ocean that drops Nao's diary on Ruth's island, but they are also metaphorically connected by their own personal tragedies: Nao's grief over her former life and Ruth's loss of her mother to Alzheimer's disease. But the mechanisms—the gyres—that bring them together aren't perfect. The connection comes in nearly unidentifiable pieces that require work and care to put together.

"Each of the gyres serves to connect us, but there's something about the movement of the gyres that breaks down the substances too, so plastic becomes degraded, and so does history and so does memory," she says.

"There's a sense of things breaking down and reconstituting as well through time. This is just another way of talking about impermanence, this idea that nothing stays the same, that things are constantly moving and changing form."

To Ozeki, this is the struggle at the heart of our modern global existence. We live in a world where, thanks to the Internet, it's easy to feel as though we know everything about each other, but the imperfections and omissions in that network often go unnoticed. Rarely is this tension between impermanence and permanence more visible than at the height of a disaster.

For the first two weeks after the tsunami, Ozeki remembers being glued to the never-ending supply of images of the devastation on the Internet. "And then about two weeks later the attention of the news media moved on and other things were important," she remembers. "Even though world attention had shifted to the next thing, the situation in Japan was ever more dire. The Internet gyre, the news gyre is very speedy. It cycles very, very quickly."

Ozeki acknowledges that remaining open to the movement of global news can be overwhelming. But she also sees it as a powerful tool to construct empathy and build the kinds of connections she writes about—when I speak to her near the end of summer in 2013, she is glued to the events in Cairo.

"We care about these things now," she says. "These images have the power to move us and to make us care. That has to be a good thing. For as much as email deprives me of huge swaths of my life, at the same time I'm glad of it."

Zen, with its emphasis on empathy and mindfulness, is a way for Ozeki to find peace with that incredible amount of information and the impermanence of life. She became interested in the practice in the 1990s, using meditation as a way to deal with her father's death.

In 2001, she met Norman Fischer, a San Francisco practitioner of Soto Zen who would eventually become Ozeki's teacher. Joining the sect felt like coming home because it was the same one her grandparents had been a part of. In 2010, she was ordained a novice priest.

Of course, this too appears in *A Tale for the Time Being*, in the form of Jiko, Nao's ninety-six-year-old grandmother, a Buddhist nun who lives in a monastery near the coast in Miyagi Prefecture. The scenes at the monastery are some of the most haunting in the book, touched with echoes of Hayao Miyazaki's classic film *Spirited Away*.

As a writer, Ozeki has used Zen to help her move past the usual blockages and struggles of the solitary profession. The practice centres on struggling toward perfection, even as you acknowledge the impossibility of that perfection, a sentiment that is familiar to any novelist.

"There's something very beautiful about making an impossible vow," she says. "In a way, every time you start to write a novel, you have an impossible idea of what this novel will be, and you know that you'll fail. There's no question about it. There's no way to write the novel that you want to write, that you think you're going to write. There's no way to raise the perfect child. There's no way to do all of these things that you most want to do in life, but that doesn't mean that you shouldn't try to do them. In a way, the more impossible the vow is, the more beautiful it is. It's about the willingness of the spirit."

That effort certainly seems to have paid off. In the autumn of 2013, Ozeki would be shortlisted for the Man Booker Prize, one of the most prestigious awards a novelist could hope for. And yet on the day that I spoke to her, just days after the announcement of the longlist, it's that song in a little bookstore in Bath that really captured the author's imagination. To Ozeki, this kind of evidence of her work's reverberation in the hearts of her readers is the greatest award. "It felt like such a precious gift that I was getting," she remembers. "It's a beautiful process."

Author Commentary

I became enamoured with Ruth Ozeki and her book *A Tale for the Time Being* just after I had returned from a visit to the Tohoku region of Japan, where I travelled to places that had been destroyed, and I collected stories with an eye to writing a book. I was searching for meaning in the unthinkable, and here was a novel that explored all the themes that had been on my mind—disaster, grief, and profound human connection over time and distance. It was as if Nao, the fictional Ruth, the real Ruth, and I were all part of this grand conversation about what it meant to be human in a time when the world seemed both smaller and larger than it ever had before. *—Erika Thorkelson, 2015*

About the Author

Erika Thorkelson was born in Winnipeg, grew to adulthood in Edmonton, answered phones in Dublin, Ireland, and taught English in a little town called Shiroishi, in northern Japan. She now lives in Vancouver, where she writes nonfiction, tells stories, and teaches writing.

Creative NonFiction

Light at a Window

Ricepaper 15, no. 1 (2010)

Terry Watada

Tomeo Shoyoma was a good-looking teenager living in the east end of Vancouver, 1941. He was at the top of his class at Britannia High School and looking forward to UBC and a wonderful career like his big brother's. True, Tommy, a UBC graduate in commerce and economics, couldn't become a chartered accountant because of the times, but it was a temporary thing for both him and his brother, Tomeo reasoned. After he graduated, he knew the world would be different, and he'd be all right in the long run.

He lived with his brother in a rented room in a house south of Powell Street Grounds, the park that formed the centre of the Japanese community back then. Their parents still lived in Kamloops, BC, not wishing to be anywhere near the big city. They consented to their boys moving to Vancouver to attend school.

Like so many others his age, Tomeo had a nickname based on some prominent characteristic. There was "Hammerhead" Nishihata for the shape of his head, "Fuzzy" Seko because of her Japanese name, Fusae, and "Windy" Gotanda who had the nasty habit of passing wind in public, hence his moniker.

Tomeo's label was appropriate enough: "Romeo." Besides the obvious rhyme, he was very popular with the girls. On a Saturday night, when most went in groups to a movie at the Palace or an old vaudeville show at the Pantages, Romeo always had a date. He looked real sharp with his slicked-back hair, wide-lapelled suit, and two-toned patent leather oxfords bought with money he earned at a part-time job at Soga's Department Store on Powell Street. The girls, too, were real dolls—Hedy Shimizu, Addie Kodama, and Helen Yoneyama, to name three. They always wore the latest styles, dresses from back east and high-heeled shoes from the women's department at Eaton's downtown. The girlfriends did each other's hair, copied from movie fan magazines, because Viola's Little Beauty Salon on East Hastings just couldn't cut it. Good for their mothers but not them.

Whenever there was an occasion, say the Valentine's Dance thrown by the Bussei, [a.k.a. Young Buddhists] in the Peter Pan Ballroom of the Ambassador Club, Romeo and his date really were a sight to behold. Of course, the music was hip: Glenn Miller, Benny Goodman, even Duke Ellington. The lights were low, and a glitter ball revolved, casting stars all over the floor. Romeo's girl always had that dreamy look in her eyes as he led her around the dance floor. They looked exactly like Fred Astaire and Ginger Rogers.

That was why none of his gang could understand his falling for Julia Sato. She was pretty enough, but in that "good girl" and plain kind of way. Her dresses were strictly bargain-basement, and she wore flats. Her hair was always in a ponytail. She never wore makeup. Most knew she could afford more. Her mother had died in a car accident, but her father was Shigeki Sato, the top judo sensei in British Columbia. His club, the Hinomaru Dojo, attracted everyone and anyone interested in the Japanese martial art from as far away as Hope, BC. He also had alleged ties to organized crime; people believing that his dojo supplied the muscle for Etsuji Morii and his Black Dragon Society. Whenever the *oyabun*, or crime boss, wanted something done, for whatever reason, he'd call on Sato and his students for help. For a high price, of course.

Murakami's Confectionery and Soda Parlour was an excellent example. The quaint shop stood at the corner of Main and East

Hastings, serving "the best handmade ice cream in Vancouver," as the sign boasted. It did a brisk business in the summer, on hot days, when a cold, tall vanilla cone was just the ticket. It got by in rainy weather with pies and coffee and sodas for the kids. It was in a prime location in any case.

One spring day, when Murakami-san himself was behind the register, Morii, a small man in a dark oversized suit and bowler hat, walked in with three judo thugs behind him. He strode to the counter, while the judo boys took up strategic positions in the place, and called over the aging owner.

"Murakami-san," he started. "You've accumulated quite a debt to me."

"Yes, oyabun," he answered with his head lowered in shame.

"You know you shouldn't gamble."

He nodded, eyes averted.

"Makes it hard for your family," he observed. "Well, at least you do it at my place and not Chinatown. Well, well, well, I'm here to help you with your debt. I'm not unfeeling after all."

"Thank you, oyabun. Thank you."

"First of all, you are no longer welcome in the Showa Club. You come in, we'll throw you out. Second, my men will be watching you, so you don't go to the Nanking gambling dens. If you go there, I'll know about it, and you don't want me to have that kind of knowledge, do you?"

"Yes, oyabun. I mean, no, oyabun," he said nervously.

"Good, good. Now, as to the matter of your debt to me, you will sign over this little place of yours to me."

"But ... but, no, oyabun, I couldn't."

"What?" Two of his boys moved. One knocked over a large jar of candy, the brightly coloured confections spraying across the floor like cherries on a pool table after a break shot. The few customers enjoying their sundaes ran for the door, leaving their dishes behind.

The third thug stood at the ready with fists clenched.

Murakami-san reached out as if to prevent the deliberate mishap. "I mean ... I mean I can't until the bank manager comes back from holiday. I'll see him next Monday and get the papers to hand over to you."

No one understood what Morii wanted with the property, because it stood vacant for the longest time after the Murakami family surrendered it. Everyone concluded that he took possession of the place simply because he could.

So maybe Romeo liked the danger in dating Julia. His brother, Tommy, as editor of the *New Canadian*, was a dedicated and outspoken critic of Morii and his political activities. But the paper never reported on the oyabun's crimes. That would've been pure suicide. Instead, the Nisei newspaper, being the voice of the younger generation, the first Canadian-born generation, focused on the criminal boss's support of the Japanese military in China.

The stories focusing on the atrocities by the emperor's army in China were bad enough for the oyabun, but the personal-attack editorials brought him to the point where he fumed at the mention of Tommy's name or at the sight of the *New Canadian*. Because of Sensei Sato's connection to organized crime, Romeo knew he and his brother were in for a rough ride if the judo master ever discovered his relationship with his daughter. He wondered what the old man would do, but then again he wasn't in a hurry to find out.

Romeo met Julia at Ernie's, an innocent soda shop where the kids hung out. It became popular after the closing of Murakami's. The jukebox always had the latest songs from the hit parade, the malts were sweet, and Ernie was friendly enough. Julia sat at a table with two girlfriends with the same conservative, unremarkable looks as she. Romeo came in after a ball game at the park with a few of his gang.

"Did you see that Yamamura guy hit that homer? I bet it still hasn't landed," Frank claimed.

"Yeah, sure. Them Asahi are one powerful team."

"Romeo, you oughta join. They could use your arm. Romeo? Romeo?"

He was distracted for the moment. "Well, lookee here," he began as he walked across the floor. "Well, boys, the Andrew sisters are in town." It was clear that Romeo wanted to tease these girls. The boys laughed, and the girls squirmed in their discomfort.

"Hey, Gladys, sing us a tune," he said to Julia.

She turned and, with her nose up in the air, said, "First of all, that's the *Andrews* sisters, and second, their names are Patty, Maxene, and LaVerne."

"Hey, Romeo, nice line!" shouted one of his gang. "You ain't dealing with no square!"

Everyone laughed out loud.

Romeo walked right into that one. Good thing he could take as much as he could give. "Hey, I'm a lover, not a fighter, doll face," he said, and then immediately offered to buy her a soda, much to everyone's surprise, especially Julia's.

From that day on, they were inseparable. If she could best him, he was heard to say, she was worth knowing. The only problem was he had to see her on the sly, once they learned of each other's families. Julia couldn't tell her father, but Romeo did seek his brother's advice.

He sat in the *New Canadian* office among the mountains of paper and bottles of India ink while Tommy worked to get the paper together. His older brother was slight in build but always commanded respect. There was such an aura around the man; all who met him knew they were in the presence of greatness.

"You look worried," the editor said, reacting to his brother's silence.

"I am, *oniisan*, I am."

"So what's the problem?"

"I got this girl, see."

Tommy nodded as he fussed.

"She's nice and all. She might even be the one for me, but—"

"But? You aren't in trouble, are you?" he asked, alarmed. "She's not in trouble!"

"No! Nothing like that," Romeo assured. "It's her *otosan*. He doesn't approve of me."

"Really? He said that?"

"Not exactly."

"You're speaking in riddles, Tomeo."

"I've never met him, but I know he won't like me. He's Sensei Sato." The revelation fell with a thud as Tommy turned to consider the consequences. "I know you and him got something going—"

"Only because he's connected to Morii."

"Yeah."

"Tomeo, you be careful."

He was careful. Romeo and Julia decided not to be seen together at community events like the annual Buddhist Church bazaar or the Obon festival every summer. Whenever a dance came up, they were careful to go with their group of friends and eventually meet on the dance floor. To arrange a date, Romeo couldn't phone her or walk up to her front door and ask for her. He instead had to stand on the sidewalk in front of her stand-alone house on Jackson

Avenue after dark and toss pebbles up at her window. Fortunately, her room faced the street, and he only did it when the window was lit.

That way they could meet for walks, a soda at Ernie's, their special place, and an occasional afternoon movie downtown on Granville Street. One of his favourite stars was Errol Flynn. When he saw *Robin Hood,* he got hooked. He saw, in rapid succession, *Captain Blood, The Dawn Patrol, Dodge City,* and *They Died with Their Boots On.* Julia tolerated the swashbucklers but really liked romantic films like *Gone with the Wind,* despite Rhett Butler's swearing.

Sometimes the theatre ushers questioned them, but the questions were of no consequence to them. Romeo just whipped out his government-issued identification card, which all Japanese-Canadians had to carry, and that was that. They weren't spotted by anyone from the Powell Street area after all. They giggled about their situation on the balcony, Romeo stealing a kiss now and then. Within the danger and secrecy, they fell deeply in love.

All went well until that fateful day when Romeo came to a decision. Late one night, he stood in his usual spot in front of Julia's house. This time, however, the house was dark; everyone had gone to sleep. It couldn't be helped; what he had on his mind couldn't wait. He grabbed a handful of pebbles and started tossing. It took awhile, but finally the light went on, and the window opened. A rather sleepy Julia leaned out for a look.

"Julia! Julia!"

"Romeo? What are you doing? It's so late."

"I'm sorry, but I just had to see you. Can you come down to the veranda?"

"Now?"

"Come on, it's important."

She closed the window and a minute later appeared at the front door.

Romeo thought he had never seen her more beautiful than in the moonlight. "Julia, I've been thinking a lot. I think we're pretty serious about each other."

"We are?"

"Aren't we? Ah, cut it out," Romeo smiled. "We're going to university soon, and it's gonna be a different world."

"What're you trying to say, Romeo?"

"I'm getting tired of all this sneaking around. I feel like some kind of ... I don't know, criminal or something. Sorry, but we oughta bite the bullet and tell your otosan about us."

"Oh no," she said, horrified.

"Wait a minute, hear me out. If we go together, we can do it. We'll present a union."

"You mean, united front."

"That's what I said."

Suddenly the porch light came on, and a Japanese voice boomed from inside. "Junko-chan, who's at the door at this hour?" It was Sensei Sato.

That was Romeo's cue to cut out of there, leaving Julia standing at her door with a looming shadow behind her.

A couple of days later, Julia sat by herself at Ernie's. At their table. A couple of minutes later, Romeo joined her. She wasn't herself; she wasn't sitting in her usual prim and proper way. In fact, her hair was down and not in its comfortable ponytail. Some of the strands partially covered her face.

"Hey, you changed your hair."

She said nothing.

"Something wrong?" He touched her arm and she flinched, revealing a small splatter of India ink underneath one of her eyes. It was a bruise.

"What happened?"

"Nothing."

"Your old man? He hit you?" His anger spiked.

"Never mind, it's nothing. I'm here to tell you something."

"What kind of animal is he?"

"Tomeo, we've got to stop seeing each other," she said insistently.

Her words went through him like an electrical shock.

"It's never going to work," she continued. "The way we sneak around is shameful and embarrassing. You said it yourself."

"Embarrassing? I never said that."

On the verge of tears, Julia took a different path. "My otosan forced it out of me ... about us, and as long as your brother continues to print those stories—"

"Wait a minute. Don't drag my brother into this. This is about you and me. Nobody else."

"No, it isn't. My father is a good friend of Morii-san and your brother—"

"What about us?" he insisted.

"Don't you see? It's no good. My father made it quite clear that no daughter of his is going to consort with the likes of you."

"The likes of me? What does that mean? What does he think I am?"

"That's my father talking."

"How does he know what my brother writes anyway? It's all in English."

"He hears it from Morii-san. His friends ... it doesn't matter. We can't see each other anymore."

"But Julia—"

"No, it's over." Her words had a sense of finality that crushed him as she rose to her feet. Sobbing silently, Julia left Ernie's with Romeo sitting stunned at what was once their table.

All Romeo could do in the days that followed was to mope around, muttering about his lost love. He had no interest in anything around him. Baseball, school, even other girls. His friends tried to snap him out of it. "Hey, Romeo, get a load of Akiko. Ain't she something? I hear she's been looking you over but good in class! What do you say? Give her a tumble?" But nothing worked.

Tommy was sympathetic and knew he couldn't do much to help except to say, "Time heals all wounds." Romeo smiled as if to thank him for that.

He finally took to going over to Julia's house at night to gaze at the light in her window, perhaps to catch a glimpse of her. He stood there every night, even as the nights grew darker and colder.

One day he started smoking, for no particular reason. He just felt like lighting one up. The cigarette did give him some comfort as he stood in the cold. So one night in early December, he shivered with a cigarette hanging out of his mouth and his hands in his jacket pockets in front of Julia's house. The light was on and the lace curtains were drawn. Her silhouette suddenly appeared facing the window. He couldn't move, mesmerized by the shadow. What he thought he heard next was like a dream come true. Yet he couldn't believe it, since it did seem like wishful thinking. Her voice called out his name, once, and not in anger but in a sad, regretful, and yearning way.

There was no time to ponder it further because someone came crashing into Julia's room, complaining loudly in Japanese. Because his parents kept him and his brother away from the Powell Street area, he couldn't understand the meaning, but he did recognize the tone. Her shadow collapsed as Romeo reacted to the sound of a loud slap to the face and a scream.

He automatically raced to the door, opened it, for it was unlocked, and stepped inside. "Julia?" he yelled. "Julia?" He scrambled up the stairs as he heard more angry Japanese.

Romeo turned the corner and approached the front bedroom. As he entered, he smelled stale liquor and found Julia on the floor nursing a cheek with her father towering over her.

"Leave her alone!" Romeo commanded.

Surprised, the judo sensei uttered, "*Nanja*?"

Without thinking, the teenager rammed his body into Sensei Sato.

"Tomeo!" Julia called out. "Stop!"

Even though he was drunk, Sensei Sato quickly recovered from falling against the dresser and grabbed Romeo's arm in a painful lock. Just as quickly, Julia jumped to her feet and pushed against her father with all her might, allowing the captive to get free.

Romeo must have suddenly realized what he was up against—he was a lover, not a fighter after all. The sensei, too, was a black belt, third *dan*. As fast as he could, Romeo fled the room and ran down the flight of stairs to the outside. He disappeared into the muck of night. Sensei Sato, bogged down by his daughter's tight grip and his dizzy head, had no choice but to let the boy go.

No one saw Romeo much after that, though everyone guessed there was some comfort in holding Julia's true feelings in his heart. He was rumoured to have talked to his brother later that night, for the last time. After explaining what had happened, he said to him, "I'm sorry, Tommy, I really put you in it this time. I've got to get out of town for a while."

Tommy smiled his characteristic understanding smile and answered, "Don't worry about me. I suspect if this hadn't happened, there would've been something else to inspire Morii to attack me. Just take care of yourself." The brothers hugged each other and, after Tommy gave Tomeo some money, Tomeo left, stifling his tears.

Morii didn't, in fact, attack Tommy and the *New Canadian.* Never had the chance. Even after World War II and its editor's departure, the *New Canadian* flourished for the next forty to fifty years. Tommy Shoyama himself eventually found work as an economist and rose to great heights in Canadian history: from Tommy Douglas's right-hand man (they became known as the Two Tommys) to deputy minister of finance in the Trudeau government.

Sensei Sato never hit his daughter again, perhaps having learned some kind of lesson that night. Circumstances soon humbled the man in any case. Julia, for her part, married a good man and moved to Montreal about five years later but never forgot Tomeo.

Throughout the rest of their lives, Tommy and Julia each said they were happy, but everyone who knew them saw a sadness in their eyes. Perhaps it was over the reckless but romantic teenager who was lost in the chaos on the Sunday following the confrontation—when Pearl Harbor was attacked on December 7, 1941.

Author Commentary

Midge Ayukawa told me a story about the aunt of a friend of mine who was dying of cancer. Before World War II, the aunt and Tommy Shoyama, future deputy finance minister of Canada, were in love—an ill-advised love. Mr Shoyama was then editor of the *New Canadian,* and the aunt's father was a known associate of Morii, the Black Dragon gangster. Tommy and the aunt knew such a relationship wouldn't survive if discovered, so they sneaked around, meeting in back alleys and dark movie houses. Unfortunately, her father found out and demanded that she end it. She did. I decided to turn it into a short story, changing the facts by adding a fictional brother, Tomeo Shoyama. Many Canadians in the 1930s and 1940s gave nicknames to one another, especially the Nisei. Tomeo becoming Romeo seemed a natural fit in a Japanese-Canadian story about star-crossed lovers. —*Terry Watada, 2015*

About the Author

Terry Watada is a Toronto writer with many titles to his credit. His recent publications include *The Game of 100 Ghosts* (poetry, TSAR, 2014) and *The Sword, the Medal and the Rosary* (manga, HpF Press and NAJC, 2013). His work has been extensively anthologized, most recently in *Vancouver Confidential*, edited by John Belshaw (Anvil Press, 2014). "Light at a Window" has since been expanded for publication as his second manga.

Notes Towards an Essay About Maria Callas

Ricepaper 15, no. 4 (2010)

C. E. Gatchalian

My Journal Entry, April 5, 1994

Homosexuality=shamanism=the chosen=antennae of the world. Further down: *Art points skyward, defies nature, transcends the muck. It is, without question, the highest human faculty.* Anthropology and Camille Paglia nudging a Filipino gay boy toward self-acceptance. The ego consolidation of a newly out sophomore. But despite a newfound Buddhist emphasis on ego-devaluation, those ideas are still with me, still motor my daily existence.

I want to write an essay about Maria Callas, the greatest operatic soprano of the twentieth century. Most modern classical music stars dwell in rarefied peaks, free from the glare of the masses, subjects of esoteric study. Maria Callas was an exception. She was a pre-Stonewall icon, the gay cultural intelligentsia's Judy Garland. To adore Callas in the twenty-first century is to retreat. Regress. Which is why I am writing this essay: to remember a fabled war-torn time. The essay I want to write is about adoration and inertia.

***

La Bohème was my favourite opera once upon a time, but I eventually tired of it, coming to see it as "opera lite." But surfing YouTube two years ago, I happened across an audio recording of Mimi's Act-one aria rendered by Maria Callas, a singer I'd never particularly cared for. Her voice emerges from my laptop—that hard-to-describe, naked sound that has always divided opinion. Two and a half minutes in, the aria swells towards its high point: "Ma quando vien lo sgelo, il primo sole é mio." The simple, virginal Mimi singing of how spring's first kiss is hers. Callas and orchestra in perfect synchronicity as the world, for a moment, lifts the veils from sensuality, and a stodgy, effete art form becomes a container for living truth. I've listened to more renowned Mimis—Tebaldi, Scotto, Stratas—but none achieve the miracle that Callas pulls off. I'm not hyperbolizing when I call my Callas moment one of existential clarity, when my east met my west, when all came to Librium.

So began my personal study—one undertaken, so it seems, by many other gay men—of the life and art of Maria Callas: ugly duckling, musical genius. The narrative of her life, informed by egomania, willpower, metamorphosis, sexual frustration and fulfillment, and, finally, tragedy, is undeniably queer: the lonely outsider who pays the price for professional and personal acceptance. But the most efficient manifestation of her queerness is her art, a masterpiece drawn from imperfection, insecurity, and a bit of hate.

Callas's voice takes me inside myself and out again—the exact opposite of what happens when I listen to a more conventionally beautiful voice. The latter is escapism—a fireworks display from which I return unchanged. The Callas voice is too flawed, too human for escape: The dark, eerie timbre; the ferocious, almost manly, chest tones; the bottled middle register; and the forced and wobbly high notes (especially later in her career) were the musical equivalents of her personal flaws and, in turn, mine. Tito Gobbi christened her "La grande vociaccia"—the Great Ugly Voice—but it was ugliness contained in the most refined and exquisite musicianship. The impeccable diction; the flawless weighing of every note; the silken fioritura; the perfectly placed portamenti—what was great was not the voice but rather what she did with it.

It was, in short, a voice from the closet.

You know the story. He's bullied and ostracized. So the young gay boy retreats to be the best at whatever he's good at. Not the best he can be, but the best, period. Just as society invokes "objective standards" in condemning his burgeoning sexuality, so the young gay boy invokes them in his quest for perfection. Callas attracts a lot of gay men because she's the best, period. And she became the very best despite a bevy of disadvantages: a broken home, a difficult mother, an ungainly figure, and a seemingly untameable voice. In *The Queen's Throat*, his brilliant and now-legendary paean to opera, Wayne Koestenbaum writes, "The listener's body is illuminated, opened up: a singer doesn't expose her own throat, she exposes the listener's interior." When I listen to Callas, every trill, every cadenza becomes a journey out of the dregs, a manifestation of her personal triumphs and, by extension, mine. In her unflinching artistry, I see my own obsessive-compulsive perfectionism; in her astonishing mid-career weight loss, my metamorphosis from willowy geek to musclebound quasi Adonis.

As a young gay boy I was shy and artsy, and while I managed to escape physical bullying, backtalk and exclusion were inevitable. Scholastic excellence was my weapon, as was success as a classical pianist (which lessened the trauma of my teenage years by significantly abridging my school schedule, including exemption from P.E.). Egos that are mutilated eventually balloon, and for most of my life it's been egomania that's gotten me up in the morning, a narcissistic search for vengeance against a world that I was convinced was against me. (Therapy and meditation are doing their job, I'm happy to report.)

I adore Callas because she avenges on my behalf. The Greek-American fat girl-become-svelte prima donna of La Scala. Each diamond-pointed gruppetto, every sweeping arpeggio is an act of revenge against gay bashers, against all who ever crossed me. Indeed, Callas's own words, "We [artists] must whip ourselves into shape like a soldier," and "I would not kill my enemies, but I will make them get down on their knees," suggest a militaristic, score-settling approach to her craft.

Her 1949 career breakthrough was one of the queerest events in twentieth-century opera. While performing Brünnhilde in Wagner's *Die Walküre,* she was asked, on a few days' notice, to fill in for a sick colleague who was to sing Elvira in Bellini's *I Puritani,* a part Callas had never before performed. She opened as Elvira to an incredulous audience. To perform, back-to-back, the heavy verticality of a Wagner opera and the florid horizontalness of a bel canto opera was an unheard of feat—akin, almost, to a skater speed skating one week and figure skating the next. This was Callas at her queerest: doing the unthinkable, defying categories. Breaking the seemingly impenetrable wall between the dramatic repertoire and the coloratura one, Callas—despite her self-declared aesthetic conservatism—was a bona fide postmodern opera star: a convention-busting, boundary-blurring *sui generis.*

There is, also, the curious quality of Callas's sexual persona. There was an affected, contrived quality to her famously genteel way of moving and speaking, a quality undercut by the unaffectedly fierce "masculine" manner in which she approached her work. Unlike her alleged archrival, the musically demure and unthreatening Renata Tebaldi, Callas attacked the music with a decisiveness normally associated with male singers. The end result was a compellingly solipsistic persona: hermaphroditic, self-completing, narcissistic.

And there is the story of Maria, the woman whose nun-like devotion to her calling ended, for all intents and purposes, when she met shady Greek shipping magnate Aristotle Onassis. The virginal high priestess of opera had lived most of her life in her throat; the extraordinarily sexual Onassis opened her up to the rest of her body, a body she'd hated, even when she lost weight, a body that, for most of her life, nobody had ever wanted.

***

My Journal Entry, August 7, 2000

Went the full nine yards, finally. Pure, total blandishment. That a man like D, with his manliness, his Greekness, his swagger, would want me, with my awkwardness, my Filipino-ness, my inexperience. He's a collector, yes; I was willing to be collected. My first real man; he left me a bit more of one.

***

Opera is pre-modern, steeped in the past, home to myth, old-style melodrama, and stereotypical notions of sex and gender. When I embrace opera, I am embracing a world that shunned me, thereby accepting the beast and consequently disembowelling it. If opera remains popular, even outside gaydom, it has little to do with the inner (i. e., plotlines) and almost everything to do with the outer (i. e., the music, the staging).

When gay men love Callas, they are embracing pre-modernism while queering it up royally. For she dragged hidden human truths out of sexist, archaic stories—out of the effete, rococo, centuries-old closet that is opera. Absolute honesty is queer; notions of normalcy are always relative. Callas simultaneously embraced the norms of bel canto singing and broke through them to illuminate the only reality that ultimately counts: human emotion. She was the most profoundly gifted vocal artist of her century, one whose polychromatic voice could encapsulate every nuance and subnuance of feeling. There is no irony in Callas-philia, as there is with Garland-philia or Monroe-philia; when gays align themselves with Callas, they align themselves with greatness. But it is greatness haunted by the omnipresence of the abyss, by intimations of what can and, in Callas's case, did go wrong. The great Callas scholar John Ardoin likens the experience of listening to Callas to watching a trapeze act. Usually there is a net below; but on those rare instances where there is not, a completely different atmosphere is created. "The very being of each spectator seems to be bound up in each step taken on high," says Ardoin, "for there is no longer any semblance of pretence."

Callas's vocal fall was legendary, ugly. Her hard-won artistic victories were Pyrrhic, unequalled greatness for a too-brief time. Pushing her voice beyond its natural Fach, tackling the most technically intimidating repertoire, giving every ounce of herself to each and every performance, she seemed constitutionally incapable of performing with a net. And while this cost Callas her voice (her career was essentially over by age forty-two), it is what gave her singing its abyss-defying, life-and-death intensity. "Singing for me is not an act of pride, but an effort to elevate toward those heavens where everything is harmony," she once said. But she could never escape the abyss—indeed, she seemed always to be staring it down. Her singing, even at its most technically brilliant, never sounded easy the way the vocalizing of her great bel canto rivals Joan Sutherland and Montserrat Caballe did. It always carried with it a knowledge of the fragility of greatness—and of the unspeakable horrors that lurk beneath it.

***

"Death ... the opposite is desire," says Blanche in Tennessee Williams' 1947 masterwork *A Streetcar Named Desire*—a startlingly prophetic précis of the late twentieth-century gay male experience, defined as it was by the polarities of erotic fulfillment and deadly disease. Physical love, in the face of sordid, mythopoeic-laden fatality, became even more intense, more transcendent—an act of ecstatic defiance against the ever-present threat of death.

Indeed, early death is the final italicization of gay-icon status. Callas died at age fifty-three in her Paris apartment, *sola, perduta, abbandonata*. Onassis, the love of her life, had left her for Jackie Kennedy, and Callas's final world tour betrayed a voice in irrevocable ruins. From *la dolce vita* and unprecedented heights of operatic artistry she had come to this: a recluse wasting away on Quaaludes and memories of a once-glorious voice. Apparently, on her deathbed she had never looked lovelier or more immaculate: undimmed beauty even in her darkest moment. As it was will that allowed her to achieve artistic greatness and physical beauty, it was will that propelled her to her early, quiet death—if not technically a suicide, then a perfectly paced winding down. To die beautiful and young is in concord with gaydom's cult of youth, with that familiar refrain of the vain club bunny, "Who wants to die an old queen?"

La grande vociaccia. The ugly voice became the instrument of the century's most sublime operatic expression. To mould beauty out of ugliness is the queerest of acts. From the channelling of deviancy into the creation of polychrome frescoes, to the transmuting of HIV-positive statuses into marks of desirability, gay men are often expert alchemists, reliant on magic to survive. In the magic of Callas's music, we see the sanctioned version of our own all-too-private narratives, our own tortuous, ferociously willed ascents to greatness. Whether these ascents are actualized or merely dreamt of is moot; Callas reminds us that, no matter how brilliant we make ourselves or how accessible become the corridors of power, disaster is always just a stone's throw away.

***

Alas, these are only notes towards an essay. To actually write one would be to regress completely to an age of masks, when passion was sublimated, when brilliance was borne of suffering. When we revered the likes of Callas because there was no out-and-proud icon to revere. When we fed off heteronormativity and built a parasitic culture out of parody and pastiche.

To align with Callas is to align with pre-Stonewall gays, the closet-dwelling, aesthetic types gays my age were supposed to have left behind. But I am attracted to the closet; cannot and will not leave it completely. For in it survive narratives whose universality not even postmodernism, with its rejection of the universal, can wish away. Narratives that will remain relevant as long as gays are a numerical anomaly. A space of shared experiences from which emerges the beautiful.

These love notes to Callas, then, are love notes to the closet, a place that inhibited action but that ignited imagination. Where unassuaged pain and suffering were catalysts for great art. Where a voice as queer as Maria Callas's could be called beautiful.

"Notes Towards an Essay About Maria Callas" is part of a book-in-progress about literature, art, popular culture, and gay male sensibility.

Author Commentary

Maria Callas was, arguably, the greatest opera singer of the twentieth century. Her narrative was of particular interest to pre-Stonewall gay men—she was, as I call her in this essay, "the gay cultural intelligentsia's Judy Garland." My own attraction to her as a post-Stonewall queer preceded any real knowledge of her status as a gay icon, so I began to wonder what continues to make her such a magnet for gay men. As I progressed through the essay, it became as much an exploration—and celebration—of pre-Stonewall gay male culture as a tribute to Callas and her enduring art.

—C. E. Gatchalian, 2015

About the Author

Born, raised, and based in Vancouver, Filipino-Canadian author C. E. Gatchalian writes drama, poetry, fiction, and nonfiction. An alumnus of the University of British Columbia's creative writing program (BFA, 1996; MFA, 2002), his plays, which include *Broken, Crossing, Claire,* and *Motifs & Repetitions,* have appeared on stages nationally and internationally, as well as on radio and television. He is the 2013 recipient of the prestigious Dayne Ogilvie Prize, awarded annually by The Writers' Trust of Canada to an LGBT writer of merit. He is currently artistic producer of frank theatre company and an adjunct professor at the University of British Columbia.

Gently to Nagasaki

Ricepaper 19, no. 2 (2014)

Joy Kogawa

For well over a decade, *Gently to Nagasaki* was a title without a book, tenacious and puzzling, a peg on the bathroom door with no garment hanging from it. In the past, it was the other way around. Books were finished, handed over, and still—no title.

Why *Gently*? Why *Nagasaki*?

In the late 1970s, I finished a draft of a semi-autobiographical novel. The book had no title, and in the end the title used was not one I thought up. *Obasan.*

For the most part, what happened to the fictional family was what happened to mine. We ended up on the prairies. But throughout the story was a mystery. A young mother had gone to Japan before the war and disappeared there. This was entirely fictional. My real mother never left.

"What happened to the mother?" the publisher who finally accepted the book asked.

"I don't know. I think she vanished," I said. "Isn't life like that? People disappear. Isn't that what happens in real life?"

"The reader has to know, Joy," the publisher said.

I took the book back into myself. The answer to the mystery arrived, mysteriously enough, and inserted itself as a clue at the beginning.

August 9.

That is the day the atom bomb was dropped on Nagasaki. That is where the missing young mother was in 1945. But where that answer came from, I have no idea. It was not a city about which I knew anything, except that it had been bombed.

On my way, these many years later, *Gently to Nagasaki,* I have come to understand that there is a specific lesson I am to learn. The lesson is this: every enemy is a beloved friend.

That treasure is in the midst of the devastation known as Nagasaki. An incomprehensible joy existed in Dr Takashi Nagai, Dean of Radiology at the University of Nagasaki. His story came to me via a thin paperback, *A Song for Nagasaki* by Paul Glynn given to me by a stranger, decades ago in Tokyo.

The book remained untouched in one bookshelf after another following many moves. When I finally did read it, I came to a swamp fire in the firmament, an inverted sky.

For many, the shape of the mushroom cloud over Nagasaki was a grotesque question mark. For Dr Takashi Nagai, it was a hell full of holiness and hope, of immense challenge and immense faithfulness.

What struck me with some fascination was the significance for Christians of August 6 and August 9, the two dates the atom bombs fell on Japan. The first, Hiroshima Day, was called in Christian calendars the Day of Transfiguration. On that day, Jesus went up a mountain with his three closest disciples, Peter, James, and John. While the three looked up in fear, Elijah and Moses, the prophet and the lawgiver, appeared on either side of Jesus, whose form had become "exceeding white." Mark 9:3 ... *and his garments became glistering, exceeding white* ... The man who healed the sick, restored the sight of the blind, and made the deaf to hear, the man from Galilee, was "transfigured." The light within him was, for a moment, made visible on the outside.

So it was that on the day commemorating Christ's transfiguration, the city and citizens of Hiroshima were obliterated. A little boy looked up and saw a white parachute against the sky. "Look at the parachute!" he cried just before a bright "glistering" light of death like no other flashed upon the world and changed us forever.

My brother, a retired Episcopalian priest in Seattle, told me that the word "transfiguration" in Japanese, *hen-yo-bo,* also meant "disfiguration." The Day of Transfiguration became then, on August 6, 1945, the Day of Disfiguration. This one word with two meanings and the two events on the same day merged in my mind. The transfigured one was disfigured. The disfigured one was transfigured.

For centuries, until about forty years ago, the story of the transfiguration was read on a Sunday that was followed three days after by Ash Wednesday, a day of fasting and penitence. The Day of Trans/Disfiguration in 1945 was followed, three days later, by an unparalleled day of ashes. The second bomb fell on August 9 with pinpoint precision, directly over the pre-eminent spot of Christianity in all of East Asia.

If ever the Christian west had friends in Japan, it was there, in a valley between mountains. That sacred place, the Urakami neighbourhood in Nagasaki, was home to Japan's Hidden Christians, a people who had survived the most grotesque tortures and martyrdoms. The surviving remnant had come home from exile at last, to safety, to their neighbourhood, and to the finally tolerated practice of their faith. There they worked in the fields as farmers and re-built their lives. The Christians that Japan failed to annihilate after two-and-a-half centuries of unimaginable cruelty, the Christian west managed to do in an instant.

"Were not these the most holy, the most tested of God's children?" Dr. Nagai asked.

An anthropologist friend, Stuart Philpott, told me that what makes humans unique is not that we use tools—other animals do that—nor that we have language—that too is an attribute of other animals—but that we are creatures who seek meaning. For many people, particularly following the Holocaust in Europe, the search for meaning is heinous. The answer to the question of meaning is that there is no meaning.

But I cannot accept meaninglessness as an answer to Nagasaki. For me, that incomprehensible event on August 9, 1945, the immolation by the Christian west of its best friends in Asia, means that a certain truth has been made starkly visible. It provides the moment for recognizing what lies behind the words of Jesus Christ. At Nagasaki, the impossible proscription, "Love your enemy" is transformed into a description, "You love your enemy." We no longer have to love the enemy. All we have to do is to realize that we already do.

The task for me then, the arduous but happy task, is to recognize this. For the rest of my life, what is required is to discover the ways in which this is true. If I move by thought or word or deed to defeat or deface an enemy, I am acting to harm a beloved friend, one who is of greatest value and to whom I owe deep loyalty. I am enjoined to go to my inner Nagasaki, by foot, by train, by air, by sea, by thought, by word, and by deed.

The Goddess of Mercy is there in Japan the beautiful, Japan the terrible, Japan the country of my ancestors. Although I fail Her lessons again and again, She teaches me patiently that the enemy is not an enemy. It is Her presence I attend as She leads the way gently, to the place where the sacred children of the Hidden Christians died begging for water.

Water, my Goddess. *Omizu kudasai*!

Dear Hiroshima Maidens disfigured on August 6, dear nuns at prayer in Urakami Cathedral on the day of ash, dear Friend who granted living water and who died saying, "I thirst," assist, I pray, the faltering feet of an old woman on her way to Mercy's throne.

***

The following two excerpts are published here for the first time.

Water (Prologue from *Gently to Nagasaki,* a work-in-progress)
If I could follow the stream down and down to the hidden voice, would I come at last to the freeing word? —from the prologue to *Obasan*

It is through water that the freeing word arrives. In the darkest light before dawn, the hidden voice comes to us, in the deepest light before dawn. God, Goddess, named and nameless, Avalokitesvera, Kwan Yin, Kannon, the Compassionate One, She who heeds the wailing in a world of weeping, comes to us.

Dancing the transition between moon and morning, and robed in the whiteness of clouds, She comes to us, a rider of the vast turtle that roams the eastern depths. Down and down She swims in our small sacs of fluid to the breath surrounding this blue-green planet. We hear her song as sunlight in the new day rising, in the first call of the first creatures, the orchestrators of waking.

I am with you, She sings. I am with you through the water, under the water, in the birthing, in the forgetting, in the terror and at the heart of what you most fear, I am with you. Through the long dark night of every absence, I am with you, therefore fear not.

***

Chapter Twenty-Seven

My mother, profoundly deaf and senile, died in 1987, aged ninety. Her last years were hallowed. People came as pilgrims to drink in the light.

Dad wrote *A Flower in the Shade—Memoir of Lois Masui Nakayama,* as his act of ongoing devotion to the woman he esteemed and in the end served. I wrote, in the preface, of my reverence for them both. I feel it still.

But it was not always so. My mother, the one who could do no wrong, had her limits. She was trapped in a vortex of anguish. In Coaldale I struggled to escape the unrelenting severity, the interminable lectures. I sat at the piano weeping, as practice became punishment. In the battle of wills, she was immoveable. I didn't know I was being required to carry a load she could not carry alone.

As an adolescent in the flat lands, I believed we were all nobodies. Less than nobodies. Especially my mother. I was wrong. We were not nobodies. Especially my mother. But thanks to her excessive humility, I never knew how exceptional she was.

She arrived in Canada, aged twenty-six, after years as Director of Kindergartens and had been honoured for her work by the premier of the prefecture. This is in Dad's one-page "Brief Biography" of her, my not-nobody Mama.

Her childhood was traumatic. Her parents separated. At age four, she was in an orphanage, which led to life-long loneliness, years of bed-wetting, and an inability to receive gifts.

Her mother came to her in the orphanage with a gift. This embodiment of love was torn from her the next day by her enraged father. Loss entered her as a permanent marker, and gifts thereafter became too terrible to receive.

She carried her parents' pain faithfully for the rest of her life.

Children do this for their parents. In Coaldale, I bought her a cheap unpainted chest of drawers with my first pay-cheque as a teacher. After they moved back to Vancouver, she, who rarely spoke, who asked for nothing, said, *Hoshi.* I want. She wanted that nondescript chest of drawers back. That one. Not the others. Not another new one. That one.

Oh take not from me what Love has given me.

She asked for it over and over and over. A water-drip torture.

She attended a special school for exceptionally intelligent children. She lived in a hostel run by English missionaries and was the only one rewarded with higher education. This, she believed, was because she spoke truth, this most vaunted of western values. The moral trajectory of her life was set by missionaries of the Church of England. She became truthful in the samurai way, unto death, without wavering. She had the determination and fortitude of magma.

"*Wherefore putting away lying, speak every man truth with his neighbour ...*" This quote from Ephesians was underlined in red in her big print Bible.

Another of her underlinings from Philippians ... "*in lowliness of mind* (she underscored this phrase twice) *let each esteem others better than themselves.*"

Oh that weighty *lowliness of mind.* I'd come home from school to find her at the kitchen table, Bible open. In silence. In prayer. I did not want any of this. I sought a house of laughter. I longed for my vibrant father who was away and away.

She must have struggled to esteem others better than herself. She dunned it into me. She praised me for nothing.

Except for Sundays, she had stopped caring what she wore and she was, to my eyes, not in the least attractive, apart from lovely fair skin, which she patted with powder. I was startled one day when I overheard a Caucasian woman say, "Oh, but isn't she beautiful!"

What? My mother was beautiful?

They were opposites, Mom and Dad. He was sunshine and rain. She was rock. In the torment of our family's shame, she went underground. She took me with her.

For the rest of her life, I could not bear her density. But after her death, in the winter of 2009 in Marpole, I returned to her. The mother of my childhood.

The last day I saw her was in their cluttered house in Vancouver's east end. Although she recognized almost no one, she knew me. I would bend close to her and suddenly there would be her sweet, sweet smile.

Dad used to say she was *fukai*, a person of depth. Now she was *kawai*, cute and sweet. One of the best things from old Japan is tenderness for the very young and the very old. He was with her all the time unless he was out shopping. Most days he sat, back hunched, right forefinger stabbing, clack clack, at the keys of his typewriter on an up-ended apple box in a corner of the dining room. Huge paper clips hung from nails on the outside of the box, with church records, mailing addresses. He served guests his specialty, *ohagi*, sweet azuki beans on small balls of sticky rice. He kept his connections to the end. But most of all, he was devoted to his wife.

She, who had served him, was in the end, served by him. The measure of a good life, I'm told, is the way it ends. Hers was a good ending. Dad took complete care of her for years. He cut up her grapefruit in the morning, blended the lunch *okazu* into a soupy mush, brushed her thinning hair, encouraged her to say a few words.

He changed her, dressed her, sang to her. He would tell me about little improvements in her memory. He would sit on the couch, holding her hand, his mouth to her ear. His voice was youthful. Deep and rich. She would sing with him. Soprano, clear and pure once. Croaky finally.

"Do you know what's happening today, Mama?" I shouted in her ear. She was not able to manage hearing aids. "Do you know that I'm going back to Toronto today?"

She turned on the couch where she sat most of the time, her body stiffly facing me, her eyes drinking in whatever I was doing. "I am connected to you," her eyes said. "I know who you are."

She was wearing one of her white sweaters, a necklace, and slacks. Dad changed what she wore every day. They had two beds side by side in his study. Many nights he could not sleep, he said, as she did not know night from day. He held her hand as they walked together from room to room.

She gazed up at me, her demeanor, as always, to the very last, dignified, her back as straight as she could manage. Even in that day before she died, she struggled to maintain her dignity. She was lucid as a dewdrop for a moment.

"Nozomi?" Her face was lit with love. "Nozomi?"

As a child I disliked the z sound in my Japanese name. Z for snoring or for sawing wood. The red zig zag across the comic book page.

"Toronto *ni iku no*?" Are you going to Toronto?

"I'll be back soon." I had no idea at the time how soon that would be.

She gazed up at me through cloudy eyes and told me she was now living in *tengoku,* in heaven. She was already in eternal life. Then she broke into an uncontrollable laugh, her almost translucent hand holding back her ill-fitting false teeth.

"Is something funny?"

"*Nannimo okashi kunai.* No. Nothing funny at all." She shook in spasms of giggles.

"Then why are you laughing?"

"I don't know." More giggles.

She choked the next morning on a piece of toast and peanut butter. Mama, my truth-loving mother, who played the organ and sang, who patched the sheets and patched the patches on the sheets, whose silence was patched over everything, was dead. Dad had gone downstairs "for just five minutes," to deliver some mail to the tenant in the basement. When he returned, she was on the floor. She was still breathing. Her last moments on earth were spent in her husband's arms while he pleaded with her not to die.

In my dream, heaven welcomed her, with singing, with dancing. But she was already in *tengoku,* she'd said. She was surrounded every day by heaven's kindness and the transition must have been seamless. The depth of forgiveness between Dad and Mama was my introduction to the infinite light.

About the Author

Joy Kogawa is the author of *Obasan,* one of the handful of Canadian novels that have become essential reading for a nation. Interned with her Japanese-Canadian family during World War II, she has worked tirelessly to educate and help redress a dark moment in our history. She is a member of the Order of Canada and a member of the Order of the Rising Sun in Japan. A book of her selected poems, *A Garden of Anchors,* was published in 2003. Kogawa has been working on *Gently to Nagasaki* for many years. She divides her time between Toronto and Vancouver.

Finding My Way Back Home

Ricepaper 19, no. 3 (2014)

Lou Villahermosa

My grandfather, Lolo, had a fascination for balete trees. This fascination stemmed from the belief that they are known to house supernatural beings in the Philippines. He took pleasure in telling us stories about the tree, to the point where we weren't quite sure what he enjoyed most—narrating these mysterious stories or seeing the wonder and terror in our eyes as he related these tales. Nevertheless, despite the fear we felt as our imaginations ran wild, we loved it. We were terrified, yet enchanted.

During my vacation back to the Philippines, it didn't come as a surprise when my dad pointed out, "Your Lolo planted that balete tree." It was a healthy sapling, standing no more than five feet in height, its roots firmly attached to a bending, tall coconut tree.

"Typical," I chuckled. "Of all things, of course Lolo would plant a balete tree."

My dad looked at me and laughed knowingly. Balete, or banyan trees, are common in the Philippines. Belonging to the fig family, a balete begins life as an epiphyte, growing nonparasitically on another plant, like some species of orchids, which take their nutrients from the surrounding environment and not directly from the host. But despite the similarity, balete trees are far less dainty than orchids—they are massive, bulky, and gnarly.

Growing fifty to sixty metres tall, the diameter of these great trees could easily extend to ten metres wide. Long, aerial, tentacle-like roots hang from every branch, extending in varying lengths toward one direction—down. When these roots touch the ground, they support the tree and gradually integrate to the main trunk, thereby encircling, entangling, and suffocating the host tree from which they grow, slowly killing it off.

The very notion of overpowering and killing its host is enough to unsettle anyone. But the notoriety as a dwelling for the *dili ingon nato* ("not like us," in Bisaya) was the very thing that made us wary of this tree. As a kid, Lolo took great lengths to tell us stories about the dili ingon nato that lived in the shadows and crevices atop and behind the long hanging roots of the balete tree. He enraptured our imaginations with *duwende* (dwarves), *diwata* (fairies), and other creatures.

He particularly enjoyed telling us about the towering dark creatures who resembled huge apes and smoked cigars, all the while playing tricks on people, causing them to lose their way. Lolo told us that the tall smoking creatures are called *kapre* and, according to local folklore, they were not always evil. They were capable of friendship and love for women. But as a little girl, that information didn't give me the slightest comfort.

Similar to kapre, the *tikbalang* is also known to lead travelling people astray. A tikbalang, a creature whose head and feet resemble that of a horse and its torso that of a human, lives in trees deep in the forests and mountains.

The only way to find your way when a tikbalang has released its magic is to wear your shirt inside out. To this day, I'm not quite sure how reversing your shirt can thwart off magic, but according to local folklore, it does.

My superstitious grandparents taught us the ways to evade the magic of these supernatural beings. During weekends and summer vacations, my siblings, cousins, and I would play and climb trees from noon to night. Lolo would always warn us to say "*tabi tabi, po*" when walking at night. *Tabi tabi, po* means "please move aside." Ending the sentence with "po" is typically used when speaking to elders and exhibits the deep respect that needed to be shown to the dili ingon nato. This allowed us to safely pass the creatures that frolicked in the dark and avoid their wrath (which some were very fond of exhibiting).

However, there were evenings when whispering *tabi tabi, po* was not enough to assure ourselves, when my cousins and I were feeling particularly eerie. We avoided the balete tree altogether. Every time we came across one, we would walk at least five feet from the tree and scurry away as fast as our scrawny legs could carry us. One of my cousins used to say that if we came too close, the roots would reach out and pull us inside the tree, where all the dili ingon nato could feast on our little bodies.

My imagination wasn't as gory. To me, the long roots were reminiscent of a heavy curtain hiding the magic that lived inside the balete tree. As a kid, I never had the courage to pull those curtains aside and see what lay behind those roots. My fear was stronger than my curiosity.

Nearing the end of my vacation, I took a walk with my dog and stumbled upon a fully grown balete tree. True to the image in my memory, the tree stood in its immensity—massive and haunting. I hesitated to approach it, as my wild imagination pictured me being wrapped in roots while a myriad of dili ingon nato jumped out of the shadows. Oh, that would've been the end of me!

But before my legs could run in comic speed at the very thought,

I reached out to touch the thick roots that hung from one of the wide-ranging branches and squeezed it.

"This is real," I thought to myself as I measured the width of my wrist against the width of the root, finding some quantitative way to measure my own reality with the tree. The root was solid to the touch and slightly bigger than my wrist. But despite the connection and the measurement of what was real, I couldn't help but still feel awed by the immensity and life of this tree. After all, it survived my grandfather.

Lolo passed away last year. There was nothing more the doctors could do as the cancer spread and took over his health. His frail body battled for his life as the cancer advanced, slowly but surely—eventually killing its host, my beloved grandfather.

As I walked back, I looked out for signs of smoke atop the balete tree, ensuring that no kapre or tikbalang was sitting on its branch, hoping that none would release its magic and make me lose my way home. Then I realized I had nothing to worry about—I was already home.

Author Commentary

This piece was written with fondness for both my grandparents. As noted in this story, inspiration arose when I went back to the Philippines and noticed the balete tree that was planted by my grandfather. It was interesting how one object or, in this case, one tree, can open up a chest full of stories. Like opening Pandora's box, my grandparents' superstitious tales of balete trees, tikbalang, diwata, and all other dili ingon nato jumped out at me—waiting to be written. —*Lou Villahermosa, 2015*

About the Author

Born and raised in the Philippines, Lou Villahermosa moved to Canada for her undergraduate degree and now lives in Vancouver. When she isn't working downtown or reading by the beach, she is studying for school to complete her postgraduate degree in intercultural and international communication.

Fiction

It Came to Eat Our Chicken Wings

Ricepaper 8, no. 1 (2002)

Derwin Mak

Her friends thought her uniform looked silly: tight little orange shorts, white tank top with a picture of an owl, shiny beige pantyhose, and white running shoes. Her father wondered what type of restaurant would publish a swimsuit calendar of its waitresses. But despite the raised eyebrows of friends and family, Kyra Ling liked working at Hooters. At least she made more money serving beer and chicken wings than she had pushing a dim sum cart.

However, there were moments when the job seemed distinctly unglamorous, like this moment, when the two college frat boys were lolling their heads, nearly unconscious.

The guy in the Cocoa Beach University golf shirt shook his buddy's shoulder as she passed by. "Hey," he yelled to Kyra. "My friend thinks Asian girls are hot."

Kyra smiled. How could she get these two drunks out? "Thanks," she replied. "Do you guys want a coffee?"

His buddy drooled as he leered at her. "I'm looking for a geisha."

Kyra shrugged. "Go to Japan."

The student was unfazed. "So do you speak Asian?"

Kyra's lips curled into a bemused grin.

"*Non, mais je parle anglais, français, et un peu de chinois,*" she replied.

The student didn't give up. "So can you teach it to me? It's one of those languages that's best taught by a ..." he mumbled before he slumped over the table.

Kyra tapped him on the shoulder.

"I think you're done." She handed the cheque to his friend. "Here's the tab."

"Oh, sure," the frat boy said as he handed her a fifty dollar bill.

Kyra took the money and pushed the change into his shirt pocket. "We better get you into a cab. Don't drive, okay?"

"Sure thing," he muttered.

Kyra motioned to Maria, the manager. They walked the two frat boys out the door and into a cab. When they returned into the restaurant, the regular customers burst into applause. Kyra curtsied to the audience.

Maria laughed. "That was great. You should negotiate the Middle East peace treaty."

"Get out," Kyra teased. "Did you hear those two morons? 'I'm looking for a geisha.' I bet he doesn't know what a geisha really is. Is that all these guys think about when they see an Asian woman?"

"You, Kyra dear, can be a lot of things," Maria suggested as she gave a bag of chicken wings to her. "You and Nicole can munch on these. Brandy called in sick, and Nicole's at the car show alone, so you can stay there and work at the booth."

"Cool, my first promo." Kyra retouched her lipstick. "How do I look?"

"You look fabulous. Don't keep fussing. It's only a promo, not a calendar shoot," Maria reminded her. "Actually, it can be fun. Come on, get going, or you'll be late."

Kyra hopped into her red convertible, threw the bag of chicken wings into the backseat, and drove onto the highways around Cocoa Beach, Florida. With clear weather and no traffic jams, she should be at the convention centre in no time.

Then she saw a bright light in the sky. A shiny, silvery object, engulfed in red flames, was falling to the Earth.

"Oh my God, is that a crashing plane?" she wondered. The object plummeted steadily until it disappeared into the horizon. The sound of a crash boomed in the distance. Curious about the object, she sped ahead.

A mile later, she stopped her car, walked on to the side of the road, and looked at a nearby swamp, her eyes widening with awe. A cylinder, like a grain silo about thirty feet long, lay at the edge of the swamp. Its silver surface was charred black in spots, and it had a few dents and creases, but it seemed mostly undamaged. Steam rose from the water surrounding the cylinder, but the fire was out.

She looked up and scanned the sky. It was blue and cloudless, quiet and peaceful. No storm or hurricane had brought this thing down.

Lowering her gaze back to Earth, she looked at the swamp again. She stood still for a long time, staring at the shiny, steaming cylinder.

A vehicle screeched to a halt behind her. She spun around and saw a NASA van beside her car. Workers holding cameras and equipment jumped out of the van, ran into the swamp, and waded towards the object.

"What is it?" she asked a man whose badge read: John Evans. Recovery Team Leader.

"I don't know," Evans admitted. "It doesn't look like one of ours or a Russian or a Chinese or any other country's."

"It doesn't have any markings," a recovery worker yelled from the swamp. Evans gasped.

"Darn, maybe it's somebody's secret weapon! Get out of there!"

"It's okay, it's okay," the recovery worker reported. "Nothing—no radiation, no biological or chemical contaminant—is registering on our equipment."

"It was on fire on the way down," Kyra observed.

"That was probably the surface burning as it entered our atmosphere," said Evans. "Thank goodness it fell in the water. If it had fallen on trees or grass, the whole countryside could be on fire now."

He pulled out his notebook and glanced at Kyra's Hooters name badge. "Uh, Kyra? May I ask you some questions? Did you see the spacecraft come down?"

The spacecraft. The NASA guy had called it a spacecraft. But it wasn't from any country in the world. "Maybe it was from beyond this world," thought Kyra.

She told him about the fire in the sky, the spaceship's constant speed of descent, and the sound of the crash.

Then she remembered the chicken wings in the backseat of her car. "Oh dear, the car show," she muttered. "I am so late for the car show. And I have chicken wings for Nicole. Can I go now?"

"Sure, and thank you," said Evans.

Kyra smiled, ran back to her car, and drove off. A few minutes later, a recovery worker pointed out the open hatch to Evans. "Someone was flying this ship," Evans guessed as he looked into the ship. "There's no one inside the ship. Where's the astronaut?" he asked. Nobody knew.

"Hey, look at this," cried Dr Steve Potter, the biologist.

Evans walked back to the side of the road. Potter led him along a streak of blue liquid that stretched from the swamp to a stand of trees, to a pair of tire tracks in the mud. The tire tracks were where Kyra had parked her car.

"What could that be?" asked Evans. "Mechanical fluid from the spacecraft?" Potter shrugged. "I dunno. I'll take a sample back and analyze it."

"Whatever it is, someone dripped it on a path from the swamp to the Hooters Girl's car," said Evans. "I hope she's not taking more than chicken wings to the car show."

"You're late," Nicole complained. She moved away from the racing car emblazoned with the orange and white Hooters logo on its hood. "What took you so long?"

"I saw a spaceship crash beside the highway," Kyra squealed. "It was so exciting. I think it was alien."

"As if," Nicole replied. She pointed at a stack of posters of the contestants of the Miss Hooters of East Central Florida bikini pageant. "Come on, help me hand out posters to horny car show fans."

Nicole sat down and began autographing the posters, which showed her flipping her blonde hair while posing in a pink bikini. She signed each poster, "Breast wishes, Nicole XOXO," before handing it with a smile to the next guy in a lineup of car aficionados.

As Kyra passed another poster to Nicole, a teenager asked her, "Are you in the poster too?"

"No," said Kyra. "But I'm on the coupon for ten free chicken wings." She handed a coupon to him. "Do you want one?"

"Awesome," said the kid. "Uh, can you sign it?"

Kyra signed it "Hugs and hooters, Kyra" and gave it back to the teenager. As he walked off, she turned to Nicole. "Don't you love it when you can make the day of a fifteen-year-old kid because he's seen a Hooters Girl?"

Nicole laughed. "Sure, love it. Hey, I think those guys want to take a photo of us."

The car show promo continued: handing out posters, posing for photos, and selling the swimsuit calendar. A newspaper photographer took a photo of Kyra reclining on the hood of the Hooters racing car.

During a lull in the show, Kyra began eating the chicken wings. "So, Nicole, are you going to continue your modelling?"

"Oh, yes," said Nicole as she reached for a wing. "I did a shoot for a travel magazine: Clothes for Hiking in Theme Parks."

"That's great!"

"And what about you? Still thinking of the State Department?"

"Yep. I figure when I get a degree in languages, I can get a job as an interpreter. Who knows, I might even get to work in an embassy in some place like Paris or London."

"Our little Kyra, in the diplomatic corps, talking to foreign VIPs," mused Nicole. "You can do it, girl."

Potter held the beaker of blue liquid up to the light. "Interesting stuff."

"What is it?" Evans asked.

"It's not mechanical fluid, that's for sure," said Potter. "It's biological; it has DNA."

"It has DNA? You mean it's from somebody's body?"

"Not somebody. Something. It has amino acids, but it's not human. I think it's something's blood."

"Blood? What animal on Earth has blue blood?"

Potter hummed. "Perhaps it's not from Earth."

Kyra and Nicole couldn't help but notice the babbling in the exhibit hall had suddenly grown louder.

"What's going on?" asked Kyra, staring at the crowd forming near the vintage Mustangs.

Suddenly, a creature stomped out from the crowd. Bellowing like an elephant, it waved its arms around. It walked upright on two legs and was the size of a man, but it wasn't human; it was a green reptile wearing a torn silver spacesuit. Its bulging eyes looked around.

"What's he trying to promote?" Nicole wondered.

"I don't think he's advertising anything. I think it's an alien, the outer space type," said Kyra. "But it seems harmless, like an overgrown iguana."

"Hey, look, I think it's bleeding blue blood," Nicole observed. "That spot on its upper arm."

"Godzilla! Godzilla!" a boy shouted. Squealing with delight, he ran to the alien, threw his arms around it, and hugged it. As he jumped up and down excitedly, he hit the alien's bleeding wound.

The alien growled and quickly pushed the boy away. Seconds later, jets of flames burst forth from the alien's head, arms, and parts not covered by the torn spacesuit.

Screams of panic filled the air. As people stampeded past them, Kyra and Nicole watched the alien run from car to car.

"There's gas and oil in those cars," Nicole realized.

"He could blow up the place," Kyra said excitedly. "We have to stop it, but how?" She saw a fire extinguisher hanging on the wall. "Why don't we use the fire extinguisher?"

"Good idea, but look at the thing," Nicole said as they pulled the fire extinguisher from the wall. "It's running around. How do we make it stay still long enough to spray it?"

Kyra glanced at the alien. "I've got an idea. I'll get its attention, and when it's standing still, you sneak up behind it and spray it."

"It's a plan," Nicole agreed.

Kyra poured the rest of the chicken wings onto a tray. Swaying her hips, she strutted up to the alien. "Hey, have you eaten yet?" she cooed the traditional Chinese greeting in Cantonese.

The alien stood still, looked down at Kyra, and reached for a wing. Kyra flinched as she felt the heat from the flames, but she held out the tray and smiled.

Still on fire, the alien began devouring the chicken wings, bones and all. Kyra kept smiling; in the corner of her eye, she could see Nicole sneaking up with the fire extinguisher. Without any warning, she blasted foam all over it, putting out the flames.

The alien roared, turned around, and threw foam on Nicole, then on Kyra.

Kyra brushed it off her hair. "You can have all the chicken wings you want, but you've gotta show some table manners!" she scolded.

The alien looked down at her and said, "Okay."

Kyra's eyes widened in surprise. "You speak English?"

Fifteen minutes later, NASA scientists and police officers stormed into the convention centre. The place looked empty, as the crowds had run away in panic.

"We heard there was a monster," shouted a police officer. "Where is it? Is anybody here?"

"We're over here," came a reply from the Hooters booth.

They went to the Hooters booth and found the big iguana eating chicken wings as the two Hooters Girls watched.

The police officers drew their pistols and pointed them at the alien. Kyra waved her hand at the guns dismissively. "Guys, you don't need the guns," she said. "We've negotiated an interstellar ceasefire here."

"A first-contact situation," Potter marvelled. "You're obviously feeding it. Does it need anything else from us?"

"Yes, he does," Kyra said. "Can you give this guy a lift back to his spaceship?"

The alien ship, a little dented and charred from its trip to Earth, blasted off from Kennedy Space Center. Kyra, Nicole, Evans, and Potter watched the ship disappear into the sky.

"Our first contact with an alien species, and it came here to eat our chicken wings," Evans said, shaking his head. "Unbelievable."

"It's actually quite believable," said Kyra. "Our TV transmissions have been going into space for years. He saw our commercial and decided to drop in and try our wings."

"And thus American consumerism paved the way for interstellar diplomacy," Nicole added.

"An amazing species," Potter remarked. "Even on its own world, it's the only species that can inflame itself to protect a wound from infection."

Kyra nodded. "Its fire wasn't intended to hurt us. It was intended to heal that nasty cut he got when his spaceship landed."

"You called it *he* early on," Evans remarked. "How did you know it was a male alien?"

Kyra and Nicole giggled. "He did what every male tourist to Florida does at Hooters," Kyra explained. "He took photos of us."

Aboard his spaceship, Argon put the chicken wings into the cryogenic suspension chamber and wandered back to the control room. He looked at the photograph of himself between the two smiling Hooters Girls, evidence of contact with the inhabitants of the blue planet. Finally, all those years of learning their language from their television signals had paid off. At the next song festival, the Science Academy would sing his praises.

He would have to visit Planet Florida again, if only to try the cheese burrito.

Author Commentary

I got the idea for this story during my travels to science fiction conventions in the US. There was a Hooters near each convention centre, and like many guys, I liked the fast, friendly service. Carl Hiaasen had used a Hooters Girl as a character in his novel *Lucky You,* and so I wrote my own tribute to the delightfully tacky, yet unrefined restaurant chain.

Some plot events came from the real lives of Hooters Girls whom I knew: going to a car show, autographing posters, and posing for photos for the customers. Other plot events came from science fiction stories; the crashed alien spaceship whose crew sneaks away is an old genre trope. Movie monster Godzilla inspired the lizard-like appearance and elephant-like bellowing of Argon. The name Argon came from the title of "The Eye of Argon" by Jim Theis, the worst fantasy story ever written. The name Kyra came from Olivia Newton-John's character in the movie *Xanadu.* Some day, I will write a sequel in which Argon returns to Earth for a cheese burrito. *—Derwin Mak, 2015*

About the Author

Derwin Mak lives in Toronto. His short story "Transubstantiation" won the Aurora Award, Canada's national science fiction award, for Best Short Form Work in English in 2006. He and Eric Choi co-edited *The Dragon and the Stars* (DAW Books, 2010), the first anthology of science fiction and fantasy by overseas Chinese. It won the 2011 Aurora Award for Best Related Work in English. His two novels are *The Moon Under Her Feet* and *The Shrine of the Siren Stone,* now republished by Weird and Wondrous Press.

Mercury, Messenger of the Gods

Ricepaper 18, no. 1 (2013)

Kim Fu

When you were seven, you talked to God as you walked to school. You had trouble explaining this later: that you didn't pray out of hope or obligation or thanks or fear. He was your friend. You read the Bible alone, on the floor, for hours with the slivered pages. Early on, you asked your mother about the God of Abraham and the God of Nahor. Were these multiple gods, different deities? No, she said—it reminds us that He is the god of each of us, individually. "You may say, 'the God of Adrian freed the Israelites.' He was their god, and He's your god, too."

Mercury, your roommate, is not named for the planet or the Roman god; his namesake is Freddie Mercury. Mercury's father comes to visit, bringing things he noticed you were missing: a plunger, a dish rack, a set of dishtowels, a good bar of chocolate, and a one-quart bag of weed. An enormous amount of weed, it seems to you.

The three of you sit by the window, smoking up and eating chocolate, in what is technically your room: the living room sectioned off from the kitchen with a curtain rod. Mercury has the one bedroom in exchange for a larger cut of the rent. His father's head sits directly beneath an arched-shaped woodcut Mercury has made of your names, MERCURY & ADRIAN, that hangs from the ceiling by a piece of kitchen string, spinning at a glacial pace.

Until you met Mercury, you assumed every nonbeliever you met had left the church as you had, and carried that wound for life. You didn't know people could be raised without religion, that your parents' generation had atheists too—a realization so obvious you're embarrassed to think of it now. You ask his father if his parents were religious.

"Mennonites!" he replies, like it's the punchline of a joke.

"The horse and buggy kind?" You're watching Mercury's mouth, his lips pursed and wet around the joint.

"I never met them. No, moderates. This might surprise you, kid, but Mennonite pacifists are easy converts to top-of-the-bus hippies." He grins. "At least I was."

Mercury cooks a lot of fish and there's no vent fan above the stove. The apartment smells like it has been wallpapered in fish skin, washed with dark, bitter oils. A stretch of silence—the whole afternoon, the fading, milky light through the dirty glass—passes.

"What shape is god?" you ask. He left you as a cartoon character busts through a brick wall, leaving his outline. "Is he shaped like a man?"

"I always pictured him as a big, glowing disc. A circle," Mercury's father says. He seems to age as he frowns, calling attention to his weather-stripped face and brittle movements. "Or a saltshaker. Sprinkling humanity onto the earth. Like it just needed a little flavour, and then." He sighs, deepens his body in the cracked armchair. "And then." Mercury stands and starts pacing, broadcasting his boredom.

Mercury is straight or, at least, it's always women who wander into the kitchen in the middle of the night, who wake you with the door light of the fridge as they poke at the shrink-wrapped tilapia filets, the whole headless salmon. More than once, they've drawn the curtain and jumped back when they saw you there, staring at them in the dark.

After his father leaves, you climb in the shower together, high. Mercury rubs your back and jerks you off with such tender efficiency that you realize, in that moment of post-ejaculation clarity, that it wasn't sexual for him. A loving ministration: You think of Jesus washing his disciples' feet.

Your mother washed her mother's feet. Your grandmother perched at the edge of the bed she'd chosen to die in, regal and unsteady. You filled the plastic tub and came running down the hall, splashing out the sides. You stood to the side as your mother squeezed warm water from a rag over your grandmother's swollen feet and curled, yellow nails, murmuring soft words of comfort.

After it was over, your mother climbed into the bed, her face red and bloated. Your father brought her juice and porridge twice a day. You woke her on the fourth day to tell her you were out of clean underwear. Her voice was hoarse and dry. "Get the Bible." You found it in her bedside table, a massive tome with a gold-painted, cardboard cover, black stripes over the spine, INTERNATIONAL GOOD NEWS in block letters.

Her pale face and a tuft of dark hair were visible, the rest hidden in a heap of blankets. "Read me Psalm 23," she said, pulling the pink duvet up over her chin, like a child preparing for a ghost story.

You knew how to find it, approximately how deep into the gilded pages the psalms begin. You balanced the book awkwardly on one of your skinny arms while your free hand flipped to the right spot, and your voice boomed in the midafternoon silence, your childish intonation unusually rich and crisp: "The Lord is my shepherd. I have everything I need. He lets me rest in fields of green grass and leads me to quiet pools of fresh water."

When your father died, your mother stood over his hospital bed and read Corinthians 1:13, from the same big, gold book. "I may have all the faith needed to move mountains—but if I have no love, I am nothing." She drove you home with dry eyes, composure at the speed limit: slow but not dangerously so.

In the morning, you went to church together, and the pastor called you both up to pray for your loss. You stood at the front with your backs to the congregation, eyes squeezed shut, as Pastor Rick asked God to welcome your father into His arms. Your mother began to wail, as she had not wailed in eighteen months of treatment, or even as you stood over his lifeless body and she pulled away from the nurses who tried to hug her. She wailed like the women on the TV news in faraway war-torn places, like the cry of an abandoned animal rising up to the high church rafters, the squares of painted glass in the skylights. And then they started to sing, the voices behind you. You were not aware of the guitar or the organ or the PowerPoint slides of lyrics, not aware of their bodies, their grotesque human sneers, only of their voices. And of eternal life. They sang, "We will meet again."

Sarah Brown, the leader of your youth group, was four years older than you. You thought her name was funny, ordinary to the point of parody, like the title of a book series. Sarah Brown, girl reporter. Sarah Brown, girl detective.

She was seventeen when she came back from her first mission in Ghana. She gave a presentation in the church basement, a cold room with a projector and a dusty foosball table. Pictures of her sitting among African teens and children in one-room schools, smiling in her bandana and khaki shorts, all with Mark 16:15–16 running along the bottom: "He said to them, 'Go throughout the whole world and preach the gospel to all people. Whoever believes and is baptized will be saved; whoever does not believe will be condemned.'"

Your legs are tangled up with Mercury's in the empty tub, trying to cram both of your long-limbed bodies in somehow, his beard and braided necklace beaded with shower water. He talks of evil and hell as though you've never thought of them, never woken in the night to pray for lost souls. "How can that be an all-loving god?" he asks.

You fumble for the words: You were going to be Sarah Brown—freckled, thick-bodied, unpopular at school, middling grades, and a hero to the people. You were going to hold babies as they were vaccinated in rural Ghanaian clinics; you were going to dig wells and weave chairs, drag suitcases full of bandages from the roadside. The God of Sarah Brown saved lives. What have you done today? Wrote a paper titled "Foreign Aid and the New Colonialism."

You tell Mercury, instead, about the first breath after rising from the baptismal pool. A temporary dissolution of fear, of thoughts you could not control. Your knowledgeless body, thinking it would drown, pushing back against Pastor Rick's meaty hand as he palmed your head like a basketball. So glad to be alive, sucking in air, the other kids—there was gossip, of course; why were you old, why did your parents wait so long?—in their white robes, afraid, and then joyous, like you.

You remember Joshua, a boy your age who had the air of a grown-up, compounded by the small, round glasses he wore at the end of his nose and his hunched-over walk like he was trying to develop a hump. He invited you to "bring a gentile" night at the Jewish Community Center. You didn't go, but you ended up eating lunch with him under the back stairs at school. He said Jews didn't believe in heaven and hell, exactly, or not the fire and torture version. He said when you died, you were either with god, or you weren't. That's all hell was, His absence.

The next day, you asked how "bring a gentile" night went. He said, "We made a map of Israel out of ice cream and ate it."

Nicolai, a boy at school you hated, who was the opposite of Joshua—an adult body, long-limbed muscles, violent, and unpredictable as a toddler—said he fingered Sarah Brown in the woods behind the bowling alley. He told this story in the boys' locker room, to his friends and anyone who would listen: She wouldn't do anything to him, but she let him lift her shirt and bra, let him slip two fingers inside her and pump. Sarah was a legal adult and Nicolai was, in spite of his height and bulk, a child like you. You didn't believe it, not for a second. Not with the faces of newly saved and sated children in Ghana projected onto a concrete wall. Not with Sarah's slender hand waving back and forth during musical devotion, tucked inside a chatty dog puppet during the children's prayer, clasping both of yours when you told her you wanted to go, as soon as you were old enough, you wanted to spread the good news.

You stand on the coffee table, wearing a crown someone made from a cardboard six-pack holder. Your not-bedroom is the party room, the electric standing fan pointed at the window to blow out the fish smell, maybe, or the smell of your unwashed knit blankets. Everyone else sits cross-legged on the floor. The vibrations of the stereo—through the wood of the table, through your feet—rattle your flabby skin from your bones. Mercury is thrilled that the music is new to you, that you grew up in the nineties and had never heard Radiohead or My Bloody Valentine, that your youth passed without the slow, sad strange music that was popular then. Did you never listen to the radio? Did you never go to the mall?

You hold out your wine glass, stupidly full with red. "I am the bread of life! Those who come to me will never be hungry. Those who believe in me will never be thirsty." A girl raises her empty mug and you pour some wine from your glass, sloshing onto the floor and her blouse.

"I am the light of the world," you say, and you feel as you used to feel, aglow from the inside. Guitar grates on itself in the background, a drum machine, a rattling sheet of aluminum. You look down at the slaves to sin, at your bare, wine-stained feet.

You wake up late for the bus, late for work at the gas station, late for maybe the last time. You look forward to a Long John donut and a stick of jerky. The location of the security camera makes them the only things you can steal.

You had Sarah meet you at the other entrance to the woods, closer to the mall, told her you were in need of guidance only the youth leader could provide. You walked together through the blackened trees, scorched and bare against a pale sky. You searched for some kind of tell. You thought once you got close to the bowling alley end, she'd tear up or wince at the memory. You talked lamely of the boys at school being mean to you, even of Nicolai in particular, hoping she'd roll her eyes and laugh, "That kid? He keeps following me around. I think he has a crush or something. How pathetic." Or better yet, "Isn't that adorable?" Putting Nicolai in the same sexual realm as a kitten or a teddy bear.

But somehow you said too much, implied more than you meant to. Sarah breathed, "Oh," and took off running. You watched her go, and it seemed like the trees closed up behind her, sealing the turns in the path, past where you could see the ground.

You were no longer welcome at youth group. In one version, you lured Sarah into the woods to rape her. You thought people would see how nonsensical this was; Sarah could have tossed you aside with one arm. In another, you flashed her. Like you'd want to stand with your pants down and your bony legs and little thread of a penis on display—Nicolai in the school showers, unabashed as a tree trunk—so a teenage girl could point and laugh or just look on in horror.

Only your mother believed you. You had her, and you had God.

Not Jesus, who was already slipping toward caricature in your mind. You had sorted too many colouring sheets for the Sunday school, where Jesus had blank doe eyes and wore a toga. He was becoming something like Santa Claus—who you still half-believed in but understood was for younger children, made real through the effort and good will of adults. Parents put presents under the tree, volunteers at the postal service answered letters, malls across America hired someone to sit in a chair. And in this way, wasn't Santa inside all of us?

You had God, the Father, the weary, bearded figure of the Old Testament, who gave the world so many chances, but it just kept fucking up. You did not blame Him for the actions of Sarah Brown; you did not think he took away your dad. You didn't blame the devil, either. You understood it as the price of free will. God sat at the end of your bed, put his arm around you, confessed that He was tired, too. Your child self would have done fine against Mercury—what of starvation war genocide rape disease atrocity—or the great philosophers of the nineteenth century and the professors who made you read them. It's the twenty-two-year-old you who falters, steals donuts as a matter of course.

Mercury asks what year you were born. He wants to find what would have been the albums of your teen years, what should have played in the background as you lost your virginity or got drunk for the first time. You tell him you liked your mom's CDs, because it's the only music you can think of. Abba and Boney M. and Ella Fitzgerald. In the chaos of his bedroom, clothes and moulding food containers nested as though for warmth, his albums are alphabetized: He chooses Massive Attack, Modest Mouse, and Mogwai in a single pull. "The first time I heard this song, I cried for three hours," he says.

"When you were a teenager," you say.

"No, I liked shitty pop punk then."

He puts his giant headphones over your head, padded but leaking sound. It sounds like anything else: a low, thrumming guitar. You shut your eyes, strain hard, wanting to be transformed as he was. You want to cry for three hours.

After a few minutes—the first song hasn't ended—you open your eyes. "Maybe we should try the shitty pop punk and work our way up," you joke. You don't say: Maybe it's like language. If it never got into your heart when you were young, it never would.

Mercury tells you about a metal club near where he grew up. They kept their side door propped open, and the smell of sweat and old beer spilled on the black-painted floor wafted out into the alleyway. Sneaking in and getting kicked out was a rite of passage; the bouncers pretended to be gruff but handled the underage kids gently. Mercury remembers his first time. The noise, the strength, the boundless energy of the band—they expressed something that had been bouncing around inside Mercury, restless and destructive. He felt released. "I'm sorry you never had that," he said, in that voice that could be ironic, could be ironic about irony and therefore sincere again.

You still had to go to church. Sarah went to Ghana for another three months. She was also ruined, somehow. They didn't want her to lead youth group; they especially didn't want her to lead the children's prayer. She was old enough now to fly to Africa with some large interdenominational organization, without sponsorship from Pastor Rick.

Your mom would leave late on purpose, to arrive after Rick made everyone shake the hands of their pew neighbours, after coffee and muffins, after the younger kids had been dismissed to Sunday school. Sometimes you'd even wait in the car until you heard the beginning of musical devotion, and you'd slip in together just before the doors closed. Singing, they could only glance at you from the corners of their eyes.

You kissed Joshua under the stairs. When you pulled back, he wiped his glasses on the hem of his shirt, put them back on, and squinted like he couldn't quite bring you into focus.

The summer you were fifteen, you went to a sleep-away camp in "followship"—how to be a leader in the secular world while remaining a servant of the Lord. You were gender-segregated for classes in public speaking and conflict management, and you stared out the window—a hole cut in a log wall—at the grasshoppers leaping in the dry weeds, their shrill leg-violins. A number of kids from your church came, warning the others that you were a pervert. Some girls kept track of when you went to the shower building; some promised, in cloying, prickly tones, to pray for you. Your bunkmate found a horror novel in your backpack and reported you as a Satanist.

Evenings contained a choice of choir or Bible study. For weeks, you practiced one-eighth of choral arrangements with a group of boys whose voices were roughly the same pitch as yours, though you noticed that some deeper singers—the misfits and the weirdos, the ones who were sent to the camp as punishment—also got lumped into Tenor Two. The group sounded hideous, lazily out of key, the sound of a fear of trying.

The final week of camp, the choir sections sang for the Bible studiers. You'd never rehearsed as a full group. Unaccompanied, the rickety upright piano silent, the choir sounded glorious. Your voice lost, part of one enormous human instrument, and you felt you understood heaven: part of the godhead, absorbed into nothingness, singing His praises forever. Beauty, beauty! Tears streamed down your face. You didn't get teased for this, later. If anything, some people—girls, again—seemed jealous of your devotion, that it had been visible, plain for all to see.

At home, back in your own church, you started to lose focus during Pastor Rick's sermons. The Bible, once so unconquerably vast, seemed to contain the same few stories again and again. Pastor Rick extracted some thin thread of meaning, practical advice, about how to raise your children or treat your spouse or file your taxes. Was anyone listening? The camp girls adjusted their headbands, looked around, fiddled in the pews. The elderly parishioners in the front row had their eyes shut, nodding in agreement or sleep. You started testing God, thinking the worst thoughts you could come up with: strangling the organist, drowning the new youth leader in the baptismal pool, and pissing into the sanctified water. Exhaustive maps of desire, your mind treading men's bodies inch by inch. Strike me down, you thought, not snide, not rebellious. Strike me down, you thought, please.

But the music. The music still got you. The hymnals and the rock ballads, the raised arms and clapping. Every song like the morning after your father died, like that last night at camp. Your last connection. "Bow down thine ear, O Lord. Hear me, for I am poor and needy."

A few months after you left for university, on the phone with your mother, she asked if you'd found a church yet. You'd met Mercury—slim-hipped, untamed facial hair; he reminded you of colour-me-Jesus, down to the cream-white skin of cheap copier paper. He was failing out slowly the same way you were, through forgetfulness. You woke together on the edge of the soccer field, unsure of the time or if you had class; you wrote papers and took exams when you remembered that you had them. A TA told you that your thoughts were unoriginal, so Mercury tipped a plate of fish entrails into her mailbox at the start of the Thanksgiving long weekend. He took you to a concert where the audience drifted in and out of sleep on beanbags and yoga mats, and the music sounded like a muted jet engine. He dropped acid and you watched. You would both start your second year on academic probation.

You said, "Not yet," to your mother.

"You still believe in God, though," she said.

A moment too long, two beats instead of one. "Of course."

That night, you screamed out your window. Until you ran out of breath, and then again. Again. The RA for your floor broke down the door to your dorm room with his shoulder. The whole building gathered in the hall to watch as he wrestled you away from the window, down from the bed where you were kneeling, hands clasped.

When you were seven, you talked to God as you walked to school. You recited psalms from memory. You told Him you lost your pencil case and were afraid to tell Mom. You told Him you wanted blond hair like the boy who sat in front of you. The rain fell softer or harder on your plastic coat.

Author Commentary

A journalist friend who writes about religious issues once referred to me as an "apostate." I laughed and said that the word sounded melodramatic, as though I had led a revolt and set fire to the church on my way out. I was a childhood Baptist, and like many people—and the main character in "Mercury"—I lost my faith slowly, over many years: first in the fallible humans who compose a specific congregation, then in dogma, and finally in god himself. The absence of god, when you once believed, can leave a wound, a pit in the dirt of your soul. For me, it was there that the seed of this story embedded itself, germinated, and grew. —*Kim Fu, 2015*

About the Author

Kim Fu is the author of the novel *For Today I Am a Boy* (HarperCollins, 2014), a *New York Times Book Review* Editors' Choice, a finalist for the PEN/Hemingway Award, the Edmund White Award, and a Lambda Literary Award, and longlisted for the Flaherty-Dunnan Prize and Canada Reads. She has written for *The Atlantic*, NPR, *Maisonneuve*, and the *National Post*, among many others. Fu is a graduate of the University of British Columbia MFA program and lives in Seattle.

Days of Being Wild

Ricepaper 18, no. 3 (2013)

Doretta Lau

That fall in New York, most of my thoughts had to do with pain or grief. I was not suicidal. Rather, my grandmother had died a few months earlier and I was slowly recovering from the loss. I did not know how to talk about my pain, so I often drank until I could no longer feel my hands or feet. Insomnia took hold of me. I lay in bed and watched movies until five or six a.m., taking careful notes for the screenplay I was supposed to complete to attain my Master's degree. Though four months had passed since the end of coursework, I was still working on the first act. No matter how many hours I sat in front of my computer, I could not advance the plot of the film. My characters were flat. Each line of dialogue I wrote felt like an affront to the English language.

Everyone I attracted during this time was equally preoccupied with various miseries. A PhD history student who lived in my building, Kenichi Kingsley, considered me his only friend in the city. I am not sure what qualified me for this honour. I had not sought out his friendship, nor had I been particularly kind to him when we first met. To be honest, I had been wary of him because he was attractive in a movie star sort of way. My mother had often warned me that beautiful men lacked a conscience.

Kenichi was on antidepressants, which made him an undesirable drinking companion—he was incomprehensibly drunk after only two beers. Yet, he insisted upon drinking with me on Thursday nights, after his course on the modern history of Japan. It was one of the few fixed appointments on my calendar. We always went to the same restaurant, and we always sat at the bar. Our friendship was a habit, like smoking or biting one's nails to the quick.

"I hate the guys in my class," Kenichi said, after a large gulp of beer. "Most of them have or want Japanese wives or girlfriends."

"Isn't that what you want, too? A girl like your mother?" It was easy for me to rile him because his fears were so similar to my own—we thought that we were doomed to become the sort of people we most despised.

"Shut up." He smacked my arm, hard.

"Is the seating in your class segregated? Does it feel like the South that Flannery O'Connor depicts in her stories, except with Asian protagonists?"

"If you're asking me where I sit—I sit with the Japanese kids." Kenichi scowled at me. He considered himself one hundred percent Japanese, though he had a British father whom he barely remembered. Kenichi had lived with his mother in Japan for most of his life and had attended boarding school in England. A few weeks after I met him, I entered the bathroom in his apartment and noticed that he had covered all the mirrors with vintage wallpaper. He later confessed that he couldn't bear to look at his reflection because he strongly resembled his father, whom he hated.

"I bet all the women in your class love you," I said. "You look like Daniel Henney or Dennis Oh."

"You watch too many Korean dramas."

"I'm attracted to tragedy."

"This is why we're friends."

I raised my shot of bourbon. "To tragedy."

We drained our glasses. Then we had another. As usual, Kenichi became a slurring mess once he finished his second beer.

"You have to catch up," he said, pushing my drink towards me. "Drink faster."

I was on my fourth bourbon. "Catch up? You're the one who's behind."

"You're not on meds." He began to slide down in his seat. "Because of the meds, I'm way ahead of you."

"Maybe you shouldn't drink."

He tried to sit up. He began staring at my face as if there was an answer to an important question on it.

"You're the only person I know who isn't afraid to be unhappy."

I didn't know what to say. Wasn't unhappiness something sensible people avoided? Before I could answer, a woman leaned in between us, facing Kenichi, and asked, "What time is it?"

"Ask her," he said, pointing to me. "I'm not wearing a watch."

This was a lie. Kenichi was wearing a watch. I could see this, and so could the woman.

The woman didn't turn. She stepped closer to him; it was clear that she didn't care what time it was. Strange women approached Kenichi all the time. They seemed to think that he might be a cure for their loneliness.

"It's time for us to go home," I said, standing. Kenichi stumbled as he stood, and took hold of my arm. I gestured towards the bar. "There's a clock over there."

We walked to our building. The sky was clear, and the air was crisp in that perfect autumn way.

"Why are you still in New York?" Kenichi's voice was steady. He sounded sober.

"I'm working on my screenplay."

"If it was done, would you stay?"

"Sometimes when I'm walking down the street, it still feels like

I'm watching the city on TV."

"It's not home."

"No," I said. I had been in New York for over two years. I couldn't pass for a New Yorker, but to most people, I appeared to be an American from the West Coast unless I said, "about" or "sorry." In those days, I said sorry as often as I said please or thank you. I have since broken that Canadian habit of apologizing for minor mishaps such as accidentally brushing against someone on a crowded subway train, but my accent remains the same.

"So, why are you still here?"

"I need to finish the screenplay."

"You could write it from anywhere."

"I guess so. I like living here. Every day feels new and strange."

In many ways, the United States remained a mystery to me despite a childhood informed with American television, movies, and books. Though we had lived in New York for several years, Kenichi and I were unable to form an opinion about Americans or their culture. The only Americans with whom we had meaningful interactions came from a certain class. The Americans we knew had attended private schools and liberal arts colleges, if not Ivy League universities. Many spoke of summers at the Cape, as if it was the only such land formation in the world. The future held promise for all of them; when they spoke of being broke, it was only a transitory state. For most, money loomed in their futures, whether through job prospects, inheritances or marriage. Once, while drinking overpriced cocktails at a bar not fancy enough to warrant the outrageous cost, a classmate spoke at length about how she "could not afford anything" because of tuition and I could not keep my eyes off her thirty-thousand-dollar engagement ring.

"Good night," said Kenichi in a sleepy tone.

"Night."

We parted ways. The first time we met, we were standing in the lobby checking our respective mailboxes when he asked me if I was the tenant who watched Wong Kar-wai films late at night. I apologized ("I'm sorry") but he said, "Oh, no, I don't mind. I live in the apartment next to yours."

"Kingsley?" I asked, remembering the name on the intercom outside the building.

"Yes. My first name is Kenichi."

"Sophie," I said.

"Sophie, do you want to go see *2046*?"

"With you?" I said.

He ignored my question. "There's an advance screening tomorrow. I have two tickets."

We went. We were ambivalent about the movie, but we liked each other's company.

I entered my apartment to find that my roommate, Sarah, was asleep. I tried to step softly past her room, but alcohol lent my gait an uncharacteristic heaviness. It didn't help that I was wearing heels and walking across a hardwood floor. Though I had been raised not to wear shoes indoors, I followed the customs of Sarah and my previous two roommates, and kept my shoes in my bedroom. Rather than bathing at night, I bathed in the morning. I had made small changes to my personal habits so as not to irk my roommates even though New York was only a chapter in my personal narrative. I knew that one day, when I was no longer paying tuition, the United States would not want me within its borders, and I would have to move on.

Ever since my grandmother died, I had been avoiding Sarah. She had what passed for happiness, and I did not want to impose on her because she was in the last stages of her dissertation. I was hardly ever home, and when I was, it was usually past midnight. Sarah was a morning person. Our schedules did not mesh.

During the day I worked on my screenplay in the library. When I say work, I mean to say I watched films in the Butler Media Center, and took copious notes. I was in possession of eleven medium-size black notebooks filled with pedestrian thoughts on hundreds of films. There was a notebook devoted to zombie movies, and another one on vampire flicks. I devoted two entire volumes on heists, trying to figure out just what made *Le cercle rouge* and *The Taking of Pelham 1 2 3* so appealing to me. No genre was beneath my notice.

Though I didn't believe that it was possible for me to fall in love, I watched romantic comedies. I knew that I would have a better chance of selling a love story than an action film because I was a woman. That was supposed to be my territory: shopping and grooming and courtship and marriage.

I was so lost during this time that I thought that seeking order and predictability would free me in some way. Therefore, the teen comedy *My Boyfriend's Back* merited the same careful attention as Ingmar Bergman's *The Seventh Seal*. I read movie reviews online and academic essays in obscure journals, believing I would find the formula for success. My compulsive research did not gain me exit from the hell that was writer's block. I began to hate opening Final Draft on my computer. The cursor on the blank screen seemed to mock me with its steady blink.

Aside from grief, during this period my other constant preoccupation was money. I had mounting student loans; my inability to finish writing the screenplay prevented my graduating in a timely manner. I wanted very much to finish. I devoted hours to sitting in quiet places, writing outlines for the second and third acts of my film. But as I sat in front of my computer, I felt like I was a failure. I would never be able to write anything worth watching. No one would ever want to buy my screenplay and turn it into a movie.

This paralysis seemed too much to overcome. When I was tired of working on my screenplay, I turned to odd jobs. This was against the terms of my student visa, but somehow it made me feel better. Each morning, I scanned job postings and emails in search of a few dollars. Though my great-grandfather had been a scholar, his fortune had been lost even before the Communist era and all the older men in my family were labourers. Writing did not seem a particularly honest way of earning a living. When I reported what I was doing to my parents, it sounded lazy. Who of their generation could believe that watching a film constituted real research? There were times when I thought I should have attended law school instead; I was an excellent reader and researcher, and I was relentless at completing tasks when I felt there was little at stake.

Most nights I could not sleep thinking that my father could have retired early had I not decided to pursue my film school insanity. This only compounded my fears of failing to complete my screenplay.

Kenichi called me, begging me to accompany him to a party a student from his cohort was hosting. "I don't want to go—but you know how it is," he said. "I have to make an appearance."

"Can't you go alone?" I could think of many things I'd rather do with my evening than attend a party thrown by one of Kenichi's acquaintances, such as defrost my refrigerator or alphabetize my DVD collection.

"I'll get you drunk before we go."

"Do you really want to have a drunk guest at a school function?"

"It's not really a school function. And since when have you been that kind of drunk girl? Besides, I'll behave better if you're there. Even when you're intoxicated, you're sensible."

"Come over with a bottle of Maker's Mark." I disliked many of Kenichi's cohort, but some of them amused me, like specimens in a freak show. After four bourbons, we arrived at the party at eleven-thirty. I was verging on belligerence. When I drank, I said cruel things about strangers and acquaintances, cutting remarks I would not utter while sober. Whether alcohol was a truth serum or demonic possession, I wasn't quite sure.

As we stepped into the living room, Jenna Kim—the girlfriend of an American named Chad or Chuck or Chandler who specialized in Joseon Dynasty history and who directed all his conversation at my breasts whenever I had the bad luck of speaking with him—was sitting in a chair in the middle of the room. Her skirt was hiked up to her waist, and she wasn't wearing panties.

She had a cigarette in one hand, and was blowing smoke out of her vagina. Jenna was famous for this at parties. She called it her "Singapore hooker trick."

"Oh, fuck, not again," I said loudly. "I need another drink." I went into the kitchen. Kenichi followed.

"Is this type of behaviour common at parties in North America?" he asked, amused.

"She's such a fucking moron," I said. "Singapore is the least likely Asian setting for this kind of desperate sex work. I mean, if she had said Thai hooker trick, I'd still be annoyed with her, but at least she wouldn't come across as utterly stupid. She has no sense of political and socio-economic realities in different Asian countries. You'd think all of Asia was poor and backwards from her estimation of Singapore."

Kenichi laughed. "She's got a cigarette in her pussy and you're thinking about socio-economic factors and its influence on prostitution?"

"Whatever. I was saying that she's a stupid self-hating attention-seeking bitch. I bet she thinks she's a feminist. She probably writes poetry using feet binding as a metaphor for her dislike of her father, even though her family is Korean."

"Let's punish her by finishing off her soju." Kenichi held up a couple of green bottles.

"I bet Chad or Chuck or Chandler brought those," I said, reaching for one. "Cheers."

And so we drank away another night.

One day, just as a chill had set in, I found a job posting asking for a Chinese speaker. Though it didn't specify a dialect, I knew they were seeking someone fluent in Mandarin. My abilities in standard Chinese were rather limited; I spoke Cantonese with my family. Since becoming depressed and broke, however, nothing shamed me, and I no longer had qualms about telling untruths. I sent an email stating that I spoke Chinese. I received a phone message in Mandarin from someone named Kay asking me to meet at Dodge Hall that afternoon.

I walked across campus, passing Low Library. When it was warm out, the stairs leading up to the entrance was filled with people. But because it was cold, there were only a handful of students sitting down.

At Dodge Hall, there was only one Asian woman standing on the steps. I assumed this was Kay.

"Hello," I said in Mandarin. "I'm Sophie. Are you Kay?"

"You're a Cantonese speaker," Kay said when she heard my accent.

"Yes," I said, switching back to English, not wanting to embarrass myself any further.

"You're in the film program," she said.

"How did you know that?"

"You're friends with Sam. You're in his films. I've seen all of them. Sam and I used to work together in Singapore."

"You're in the visual arts program."

Kay lit a cigarette. "And how did you know that?" She exhaled.

"I think it's your glasses," I said. "Actually, you were in my international student group for orientation last year. I was the peer mentor." Kay was one of the people I often saw in Dodge Hall whom I wanted to befriend, but had never figured out a graceful way to do so.

"I can't see without them."

"A blind artist," I joked.

"Colour and motion are okay. I don't photograph, and I don't do fine drawings or detailed paintings."

"Sculpture?"

"Installation, mostly. Some video." She peered at me closely. "How tall are you?"

"Five-two."

"Hmm." She continued to stare at me.

"I think we're the same height," I said.

"Come by my studio." She handed me a card with her name and a telephone number embossed on it.

"You know where the studios are, yes?"

"Prentis."

"Right." She put out her cigarette, and left me standing on the stairs.

A few days later, on my way back from grocery shopping at Fairway, I decided to stop by Kay's studio.

I called her.

"Yes?" she said.

"It's Sophie. From the interview."

"I was wondering when you would call."

"I'm at Prentis, but I don't have swipe access to the building. Long story, but I keep losing my ID card. The guard is away."

"I'll be right down."

Kay opened the door for me. She was wearing what appeared to be layers of burlap.

"Isn't that itchy?" I asked.

"I'm wearing it over clothes," she said. "The burlap isn't touching my skin. It's a bit cold in my studio, and this was lying around."

As we walked up the stairs, I began to feel apprehensive. I had not yet seen her work, and I was worried that I might not like it. Though it was irrational, if I didn't like someone's artistic output, I found it difficult to be civil. I was lucky to have friends that could abide my pretensions and neuroses. When we entered her studio, I felt relieved. There was no evidence of mediocre work, only projects in progress that held promise.

"Would you like a drink?" Kay asked. "I have tea, coffee and Scotch."

"I'll have a Scotch," I said.

She handed me a generous glass of the liquor.

"Where are you from?" she asked.

"Vancouver," I said.

"I hear it's beautiful."

"In parts," I said. "But when I think of it, I only think about the areas that are picturesque, like the water and the mountains and the forests."

I walked over to a wall covered in photographs. "I thought you didn't take photographs."

"That's documentation of a performance I did last year. I don't photograph with the intention to show."

"They're good," I said.

"I didn't take them," Kay said, laughing. "I paid someone to document the piece for me."

I nodded to show that I understood, and took a sip of my drink.

"So, I guess you know that I don't speak Mandarin very well," I said.

"It's okay," she said. "There's no job. I wanted to see who would answer the ad. It's part of a project I'm working on."

I felt relieved that I wasn't going to be called on to be an interpreter.

"Your friend, Kenichi," Kay began.

"Oh, you know Kenichi?" I asked.

"We all know about Kenichi—all the women in my program, and some of the men, have tried to talk to him at some point," she said. "But no one knows him. Except for you."

"He's my neighbour," I said.

"He's not your boyfriend?"

"We're just friends."

"How can you be just friends with him?" she asked. "Are you blind? I think you need to get your eyes checked. I'm not the only one with poor vision." She smiled.

"Are you interested in him?" I asked.

"No, he's not my type," she said. "But he seems to be yours."

"I don't know about that," I said.

The next week, Kenichi's therapist upped the dosage on his medication. He called to cancel Thursday night drinks because he had slept through class and didn't intend on leaving his apartment.

"Why don't we go have dinner instead?" I said, concerned that he was slipping into a deeper depression. "If you haven't been outside all day, it might be good to get some air. Have you eaten?"

"I'm too tired," he said. Then he hung up.

I watched two movies, and took notes. By midnight, I was exhausted, but I couldn't sleep. I called Kay. I had discovered that I could always count on her to be awake at odd hours. Her studio didn't have windows, and she often lost track of time. As well, her schedule remained fixed to Singapore time despite the fact that she had lived in New York for over a year. I had never thought to question why she had not acclimated to Eastern Standard Time.

"Are you busy?" I asked.

"Come over," she said.

I was also privy to the knowledge that Kay was grieving, but she had never told me for whom. I was too polite to ask, and she was too private to talk about what was bothering her. Sometimes we sat in her studio drinking tea in silence. It was enough to know that someone else was going through the same thing.

"I'm worried about Kenichi," I said when I reached her studio.

"Why?"

I told her about his missing class, and cancelling our standing appointment. But then I began to talk about my inability to work, because that was also worrying me. I began to speak as if I was delivering a monologue.

"Perhaps I'm defeating myself," I said. "What is grief? It's just a transitory thing. I wish I could think myself out of all this and just write. It feels as if I'm using it as an excuse not to work."

I was determined to start afresh. I scrapped the screenplay I had been working on and started on a new one, a romantic comedy. But every line I wrote seemed false. My protagonist was too much like myself, too afraid to be vulnerable, too afraid to love. Kenichi called. "Why are you like this?" he slurred.

"Like what?" I asked, curious.

"Never mind," he said. "I need to go back to sleep."

"Good night," I said. When I hung up, I wrote our conversation into my screenplay.

Thanksgiving came and went. One morning I woke up at eight a.m. and felt buoyant. I don't know what had changed, but something was different even though nothing had happened to warrant a change, except perhaps the passing of time.

Maybe the day was particularly bright, or I was clearheaded for the first time in a long while, but there was a sense that I had attained a freedom of some sort. Rather than plan my day around drinking, I made myself breakfast and sat down and wrote twenty pages. Later, I threw out those pages. There was nothing worth reading, but it was enough. I called Kenichi. I called Kay. I bought groceries and called Sarah to tell her that I was going to cook dinner, and that she should join me. That night, the four of us ate together, telling funny stories about our childhoods and drinking two bottles of wine. Sarah went to bed early, and Kay had to return home to make a phone call to Singapore. Kenichi and I began walking to the bar we always went to on Thursday nights.

"Did you get a haircut?" Kenichi asked me as we walked down the stairs.

"No," I said.

"You look different," he said. "Better."

Out on Seminary Row, I had an overwhelming urge to hug Kenichi. I put my arms around him, and buried my face into his coat. He smelled so deliciously clean. He put his hands at the small of my back, and it felt as if he was holding me up, preventing me from sinking into the ground. Snow was falling, and gathering on our clothes. The tears I had been holding back for months came up like a tsunami, unstoppable. My grandmother was dead. But I was alive. I would live. "I think this is what it's like to feel happy," I said.

Reprinted with permission from How Does a Single Blade of Grass Thank the Sun? *by Doretta Lau (Nightwood Editions, 2014).*

Author Commentary

I began writing "Days of Being Wild" in 2008 during my lunch break at work. I had just moved back to Vancouver from New York and I was hoping to complete a book manuscript, but I found that I no longer enjoyed writing. My initial inspiration was Mavis Gallant's short story, "When We Were Nearly Young." I was also thinking about Banana Yoshimoto's novella *Kitchen* because my grandmother had died the year before. I wanted to write a story about grief. I also wished to examine the friendships of a group of people who feel foreign no matter where they are in the world. I must have rewritten the opening pages fifty times. I had no clue how the narrative would end, no image to work towards. I was lost and frustrated. So I set the story aside and came back to it in 2011. That was the year I decided that I had to like writing again or give it up and find another office job. Over the course of two months, I mapped out my short story collection, finished this story, and immediately worked on another piece. I rediscovered my love for writing. *—Doretta Lau, 2015*

About the Author

Doretta Lau is a journalist who lives and works in Vancouver and Hong Kong. She completed an MFA in writing at Columbia University. *How Does a Single Blade of Grass Thank the Sun?* (Nightwood Editions, 2014), her debut short story collection, was shortlisted for the City of Vancouver Book Award, longlisted for the Frank O'Connor International Short Story Award, and named by *The Atlantic* as one of the best books of 2014.

Lao Yang

Ricepaper 18, no. 3 (2013)

Ying Kong

He was called "Yang Senior Engineer" at work and "Yang Gang" at home before coming to Canada. He and their daughter came to join his wife, a graduate student at the University of Manitoba. Now, a year later, he no longer carried his title as an engineer because he was never hired as one, and still he was not used to being called by his first name, Gang, as was the practice in the new country. He didn't like to be called "Gang Yang" either, because the reverse naming didn't make any sense in Chinese. He liked his name to be used in the Chinese way—family name first, then given name.

He was proud of his Chinese name because Yang Gang happened to be a Chinese idiom for "hard, rigid, firm, unyielding, strong, indomitable," and, finally, "manly." So for a long time, he did not have a clear name. After many months in Canada, it became confusing.

"How about an English name?" his daughter suggested. She chose to be called Linda not long after she arrived. Her Chinese name had been Lida.

"No way!" he had retorted. "I will feel out of place. Besides, I don't want to worship foreign things."

He finally settled on Lao Yang. "Lao" in Chinese means old, and Yang is one of the most popular Chinese last names. So he was choosing, in effect, to be called "Old Yang." However, Lao Yang was not old at all. He was in his late forties. When he moved to Canada two years before, he had often been mistaken for his wife's son or his teenage daughter's boyfriend.

Inside, he felt too old to start a new life in this new country. When he explained to Elaine, his English tutor, what Lao Yang meant, she was curious. "You're not old at all. Why do you want to be called Lao Yang?" Elaine was in her forties, only a bit younger than he.

Looking at Elaine, he said, "I am old; you are young. So I don't want you call me 'Xiao Yang.'"

Elaine laughed. "I'm not as young as you think." Realizing Lao Yang's problem in identifying himself in this new culture, she tried to help him. "How about if I call you 'Gang'?"

"No, no!" he refused immediately. "It is too close. Only my mother calls me Gang."

"What does your wife call you?" Elaine continued in her effort to help him.

"Yang Gang."

"Hmm, that sounds too formal to me," she said, adding, "Tell me, how do people decide between *Lao* and *Xiao*?"

"Age."

"Does age really matter in China?"

"Yes, in job, we say, 'Old ginger is hot.'"

"Old ginger?"

"People say baby ginger no good for cooking; it is not hot. Young people don't know lot about their job," Lao Yang explained. He enjoyed talking about his own culture.

"Oh, I understand; someone older has more value because he has more experience," Elaine said.

Seeing Elaine understand him, Lao Yang smiled. "Older good for move up and salary raise."

"Oh, that's interesting."

"I become senior engineer when I am over forty years old," Lao Yang said, with pride. Suddenly, his smile disappeared. He sighed sadly. "When I go back to China, it is very hard for me find good job."

"Oh, you would leave your wife and daughter here?"

"I don't want live here all my life," he told Elaine firmly.

"Can you tell me more about your feelings of living here?"

"My English no good. I don't find good job here."

"Yes, I understand." Elaine nodded with empathy. "But, I'm sure you will learn English."

Lao Yang seemed not to hear her. "China change now. When look for job, young people easy to get job. Hire cheap. Bosses must pay me more because I am senior engineer. If I don't go back soon, I will be too old to find good job."

"Do they ask your age when you apply for a job?"

"They ask age. Job poster always say 'No People Over Forty-Five.'"

"Oh, they can't do that here. That's age discrimination."

"Dis-what?" asked Lao Yang, frowning as he attempted to repeat the word.

"Age dis-cri-mi-na-tion," Elaine said slowly. She wrote the word on paper. Lao Yang recognized the word at once. "I know what that word mean."

Elaine continued, "When you look for a job here, a company can't say, 'You're too old. We don't want you. '"

"I know," said Lao Yang. "At my work here in cafeteria, my boss don't know my age. She ask me do this and that. She think I am very young. I am not! This young woman don't respect me. When I am work, she always say to me, 'Faster, faster!' I think this is age dismation. They don't respect old people here."

"I see." Elaine acknowledged his feelings. "I never thought of discrimination like that! Do you want to tell me how old you are?"

"No problem. In China, we don't tell lie for age. I am almost fifty years old," Lao Yang said loudly. He was proud of being so close to fifty, a venerable age.

"Fifty is not old at all," Elaine said cheerfully. "I can still call you Xiao Yang."

"No! Call me Lao Yang. I like that," he insisted.

"Okay, Lao Yang!" she said and then changed topics.

"Do you know what the date is today?"

"Wend-day," Lao Yang replied immediately.

"No, I mean DATE, not day."

Lao Yang corrected himself. "Ah, FE-BU-REE."

"Yes, it's FE-BROO-ARY. But, what is the NUMBER on the calendar?"

"Fourteen."

"Yes, February fourteenth." Elaine looked at him, and then gave him a hint. "Is there anything special about today?"

Lao Yang looked blankly. "I don't know."

"Do you have Valentine's Day in your culture?"

"Valen-Day?"

"ValenTINE's Day. On that day lovers give gifts and love messages."

He seemed to remember. "Oh, we call it *Qingrenjie*. That only for young people, not married people."

"But married couples can also celebrate their love," Elaine said with a smile.

Lao Yang didn't agree. "My wife and me too old for that. We old couple, don't play that game."

"But Lao Yang, you're HERE now. Don't you want to express your love for your wife in the Canadian way?"

"What I do then?"

"Buy her candy."

"Chinese don't like eat sweet things."

"Then buy her flowers."

"No use for flowers. They die two or three days."

"Take her to her favourite restaurant."

"She likes Western food, I no like."

Elaine paused and then said, "What food do you like?"

"Chinese food!"

"Then take her to a Chinese restaurant," she suggested.

"Chinese food in Canada too Western," Lao Yang started complaining. "Everything deep fried, too sweet. In China, no lemon chicken, sweet-sour pork, ginger beef. Canadians more big bodies, Chinese small. We different bodies."

Elaine persisted, "Then what can you do for her for Valentine's Day?"

Lao Yang paused and then said, "I cook her real Chinese food!"

"Like what?"

"Rice and *mapodofu*."

"That sounds great, Lao Yang," Elaine said, feeling satisfied that he had come up with something for himself.

When Lao Yang got home, he was surprised to see his wife, Mei, already there. She was home earlier than usual. His daughter, Linda, was practicing the piano. He was relieved he was finally home again, where he could speak Mandarin.

"I thought I would give you a surprise today when you came home," Lao Yang said with a smile.

"A surprise? What?" said Mei.

"For VALEN-DAY," said Lao Yang loudly, using the new English word he'd learned.

"Oh, Valentine's Day! You've started to celebrate *lao wai*[1] festivals." She sounded excited. "I'm so happy to see you have accepted the cultural customs here."

"I didn't know that it was Valen-Day today," Lao Yang said honestly. "Elaine told me and she tried to persuade me to buy you flowers. That's not practical."

"Don't say that! I like roses," she said, adding, "I know you will get used to it here sooner or later."

Lao Yang's smile disappeared. "I'll never like it here."

"You will. Once your English improves, you will find a good job," his wife cheerfully said. "Then you will like it here."

Lao Yang sighed. "I'm too old to learn English now," he said. "If I were ten years younger, I would like to go back to school, learn this damnable language and get my engineering certificate."

"Don't say you're old. All my friends say you look much younger than me. Look at me, I'm still a student. And I don't feel old at all."

"Men are different from women. Their life spans are shorter than women's. Also, women are better at resisting aging psychologically, and—"

"Okay, stop!" Mei interrupted. "Remember, it's Valentine's Day today."

"Do you also want to follow the customs here? You know I don't like candy or flowers," Lao Yang said.

"I know that. So I got you something else." Mei took out a wrapped gift from her purse and handed it to Lao Yang.

Lao Yang took the wrapped gift, looked at it and then shook it near his ears, trying to guess what was inside. As he did this, Linda came up to them to see what Lao Yang had gotten. Lao Yang turned to his daughter and said, "Your Mama has learned the

1 *Lao wai:* a good-humoured nickname for foreigners.

lao wai's game very quickly. She's never bought me anything for Qingrenjie before."

"Do in Rome as the Romans do," Linda quoted, adding with excitement, "Ba, open it and see what it is!"

"No," Lao Yang said, setting the gift down on the table. "I think I'll open it after dinner. I'll prepare our dinner first."

"No, Ba, open it now!" Linda said. "The custom here is that you have to open the gift in front of the guests, and then say thanks."

"Okay, okay." Lao Yang began tearing off the wrapping paper. There was a box. He opened it, and saw a leather wallet with many pockets for credit cards inside. Looking at it, he said, "This must be very expensive. You don't have to spend big money on unnecessary things."

"But you need this wallet for the credit cards and your bank card," Mei said.

"Let me have a look." Linda took the wallet from him. "Wow, it's a good one and it's a brand name, Crocodile. Look, there are lots of holders and you can put in all your cards, especially your credit cards."

Lao Yang frowned. "You know I don't want to use credit cards. I don't feel like I am actually spending money when I use them. It's deceptive. The credit company charges high interest if you fail to pay on time. That's why people here have such high debt. I want to use cash. Using cash makes me aware of how much money I really have to pay, and I will never owe banks money."

"Ba, people here don't use cash as much as we do back home," Linda said, nudging him. "Please say thanks to Mama."

Lao Yang said in a dispirited tone, "Thank you, but I want you to know that my heart aches when I see you spending money on me like this. This must have cost my whole day's wage. You two women don't work as a *dagongzai*[2] here like me. If I continue with these dead-end jobs, I'll be a dagongzai forever. I'll go crazy!"

"Stop talking like this!" Mei admonished. "It's Valentine's Day today."

Remembering his promise to Elaine, Lao Yang said, "Actually, I was going to cook our favourite dish for our dinner tonight. That's my Valen-Day gift for you. I am going to cook now."

With a smile, Mei replied in English, "Thanks, my dear."

"Don't say 'my dear!'" Lao Yang snapped. "I get 'chicken bumps' when I hear you call me 'my dear.'"

"It's not 'chicken bumps,' but 'goosebumps' in English," Linda corrected him.

"I don't want to hear any more English today. I've had enough!" Lao Yang said, exasperated.

"Listen, I don't want you to cook today. We'll save it for some other day. Let's go out for dinner," Mei suggested.

"But I don't like to eat out," Lao Yang protested.

"Why? Not even for today?"

"I hate to eat in restaurants," Lao Yang said in a loud voice.

"I know you don't like Western food, so let's go to a Chinese restaurant."

Lao Yang became really angry now. "It doesn't matter what restaurant it is. It all reminds me of the boring dagongzai job like the one I have. It's a shit-hole where I work. I peel onions and carrots, all day. My job is never done. There is always another thing I have to peel or cut. I want to finish as quickly as possible so that I can take a break. Chopping, peeling, and cutting, I'm sick of work like this! Screw this job! When will I ever leave this hell?!"

2 *Dagongzai:* a labourer.

"I'm sorry," Mei said. "I didn't realize it hurt you when we eat out in restaurants."

"You never think of my feelings. All you think is how lazy I am in learning English. How can I have energy to learn it after a day of tedious and boring work?"

They ended up having dinner at home. Lao Yang prepared delicious plates of mapodofu, *disanxian*[3], homemade salad, stewed chicken with dried mushrooms, and vermicelli he bought in Chinatown, all of which were Mei's favourite dishes. But there were no festival feelings around the dinner table, only a subdued silence.

That night Lao Yang couldn't sleep. It was the beginning of his second year in Canada. He never felt at home, not even for one day. He remembered clearly the first day of his arrival in Canada.

It was late summer. He came with his then seventeen-year-old daughter, Linda, to this prairie city he had never heard of before his wife became a graduate student there. When he and his daughter got off the plane, it was already midnight. At the airport Mei gave both him and their daughter big squeezing hugs.

He immediately felt embarrassed. His face flushed; he looked around and gently pushed his wife away, saying, "Be careful! People are watching us." Then he turned to his daughter. "Your mama seems to be Canadianized."

On the way to the apartment Mei had just rented for the family, Lao Yang looked out through the car window. "We seem to be driving in the countryside. There are no buildings along the highway. This doesn't feel like a city at all."

"Yes, on the prairies, you don't see as many high-rise buildings as back home," Mei replied.

3 *Disanxian:* stir-fried eggplant, green peppers, and potatoes.

When they got to their one-bedroom basement apartment, Lao Yang remarked, "What a hole, not even a rabbit would shit in a place like this."

Mei was shocked by the comment, but did not say anything. In the small apartment, Lao Yang was surprised to see the kitchen open to the living room. He recognized the refrigerator and the stove top, but he didn't know what the oven was for. He was surprised that there was no fan above the stove. He asked his wife, "How can you cook without a fan?"

"I seldom cook."

"Then what do you eat?"

"In the morning, I only have milk and cereal; I take sandwiches for my lunch at school. If I cook in the evening, I usually boil meat and vegetables. Sometimes I have noodles," Mei replied.

Lao Yang felt sorry for Mei, who used to live a comfortable life in China. "What a simple life you lead here! Don't you miss your life in China?"

"A little bit. But I'm used to the lifestyle here now."

"I've brought lots of things from home to fry your favourite dishes. You'll enjoy my cooking, won't you?"

"For sure! I missed your cooking," Mei said. "However, there is no ceiling fan in the kitchen and the smoke detector is connected with the city fire system. So, we can't stir fry like at home."

"Screw this place!"

The next day was Sunday. Lao Yang woke up very early, but stayed in bed with his wife.

Seeing her husband exhausted, Mei said, "We can sleep till noon, you know. In the afternoon, we'll go to the mall."

"I want to go in the morning so that I can cook you a Chinese dinner today," Lao Yang said, getting out of the bed.

"But the mall won't be open until noon on Sundays," Mei explained. "So we can sleep in today."

He was reaching for his slippers on the floor. "I'm used to getting up early in the morning. I might not be able to enjoy this kind of lifestyle. How can businesses make money if they close on Sunday mornings?"

"Even if they are open on Sunday mornings, there won't be many people."

"Why?"

"They go to church. If they aren't at church, they're resting at home or taking kids to hockey or soccer practice," Mei tried to explain.

"Church? Do you go to church, too?"

"Sometimes."

"What do you do there?"

"I like to meet friends there," Mei said. "Next week, I'll take you to a church where my friend is a minister."

"I don't think I'll like it. I won't understand a word of it."

"It doesn't matter. We'll see some of my friends there. You can also learn English by talking with native speakers."

"I'm too old to learn English," Lao Yang responded quickly.

"No, you're not too old. People here go back to university even after they're retired."

"They're different from us. They are stronger and have more energy than us Chinese. They eat cheese, dairy products, and beef."

"We can eat the same things here," Mei encouraged.

"It's too late. We're congenitally deficient in nutrients. My mama said that when she was pregnant with me, she could only afford cucumbers, which were cheap because they were in season. After I was born, there was the famine. Our family never had enough to eat before I went to primary school. After middle school, we were forced to go to the countryside. You remember what we had as food on the collective farm? *Dachazizhou,*[4] *fentiao,* [5] and *xiancai*[6] every day."

Lao Yang went to the bathroom. Mei called out after him, "But now we can make up for what we lacked before; we can eat as the Canadians do."

Later, in the kitchen, Lao Yang asked Mei, "What's for breakfast?"

Mei opened the fridge. "I have milk, cheese, juice, bread, cereals, and also fruit."

"Do you have corn flour? I want to have corn flour porridge with pickles."

"Sorry, no."

"Screw this place!"

That first weekend, Lao Yang, his wife, and daughter were kept busy. Mei gave Lao Yang and their daughter a tour of the neighbourhood—the campus, shopping malls, and downtown. That Sunday, which was the first anniversary date of Mei's earlier arrival in Canada, the reunited family had dinner together. On the dining table were plates of fried dumplings, stir-fried vegetables, and crispy shrimp. Mei was very happy with the delicious dishes that Lao Yang cooked even though the apartment smelled of smoke. By putting a wet towel on the smoke detector, Lao Yang managed to do his Chinese cooking without setting off the alarm. He enjoyed the family being together.

The first few weeks, Lao Yang stayed in the apartment with his daughter, watching movies brought from China and chatting on MSN with family and friends back home. One evening, when

4 *Dachazizhou:* thick porridge made of crushed corn.

5 *Fentiao:* noodles made of potato starch.

6 *Xiancai:* salt-preserved cabbages and turnips.

Mei came home from school, he was on the phone with a friend. Knowing his wife was in the room, he continued his conversation.

"Life is so dull here," he said loudly. "Inside the apartment, I am facing the white walls. There is nobody to talk to, and here they don't allow smoking inside the building. Where we live, it's far from downtown. Outside the apartment, the only company I have is rabbits and squirrels."

He paused, then continued, "No, nobody hunts them. I was told you need a hunting licence. Even for fishing, too. There are more rules and regulations here. No, this is not a country as free as you think. A lot of dos and don'ts. Even if you cough and yawn, you have to say 'Excuse me.'" There was another pause. "Yes, a few of her friends invited us to dinner at their homes. I don't like going. I can't understand their talking. There are a lot of ridiculous rules even for eating. It's not good to eat noisily, to talk with food in your mouth, to take your bowl in your hand, to scratch the plates. Lao wai are so used to using knives. Even when the meat is too small to cut, they still try to cut it."

Mei started to prepare dinner in the kitchen; Lao Yang was still on the phone. "Yes, she has several Chinese friends. The only fun they have is potluck parties. Every family brings a dish of food and they eat together, but I like to be with the Chinese families better than with lao wai."

While glancing at his wife, Lao Yang walked to the bedroom with the phone to his ear and lowered his voice. "It's very hard. I've sent my résumés to several places. After interviews, you seldom hear from them again. However, two companies wrote to me afterwards, saying I could go for another interview if my English improved. I'm telling you, I'm too old to learn English."

After a month, Linda started high school, and Lao Yang was home alone. Mei only allowed him to cook one Chinese meal per day. He tried all kinds of recipes and enjoyed the task of cooking dinner for the family, but after that, he had nothing more meaningful to do.

After he failed several job interviews, Mei asked suspiciously, "What do you do during the daytime?"

Lao Yang replied coldly, "I read newspapers online."

"Free Press?"

"No, *Shenyang Daily*, *Yangcheng Evening* paper, and some Chinese websites."

"Why do you still read those papers since you are here in Canada?"

"I want to know what's happening back home. Oh, today's paper says that the price of the pork is higher than the same time last year. And the—"

"I'm not interested in what's happening there, but what's happening here," Mei interjected. "I'm not the kind of person who lives in the Cao camp with his heart in the Han camp."

"Well, I'm the kind of person who doesn't forget the past easily," Lao Yang retorted.

"I didn't say you should forget the past, but at least you should base yourself in the present reality."

He stared at her angrily. "What is the present reality?"

"To improve your English so that you can feel at home here!"

"I'll never feel at home here!" Lao Yang said loudly.

"We can't afford to argue any more on this issue. How about we speak English at home so that you can get used to English?"

"No way! I stay at home alone the whole day, and I wait for you and Lida to come home early so that I have somebody to talk to. If you all speak to me in this dumb language, how can I find any pleasure in living here?"

Lao Yang's face turned red. He was frustrated and angry.

After six months, with the help of Mei's friend, Lao Yang started work as a kitchen helper at the campus cafeteria. The first day Mei went with him to meet the head cook and the manager. After she interpreted his duties and responsibilities to him, Lao Yang managed to work there with his limited English.

Two weeks later, Lao Yang got his first paycheque. He proudly showed it to Mei and Lida at the dinner table. "The money is good," he said. But while Mei and Lida were looking at the cheque, his face turned dark.

"But the job is too hard for me physically. And it's demoralizing when the boss tells me to work faster, faster!"

Mei felt sympathetic for him, but she said, "It's hard on anyone to work eight hours every day like that, but you only work three days a week. The other two days, you can go to a class to study English."

"It's okay for now. But I can't be a dagongzai forever."

"Ba, you won't be a dagongzai forever," Linda said cheerfully. "You're a senior engineer, and they need engineers like you here."

Mei also encouraged him and said, "Nobody says you have to do it forever. Once you improve your English, for sure you'll find a better job. But think of this—compared with our life and those years on the collective farm, life here is much better. We don't have to work in the fields from morning till night. There are lots of varieties of food to choose from if you don't like Western food."

Lao Yang stopped eating and put his chopsticks on the table. "But for me, life here *is* worse than the life we had on the farm. What's the difference between working in the kitchen and in the fields? They're both labourers' work, only using the hands and not the mind."

"They *are* different," Mei said impatiently. "We were *forced* to go to the country to be re-educated by the peasants."

"But here we have to be re-educated by lao wai. We have to learn their language and their culture. When we lived in the country, we didn't have to worry about jobs, bills, or tuition."

"Don't you understand that we didn't have any choice for jobs? All of us had to work in the fields. It's true that we didn't have to pay the bills, because there was no water or heat in the house, and all the schools were closed because education was banned. It was terrible!" Mei argued. "Don't you remember?!"

"At least I was not lonely," Lao Yang complained. "In summer, we worked in the fields together. In winter, we prepared programs of entertainment for the local farmers. That was fun." Lao Yang paused. He remembered that it was on the farm that he met Mei. She played the pipa and he played the flute in the same youth performing troupe. So they had literally made music together as a couple. Lao Yang could have been truly happy then, but of course, the terrible thing was that the Cultural Revolution denied young people further schooling at a crucial point in their lives. Dreams of living a better life could not be realized.

"I don't remember you having any fun while we were on the farm," Mei said, interrupting his reverie.

"Well, of course I was not happy," Lao Yang snapped back. "We were deprived of the opportunity of going to university."

"But then when you were accepted into university after the Cultural Revolution, you were not happy then either," Mei pointed out.

"I was unhappy because I was assigned to the university I didn't like."

"You could have refused to go if you didn't like it."

"You're talking nonsense!" Lao Yang fired back. "You know that I couldn't take the risk. I might have lost the opportunity to go back to the city if I refused the admission."

"I have never heard you say when you were *ever* happy," Mei said angrily. "Don't think of the past! Think of the present!"

"Nonsense! Nothing of the present for me is worth thinking about! I have no profession, no money, no dignity here!"

"You don't have to lose your dignity just because you have no profession or money."

"I feel ashamed that as a man I can't even support my family," Lao Yang said in a subdued voice. His face twisted in misery.

"That's only temporary. You'll have a better job when you improve your English."

Lao Yang stood up. "Stop talking about English! I'm too old to learn English!" He stomped off to the bedroom and slammed the door.

Looking at her mother, Linda said, "You and Baba shouldn't have talked about this at the dinner table. I don't feel like eating now."

"Sorry," Mei said regretfully. "I don't feel like eating now either. If you want to have dinner later, ask your Baba to have it with you. I'll go to the library now and will be back late."

All the untouched dishes were left on the table: vegetable stir-fry, shrimp, tofu stewed with pork, and three bowls of rice. Linda covered everything with plastic wrap.

After that Valentine's Day, or what he thought of as the Qinrenjie disaster, Lao Yang left his wife and daughter for the hometown he had been longing to return to. He had worked in the cafeteria for a year and a half. He had gone to Elaine for English lessons two hours a week. She had taught him enough English to work well as a kitchen helper.

But after struggling for two years with the choice between studying English and going back to China, he chose China. Before the Chinese Spring Festival, he left his wife and daughter for the hometown he had been longing to return to for two years.

Two months after leaving, he phoned his wife. Without even greeting Mei, he said, "I want to come back to Canada next month."

"Why?"

"I miss you and Linda."

"We'll go back this summer to visit you and the family."

"I still want to come back," Lao Yang stated, a hint of desperation and despondence in his voice.

Looking out of his condominium window in Dalian, he saw the public square full of young people, laughing and playing in the morning sun. He held the phone close to his ear, walked to the dresser, and sat in front of the mirror. In flannel pyjamas far too loose for his small body, he saw in his reflection the abundance of white hair on the sides of his head. White hair that had not been there months ago.

"Mei," he said, looking at the mirror. "I'm too old to find a job in China."

Mei did not answer.

"Mei?" Lao Yang said loudly. "Can you hear me?"

There was no answer. Just silence.

"Mei?" Lao Yang said. "Can you hear me?"

Author Commentary

For the past ten years, I have taught literature and culture in Canadian and Chinese universities, and I always find myself trapped in "mainstream" literature and culture. I once included works by Amy Tan and Maxine Hong Kingston, only to realize that the Chinese culture reflected in their works was too traditional to reflect today's immigrants to North America. As a new immigrant, with my own experience of cultural orientation, adaptation, assimilation, and, finally, accommodation, I started writing fiction about Chinese immigrants. "Lao Yang," part of a trilogy, is the story of a former engineer who takes on all kinds of menial jobs to survive and finds himself returning to his home country. By writing about Chinese immigrants, I have enhanced my knowledge and sensitivity to Chinese and Western cultural traditions and practices, while hoping to move Asian-Canadian literature and culture from the margins to the mainstream. —*Ying Kong, 2015*

About the Author

Ying Kong is a Chinese-Canadian currently teaching Chinese culture and literature at the University of Winnipeg. Before coming to Canada, she was a professor of English in a Chinese university. After obtaining her PhD in literature at the University of Manitoba, she travelled and taught for universities in China and Canada. She has published three pieces in *Prairie Fire*. "You Can't Go Home Again" was recognized in 2008 as one of the best creative nonfiction pieces on the theme of home.

Lucky in Saigon (novel excerpt)

Ricepaper 18, no. 4 (2013)

Yasuko Thanh

Chapter 1

Georges Minh thinks: *Killing a man is easy. Life is fragile, for one. And the world is poisonous, for two. How poisonous? Cobras, mushrooms, stonefish, apple seeds. Consider the datura plant.* Datura stramonium. *White flowers the shape of a trumpet and the size of a human heart. The seeds, crushed with a mortar and pestle, are easily processed. Thieves and prostitutes favour its killing properties. He's seen the results in his practice and has such a flower blooming in his courtyard.*

Six men plotted in a circle, cross-legged, on Georges Minh's bed. Six men, none of them yet thirty-five. Six men on Georges Minh's command centre, where he ate, slept, played cards, and officiated the weekly nationalist meetings.

Carved out of the rarest red wood, with no mattress in the Chinese style, Georges Minh's bed took up half his bedroom.

"Mysterious Scent of the Mountains," said Khieu, who owned an inn with his wife and spent his spare time painting poetry on to the inside of rice paper sun hats. *Had it not been for winter, the falling snow might have been cherry blossoms.* One day he would close the inn and just sell the hats whose words could be read only when they were raised to the rays of the sun.

Khieu wore the same type of linen suit as Georges Minh except that Georges Minh's was ironed. Khieu's knees sloped in the linen pants, and the collar of his white shirt, where it met the dark line of his unshaven stubble, was wrinkled as the rings of a pineapple tree.

Smaller than Georges Minh with a thin mouth and powdered hair, he sat to Georges Minh's right, so close their knees touched. Georges Minh thought Khieu's swimming irises appeared somewhat lecherous.

"No, no, no. I still like Fighting Dragon," said the engineer, who flirted with laziness. He was slightly walleyed and laughed so his belly moved.

Long looked at the back of his hand, examined his nails. "Or, like I said before, we can make a poison."

"How's your brood, Khieu?" Georges Minh asked.

"I don't know."

"You don't know?" Georges Minh stared at Khieu's thick betel-nut-coloured hands rolling a cigarette, shielding the tobacco from the wind of a small oscillating fan.

"Haven't seen her in a year. Didn't you know?"

"Mysterious Scent of the ... *whatever* is ... too ... too, too ..." the engineer waved his tea cup, trying to catch the right word. "It sounds like something from a song. We're a revolutionary organization—not a *minstrel* group."

The French-style villa was distanced from the neighbouring houses by a property considered expansive, even for the Thao Dien area, and guarded by the noise of the river out back.

"Not even the kids?" Mostly they kept their private affairs private. Still the revelation shocked Georges Minh because Khieu had been married to his wife for seven years; they had four children together.

"Nope, but, I suppose that's how it goes sometimes," Khieu said. Georges Minh thought of Mai, whom he'd met once or twice, running the inn alone. "Oh, well, these things happen." Like a storm that washed your memory of a family the way a rain washed a road in a sudden burst? Or did they happen the way a thief with a bludgeon attacked a family leaving death in his wake?

Georges Minh looked down at his cards as if it was his hand that troubled him.

"How many soldiers can there be?"

"Thirty or forty?"

"I heard fifty," said Khieu.

"You're both wrong. The exact number is eighty."

"Do you know nothing? They number over two hundred!"

"We will drive out the French bandits."

"We will restore Vietnam."

"We will create a democratic republic."

"No, a monarchy."

Their hearts were in the right places, these members of the MFYM, Mysterious Fragrance of the Yellow Mountains, who didn't yet have a name, in spite of the fact that most of their meetings were spent drinking and playing cards. They discussed lofty ideals. Drank.

Outlined what a free and democratic Vietnam would look like. Drank. Compared international political systems. Drank. Cited historical precedents. Cursed the French.

Each man held some playing cards and a glass of mulberry wine. They were tea cups, not wine glasses, and none of them matched, but Georges Minh liked to be thought above the man who cared about such trifling matters and superficial details. He could have afforded matching wine glasses, but only shallow men cared about such worldly things.

"If we can't agree, let's move on," suggested the horticulturalist who raised moonflowers for an exclusive clientele. "Let's talk about what we're actually here for, as our esteemed colleague Long suggested earlier, when he brought up a rather interesting idea. Why don't we talk about that?"

Long was the son of the Junior Minister of the Annamese Cabinet of Cochinchina. "And High Class Resident of Saigon," Long would smirk and say, even as a teenager. Though the Le family was powerful, the power parroted the French establishment, and the Le family knew it and flaunted their wealth, as if that could repair the insult. The two had known each other since grade school. Long and Georges Minh, who were best friends. Long, whose family's power fecundated Saigon's alleys and open sewers and jackfruit trees and feral animal population.

Long hated the sell-out, the collaboration of his family with the enemy that included his name, "Henri," but he stopped short of hating the urchins who called to him across the alleyways of Cho-lon: "Hon-riii, Hon-riii, give us a tai-an, give us your tie," who worshipped anything French, giving themselves French nicknames for fun.

"Chosen well, a good name helps define a group's beliefs, bestows desired traits," Georges Minh said, because Long was the kind of person who as a child had given away his pencils and schoolbooks to those same urchins, and now sat with a cracked tea cup of wine in his hand goading him. Georges Minh shrugged his shoulders. "Look at all the fuss and divination that goes into choosing a child's name." Georges Minh would go to as much trouble when he named his son. When he had a son. When he found a woman. When he got married. Which he would. Any day now.

"Not a *monarchy*, a republic," Khieu said. "Haven't you read Rousseau?"

"They should die like dogs."

"They should die like a snake under a rickshaw driver's wheels."

"They should die like an iguana in the mouth of a hungry dog, swelling at head and tail until they burst under the pressure of his powerful jaws."

"They can die like a lover in the arms of a woman," Khieu said. "I don't care. So long as they die."

Making a poison strong enough to kill a man is easy. Remove the seeds from the stamen. Crush them with a mortar and pestle until the dry seeds stop crackling. The powder is now so fine as to be invisible and weightless. Season chicken, shrimp, or buffalo with the dust. Steeped in fish sauce, the poison is tasteless.

Because he was a little drunk, Georges Minh fell against Khieu. He righted himself and dabbed at the spilled wine on the wooden bed slat with his thumb. "I don't mind talking about the group name some more. A thing becomes its name and vice versa. Can you imagine a militant group with the word 'bananas' in its moniker?"

"Bananas is definitely out."

"I second."

"Third."

"Obviously."

"This is absurd."

"What was that name you said? Mysterious perfume ..."

"Mysterious smell."

"Fragrance."

"No, it was mysterious scent, but I like perfume better."

"Me too."

"Perfume then," said the court translator and lover of books, "but mysterious is the important part, because it's how we must remain. Elusive. As in impossible to catch. By soldiers, police, any and all enemies."

"Well, perfumes are important, too," said the horticulturalist, who would have said such a thing.

"Sweet, right, because *that's* what we want to be," the engineer said, facetiously.

"Maybe you're not that much of a block head," said the translator. "Sweet as a flower that rises in the spring. In the spring there's hope. Especially in the north."

"Where at present," said Georges Minh, striking a serious face, "the news is one in three women are now prostitutes, because of the regime. Did you know they're starving in Tonkin? Picking individual grains of fallen rice from between stones with their fingers. Eating farm animals dead of disease."

The men sympathised with silent nods. "Invisible as a fragrance, invisible as hope, invisible as a guerrilla fighter." The court translator continued, "Mountains, of course are a symbol of strength. Where were we then, mountains?"

"Don't forget, prayers are invisible, too," said the pipa player.

"True," said Georges Minh.

"Like the fart I just let out?" the pipa player said.

"God." The horticulturalist groaned.

Long took a sip of his wine, then drained the cup avoiding the chip on the rim. After lighting a cigarette he said, "If we're not going to move on to the poison until after we choose a name then I say let's add 'yellow,' Mysterious Perfume of the Yellow Mountains. Makes us sound like poetry."

Was Long playing it straight with the group? Yellow? Georges

Minh couldn't tell much about the man these days. Long had accompanied his father on business trips to the Dutch East Indies, France, and Switzerland when his father had still thought Long might be sane enough to follow in his footsteps and enter the cabinet himself. But Long had recently started growing his hair long again, like some of the Hindu holy men in the marketplace. Long had discarded his topknot and traditional turban in favour of clipped hair long ago, but now he no longer kept it sleek, no longer washed it. He wore his hair unkempt and ran around the marketplace pushing a broom or borrowing rickshaws that didn't belong to him. This, in itself, wasn't completely new. But he'd changed since the hauling of those French contraptions of horror into the square, the guillotines.

Georges Minh hated the French—he could say those words. But could he write someone's name in poison? Georges Minh didn't know if he could kill a man. Maybe one man. But could he poison a whole garrison? *Poison*. Long's words of earlier hung in the air along with Long's cigarette smoke waiting for Georges Minh's response. The truth was, ever since that day as a schoolboy, when Long with his one green eye that emphasized his craziness had stood nearly naked in the marketplace in Cho-lon, Georges Minh had admired him because he was everything Georges Minh was incapable of being by nature, lacking the inner rigour. A few years later, as a teenager, when Long stole a driver's rickshaw one afternoon and pretended he was a coolie, returning the rickshaw and all his earnings to the rightful owner that evening, Georges Minh had wanted to be him. Long, who had a neck as solid as an Iron Wood tree, was strong. Even now, as an adult, when he returned to Cho-lon and swept the streets with a broom or collected garbage, barefoot as a peasant, for the love of work, or to prove a political point—Georges Minh wasn't exactly sure—everyone knew him by name. Now Long was looking at him, and Georges Minh could feel whatever small admiration he'd built up for himself in Long's eyes over the years slipping away by degrees like a small village slipping down a water-logged hillside during the monsoon rains. Long, looking again with that provocation in his eyes. Georges Minh decided the look was Long's way of mocking him, for being weaker than him, teasing him for his reluctance to get involved. Provoke him into being more than the wimp he always was. Making a stand.

Long still loved mathematics, detective novels, and astronomy, searching with his telescope for alien life in the skies, but another part of him had evolved into something Georges Minh no longer recognized after hearing men screech nationalist slogans, watching the blade fall, heads tumbling into baskets. The heads were then collected and mounted onto spikes as warnings to others, with punishments distributed to Vietnamese who tried to remove the heads too soon. Even as he sat there now, with Long waiting for his response: Would he or would he not make a poison to kill the soldiers stationed at the French garrison of Saigon? He knew he was disappointing his friend. And his country by extension. He was the natural choice. The doctor of the group.

Georges Minh looked out the window. Subterfuge. An irrational ploy. Smile and no one will bother you. Look away and what you don't want to see turns invisible. Gazing at the river that flowed out back. Now the shade of a ball bearing. Now the shade of dirty cotton. Now the shade of belly button lint. He could pretend the river was something fleeting. A minnow, a swordfish, a dragon. Then the dreaded thing happened. It must. It had to.

"Yes, of course. He could make the poison."

"Naturally, he's a doctor."

"What do you say?"

"Georges Minh?"

"Aren't you listening?"

"He's drunk."

"Could you or couldn't you?"

"Daydreaming."

"No, I was paying attention. Poison."

"Well?"

"There are many ways to poison a man."

Could you?

Georges Minh stared into Long's one green eye and didn't answer. Mulberry wine made all the fish in the near dark leap out of the river and hover over the water.

They spun and danced, a synchronized ripple, the way the water puppets shimmer and perform boisterous art over *Song Saigon* currents. Fish galloped through the air—Georges Minh had witnessed his first miracle.

An excerpt from Mysterious Fragrance of the Yellow Mountains, *to be published in Canada by Penguin in 2016.*

Author Commentary

I visited my Vietnamese uncle in France when I was seven, and again at nine. He used to listen to jazz records. Smoked long cigarettes, cool and elegant, blowing out trumpets of smoke. My father had told me he plotted, across mysterious lines of communication, about different ways to overthrow the Communist government of Vietnam. Imagine! A counter-revolutionary in my own family. Years passed, I grew older, and I read nothing about a coup d'état. Disappointed, I conceded in my imagination that most "meetings" had probably deteriorated into drinking parties, but, intrigued enough, armed with other family stories, I decided to

write a historical novel set in Vietnam. A what-if set the first chapter into motion. What if such a group of men managed, in spite of themselves, to spark some sort of political action into motion, which then took on a life of its own? This excerpt is an early draft of *Mysterious Fragrance of the Yellow Mountains* which had the working title *Lucky in Saigon* when it was published in *Ricepaper*.
—*Yasuko Thanh, 2015*

About the Author

Yasuko Thanh is the author of the short story collection *Floating Like the Dead* (McClelland & Stewart, 2012). "Lucky in Saigon" is an early draft from her first novel, *Mysterious Fragrance of the Yellow Mountains*, set in French Indochina. It is forthcoming in 2016 with Penguin Canada, Hamish Hamilton, and Editura RAO, Romania. She was one of ten CBC Books' writers to watch in 2013, a *Quill & Quire* Best Books pick of 2012, and she won the 2009 Writers' Trust Journey Prize.

Porcelain Legs

Ricepaper 18, no. 4 (2013)

Corinna Chong

A single hair.

It grew, long and wiry, right out of Mom's eyelid, just above the crease of her almond lid. The kind of hair you'd expect to see on a toilet seat and not on someone's face. *Did she know it was there?* Queenie wondered. *Didn't she care?*

When the hair first appeared, it looked like a tiny check mark drawn with a mechanical pencil. You could mistake it for a stray eyebrow hair, plucked that morning, escaped from the swipe of her hand. But then it grew longer, thicker, started to catch the light the way a beetle's back shines. Soon, the end of the hair hooked into a coil, twisting itself into a crimp along its length. Then, another crimp. It grew long enough to dangle, to rest against her eyelashes.

"Your dad was at the recital, did you see him?" Mom ladled black bean sauce over Queenie's rice.

"Yeah," Queenie said, taking the ladle from her hand. "I want more pork."

"How come you keep looking down at the table? It's rude. You look at people when they talk to you." Mom set her bowl down, picked up her chopsticks. The hair jogged along her eyelashes when she blinked. She absently whisked her palm across her face, the chopsticks sticking out of her fist. "Why were none of your friends there?"

"It's just Kiwanis, Mom. Lots of kids had recitals. No one cares."

"No one cares. You always say that. What kind of friends do you have?"

Queenie shrugged. "They have other things to do on weekends. Soccer and dance and stuff."

"Hmm," Mom said, looking over her bowl that she held under her chin. The end of the hair was now combed between two eyelashes, hovering in front of its reflection. It tugged gently on her eyelid each time she lowered her eyes back to her bowl. Mom chewed her rice thoughtfully, smacking her lips. "We talked to your teacher after."

"I know. I saw."

"She didn't believe that your dad was actually your dad." She snickered, revealing a ball of rice between her teeth.

"No one ever does."

"Anyway, she said your rhythms were excellent."

"That's good."

"Weren't you having trouble with the rhythms before?" Mom put down her bowl, swept her eye twice with her fingers.

"No."

"I thought you said the rhythms were hard."

"No, I said the time signatures were hard."

"Oh," she shrugged. "I thought it was the same."

Queenie rolled her eyes.

Mom sighed, picked something out of her teeth with a long pinky nail. The hair rested against the fan of her eyelashes. "It was nice of your dad to come. He said it was really good. He thought you were so good."

The hair was still there two days later, longer, crimpier. It spent most of its time brushed across her eyelid, clinging to the skin. Every so often it wandered down, dangling, threatening to fish in the wet of her eyeball. When Mom got home from work, she went straight into the kitchen, heels clicking against the tile, and started unpacking her lunch bag like she always did. Queenie was sitting at the kitchen table eating Ritz crackers and cheese. Mom took out her Tupperware and placed it in the sink, paused to rub her eye. The white was bloodshot.

"My eye is itchy," she said, pointing it at Queenie. "Does it look infected?"

Queenie picked up a cracker, nibbled the edge. "There's a hair there."

"What? What do you mean?" Mom walked right up to her, brought her face level with Queenie's.

"Right there." Queenie pinched the hair between thumb and finger. The feel of it reminded her of the dog hairs she always had to pick off her sweater after she walked the neighbour's German Shepherd. The eyelid skin tugged.

"Ow." Mom jerked back. She fingered her eyelid, pinching at the skin. Finding the hair, she pressed it between her thumb and middle finger, gliding them down its length. "It's so long," Mom said, half-smiling. She released the hair suddenly, pulling a chair right up to Queenie's and sitting next to her. "Pull it out," she said, thrusting her face forward and closing her eyes.

"Pull it out?"

"Yes, just pull on it."

Queenie's fingers pressed the hair firmly. She pulled. The skin stretched.

"Ow, ow. Get it. Ow. Pull it."

"Ew. It's not coming out," Queenie said, releasing the hair. It stuck out straight.

Mom clucked her tongue and huffed. She hurried upstairs, leaving her shoes standing at the bottom of the stairs.

Queenie and Erica had the cubbyhole that day. The cubbyhole was really just an alcove in the brick wall on the outside of the school. There was a red door at the end of it that was always closed. It was dark in there, and deep enough that a dozen kids could huddle inside it to escape the biting winter wind. But over the years it had become tradition for the grade sixers to use it for escaping the eyes of teachers instead.

Way back in September, Erica had worked it out with Ryan, Jesse, and Aaron that the boys could have the cubbyhole on Mondays and Wednesdays, and she, Becky, and Queenie could have it on Tuesdays and Thursdays. The boys said no way at first, but Erica had made them all gather around her in the cubbyhole, making a wall with their bodies. Make a wall, make a wall, she had said, and they all asked her why, what was she doing, but she just giggled and kept motioning with her hands. Once the three boys, Becky, and Queenie had surrounded Erica, blocking the light so that only the dim glow pouring over their heads shone on her body, she grabbed the hem of her skirt and whisked it up, holding it in clenched fists under her chin.

They all gasped.

Erica stood motionless, her eyes gazing directly ahead, a tight smirk stretched across her face. Her panties were white and patterned with tiny red hearts, but the fabric was worn thin, so that her skin showed through in patches, and some of the hearts had turned pink. Queenie could see the faint grey line down the middle of her crotch.

Ryan and Jesse clapped their hands over their mouths and burst into hysterical laughter. Slivers of light filtered through the gaps between their legs and danced about Erica's naked thighs, illuminating the tiny white hairs stippling her skin.

An image flashed in Queenie's mind: the porcelain doll her aunt had given her years ago. The doll had black hair and dark brown eyes, just like Queenie's. She stood out on the shelf among Queenie's other six dolls, her flat brown eyes staring. "It's a Chinese doll," her aunt had said when Queenie opened it. Yes, Queenie could see, the doll's eyes were slightly upturned at the corners. But when she lifted the doll's yellow taffeta skirt, she saw her white porcelain legs. So white, so smooth, so thin, Queenie was afraid they'd shatter if she held them too hard.

Queenie looked at Becky. Becky wasn't smiling. She was staring, eyes vacant, at Erica's face, her lips parted slightly. Queenie thought Becky looked worried. Scared.

Erica opened her fists and allowed her skirt to drop. Her smirk cracked into a big smile as the boys ran away, still hysterical with laughter. With the boys now gone, the light poured into the cubby hole, glinting against Erica's glossy teeth.

Queenie and Becky stared at her, holding their elbows.

"What?" Erica said, brushing her palms together. "Now it's a deal."

The boys let them have Tuesdays and Thursdays after that, and Fridays were for whoever could get there first. The last two Fridays, Queenie had got the cubbyhole because she was the first one let out of class, having finished her assignments early. So now Erica and Becky called Queenie "the champion," patted her on the back when the boys came around sneering. Erica and Becky had also let Queenie hang out with them for the whole recess every day last week and this week.

Today was Thursday, and Becky was at home sick. It was a cold December day. Queenie and Erica leaned against the wall of the cubbyhole, taking their snacks out of their jacket pockets with mittened hands. Erica's legs were so long that she could plant her foot against the opposite wall and hold herself up. She liked to show Queenie and Becky, and she always made them try too, even though neither of them could ever do it. Without Becky there, Erica put one foot up against the wall, but she didn't ask Queenie to try.

"I'm doing this fashion show thingy at the mall," Erica said. "On Saturday. Wanna come?" She poured a little pile of Wheat Crunch in her mitten and tossed it into her mouth.

Queenie reddened, her eyes growing wide. "Well, I don't really know anything about modelling."

Erica giggled. "No, I just meant to watch. You have to be *recruited* to model." Her pillowy bottom lip puckered out when she said "recruited." "It gets kinda boring in the breaks between shows. They make us stick around, but we can go walking around the mall if we want."

"Okay, sure," Queenie replied, tearing open her fruit snacks. "I'll just have to ask my mom."

Erica wiped salt from the corners of her mouth. "Your mom's not the Chinese one, is she?"

"Yeah, she is."

"I always thought you lived with the white one."

"Well, I go to my dad's house practically every weekend."

"Ohh, okay. Cool."

Queenie nodded.

"So, do you like, talk Chinese at your house and everything?"

"No," Queenie said, shaking her head. "Never. I don't even know any Chinese. We only ever speak English."

"But weren't you born in China?"

"No. I was born here. And my mom is actually from Malaysia. There's Chinese people there too."

"Oh," Erica said. "Neat." Her lips, irritated by the salt, blushed dark pink.

Queenie inspected a cherry-shaped fruit snack that was missing its stem. Mom would only buy the generic brand, and half of them were always deformed. "What does it matter," Mom had said when Queenie complained. "Food is food." Just to get Mom to buy fruit snacks in the first place was hard enough. "Why do you want to eat this gummy stuff when you can have a banana or a bao-zi?" Mom had asked. Queenie didn't bother trying to explain how they traded at recess, and no one would trade for a deformed cherry fruit snack. No one would trade for a generic fruit snack either; it had to be Sodalicious or Gushers. Ryan had once traded a Gusher for one of Wendy's paper-thin pieces of seaweed. He and the other boys had laughed as he tore off a little square of the seaweed, opened his mouth wide, and gently placed the square on the tip of his pink wet tongue before curling it back into his mouth. "Eeeeuuch," he garbled, grimacing. The boys laughed and laughed. Wendy laughed. Queenie laughed, left her little saran-wrapped package of bao-zi in the bottom of her backpack, squished beneath her binder.

"Saturday?" Mom said, without looking away from her reflection in the bathroom mirror. She was staring at her upper lip, tweezers poised. "Saturday's no good. Jan asked me to babysit Max for a couple of hours. And I have to do it, no choice. She watered our lawn for two weeks in the summer, remember?"

"So?" Queenie said, looking at Mom's reflection.

Mom pushed her tongue under her upper lip, tilted her head to catch the light. Little black hairs stuck up along the edge of her lip like centipede legs.

"Why does that matter?" Queenie asked, turning away. She couldn't watch Mom doing that, plucking away and looking like a gorilla with her tongue sliding under her upper lip—her *hairy* upper lip. "You can still babysit."

"And carry that crazy baby up and down the mall? Ha, I don't think so."

"You can just drop me off at the mall."

Mom snickered, plucked a hair from her chin.

"I'm almost thirteen now. Everyone else is allowed to go to the mall without their parents."

"Aren't you supposed to be at your dad's on Saturday anyway?"

"He can't on Saturday. He said I was old enough, I should just go to the mall alone."

"I see." Mom put the tweezers back in the medicine cabinet, swung the door shut. "Fine. We'll go to the mall on Saturday. But you're not going alone."

Santa's Village was set up in the mall's main foyer. Kids and their parents lined up behind the red velvet ropes. It wasn't quite noon, and Santa's throne was empty.

Once, when she was little, Queenie went with her dad to get a picture with Santa. Santa's Village still looked the same as it did then. She remembered lining up between the velvet ropes, her eyes glued to the curtain behind the throne, where she knew Santa would soon pop out. She felt Dad's hand suddenly grip her shoulder, and when she looked up at him, she noticed a man standing beside them, on the other side of the ropes. The man was old, with a long grey beard. He wore a tie that looked like the keys of a piano.

"That's a wonderful thing you did there, sir," the man said, tapping Dad on the shoulder. His eyes were light blue, and Queenie could see the whites all the way around. He nodded, looking at Queenie.

"I'm sorry?" Dad said, smiling at the man.

"If people like you weren't around, I don't know what would've happened to these ones." He patted Queenie on the head with a large, white hand.

Dad pulled Queenie closer as the man reached inside his pocket. The man retrieved a five-dollar bill.

"Here," he said, holding it out to Queenie. "To show my appreciation. I did my service overseas, mind you, but I never did my part for those poor children over there." He smiled, showing teeth lined with grey gums.

Dad laughed, gently pushed the man's money away. "Oh no, sir. That's not—she's mine. She's my daughter."

Queenie hadn't understood what was happening. She wanted the money; nobody had ever given her five dollars before. She wanted to reach out and take the bill from the man's hand, but she could tell her Dad would get mad if she did.

"Yes, of course. She's your daughter. People said we didn't win the war, but was that any excuse to let the children suffer?" The man shook his head gravely, still holding out the money.

"No, I'm sorry, you don't understand—" said Dad.

"Please. I insist, a token of my admiration." The man took Queenie's hand, pressed the five-dollar bill into her palm, and walked briskly away.

Queenie had forgotten about that man until now. Remembering him made her jaw clench up.

"Where is this show supposed to be?" asked Mom as they paced through the mall. She carried Max on her hip because she hadn't wanted to ask Jan to borrow her stroller. "I shouldn't be taking the baby to the mall, anyway," Mom had said. She held Max like a sack of vegetables, one arm around his back, her hip sinking under his weight.

"I don't know where. Erica didn't say."

"Well, what are we doing then? Where do you want to go?"

"I guess we'll just walk around. We'll probably see it." Mom sighed. She shifted the baby's weight higher on her hip, quickened her pace. They came to the end of the hallway, turned left. For a brief moment, Queenie considered the possibility that there wasn't any fashion show.

"You carry him for a while," Mom said, putting Max in Queenie's arms. Mom rubbed her lower back. "*Ai-ya*, I told you I can't carry this baby around like this."

She continued walking, Queenie trailing close behind. Here at the mall, without the baby, Mom looked different from at home. Hunched. Small. Her shoulders curved, her arms dangled. She looked like a small old lady as she walked through the mall's grand, white-tiled hallways, past all the mannequins wearing leather skirts and silk blouses and tight jeans and T-shirts that said *Guess* in sparkly rhinestones. Passing, but not looking. Mom wore white sport socks with her shiny black shoes; you could see them because her pants were too short. Her pant-legs flapped around her ankles.

They passed a girl sitting at a jewellery booth wearing huge hoop earrings and bright pink lipstick. Queenie suddenly wished she hadn't worn the T-shirt she was wearing. She had saved it for this day because it was her favourite one: a souvenir T-shirt with a killer whale jumping above the word *Vancouver*, which was printed in glittery letters. It was her favourite T-shirt, but now it felt stupid, kiddish. It wasn't the right shape, either: square and too big, not like the tight, stretchy shirts that Erica always wore. Queenie pulled the flap of her unzipped fleece jacket over her shirt, tucking it under the baby, but then she didn't like the feel of the fleece jacket, either. It was lilac, with a little squirrel stitched into the chest. She shifted the baby to her left side to cover the squirrel.

The stage came into view as they approached the food court. An audience filled the first three rows of chairs, adjusting themselves in their seats and taking off their coats. Queenie sat at the back with Mom and Max as the dance music started. Red and blue lights flashed on the stage.

Erica was the first girl to step out, but Queenie didn't recognize her until she had sauntered halfway across the stage in her white high heels. Her curly hair was poofed up, bouncing about her shoulders as she walked, and her bangs were styled in a swoop across her forehead. She wore a denim pantsuit. The whole thing was one piece, and it had a big shiny silver zipper right down the middle, zipped up from her crotch to the v-neck at her chest. It was so tight that it looked like her skin was made of denim. Two small breasts rose from her chest, hugged by the taut fabric. She stood in the middle of the stage, one hand on her hip, showing gleaming white teeth between two bright red lips.

Queenie wondered what Erica's skin felt like beneath the denim. She thought of Erica's bare white legs, fuzzed with those tiny, delicate hairs. She thought of Erica's panties, the skin showing through, the little red hearts disappearing into the shadow where her thighs came together.

Queenie sat through the remainder of the fashion show, not noticing when Mom took the whining baby off her lap and out of the audience. When the music ended and the lights faded out, she spotted Mom way off to the side of the stage area, sitting with Max wriggling in her lap at an empty table in the food court. She looked tired, fed up.

"Your friend was really good," Mom said over Max's crying, her head dodging his flailing fists. "Do you want to talk to her?" She pointed to an area behind the stage where Erica was standing with a girl, another model. They were both smearing sticks of pink Lip Smackers across their mouths.

Queenie approached them, smiling at Erica, unsure if *this* Erica, the model in the skin-tight denim suit, would even know her.

"Oh," Erica said. "Hi." She looked at Queenie, head to toe, glanced at the girl next to her.

"You were so good," Queenie said, pulling on the flaps of her jacket and hugging her ribs. Up close, Erica's eyes glowed sky blue beneath the dark furl of her fake eyelashes. Queenie could only glance at them, and then look at the ground. She was afraid her cheeks were red. Erica was wearing green eyeshadow.

"Thanks." Erica tossed her hair. "Actually, I don't get a break like I thought. I have to stay here. Sorry."

Queenie shrugged, still smiling. She felt like a dwarf standing in front of Erica, whose white high heels made her look lengthened, like bubble gum stretched into a thin strand. Queenie looked down at her own thighs, draped in baggy corduroy, at her own old running shoes, once white, now yellowish-grey, scuffed along the toes and riddled with dirty cracks. "I guess I'll see you at school then."

"Yep. Bye."

Queenie stood there, staring. Max's babbling cut through the ambient noise behind her. Erica bit her nail, stared back. Then she turned to the girl beside her, asked her if she wanted to go back to the dressing rooms.

When Queenie turned around, Mom was coming toward her with the baby. Max had grabbed the breast pocket of Mom's shirt and was pulling, pulling, exposing pods of bare skin between her buttons. Mom ignored him, kept on walking straight ahead, straight towards Queenie.

The hair had grown back. Queenie could see it, black and coarse, sticking out of Mom's eyelid like a cockroach antenna. It was thicker than before, Queenie was sure. She wondered how long it would grow this time. She wondered how long it would take for Mom to notice, if she ever looked, *really* looked at herself in the mirror.

Queenie had dreamt about the hair. In her dream she saw Mom with the tweezers in front of the mirror. But when Mom pulled on the end of the hair, it didn't come out; it kept getting longer. It had been hiding beneath the skin, its length reeled up in a little ball inside her head, and as she pulled on the end, the hair unravelled. She pulled and pulled, drawing the long, black, wiry hair out like thread from a spool. She drew it out until her arm couldn't stretch any further. The hair dangled listlessly, reaching almost to her knee.

Mom put a cold shrimp bun on a plate for her breakfast and sat down next to Queenie, who was eating her cereal at the kitchen table.

"Are you going to your dad's this weekend?" Mom asked. She took a large bite of bun. Crumbs fell to the table. She chewed with her mouth open, pressing an oily finger to the crumbs and then shedding them off onto her plate.

"I dunno. He hasn't called." Queenie stared into her cereal bowl.

"Well, it's been three weeks," Mom said. She looked at the calendar on the fridge. "More than three weeks. You can call *him*, you know."

Queenie shrugged. "It doesn't matter." She looked at Mom bending over her plate and shoving the bun in her mouth.

Mom finished chewing, narrowed her eyes. "Why are you looking at me like that?"

"Like what?"

"Like *that*. Like I have something on my face."

"Well, you do. You have that hair again." Queenie pointed to her own eyelid. "There."

Mom touched the hair. She sighed. "It just grows back, always grows back."

She left the house after breakfast without bothering to pluck it out.

Queenie was the champion, and now they called her the champion for two reasons: She got the cubbyhole for the fourth Friday in a row, and she was undefeated in the staring contests they had started doing during recess. She had beat Vicky, Sam, Nora, Becky, Travis, Jesse, Ryan, and Graham, and now she was up against Erica. Erica hadn't wanted to do it; she'd said, "I'm the best at staring contests. We have to learn to stare in modelling. I'll just beat you—I know I will—I don't want you to feel bad," but finally Ryan and Jesse had convinced her. Ryan promised Erica three Gushers if she won.

Now they all crowded in the cubbyhole, surrounding Erica and Queenie. Erica stood right in front of Queenie, so close that Queenie could see little cracks in her lips, filled with caked lip gloss. Her breath smelled like sour cream and onion. The skin along her jaw was so white and smooth that Queenie would have believed it was just bone, not skin at all. The dim light that shone into the cubbyhole covered only half her face, so that the other half was shadowed, darkening her eyelashes and making her blue eyes gleam.

"Ready?" Ryan asked.

Queenie nodded.

"Okay, go!"

Queenie opened her eyes wide, stared straight into the blue of Erica's. Tiny gold flecks swam around Erica's irises. Queenie felt goosebumps creep through her body.

Erica's eyes held for a moment, but then dropped away.

"Oh my god!" she cried suddenly. "You've got little hairs there!" Erica pointed at Queenie's chin.

"What?" Queenie said quietly. "No, I don't." She felt her chin with her fingertips.

"Yeah, you do! Little black hairs. It's like a beard." Erica squealed, started laughing, still pointing. The others started to laugh, too. They all tried to look at Queenie's chin.

"Don't," said Becky, trying to hide her smile with her hand. "That's mean."

Queenie didn't know if she should say something, or what she should say. She didn't know if she should ignore Becky or look sad or walk away or get angry or say, "Yeah, I knew those hairs were there." But she didn't do any of those things. She just laughed, too. Laughed along with the others, along with Erica, tried to copy the sound of her giggling, the look of her open mouth.

Author Commentary

In writing "Porcelain Legs," I wanted to explore, through the character of Queenie, the internalized oppression that mixed-race youth who grow up in a white-dominated community often experience—a conflict I battled myself throughout my childhood. Like all kids, I just wanted to fit in but found myself unable to reconcile my own mixed racial appearance with those of the fully white and fully Asian people around me. In addition, the media images that surrounded me told me that only white people could really be beautiful, popular, and successful. While Queenie's veneration of Erica is an extension of her idolization of her white father, her rejection of her mother's unapologetic "Chineseness" reveals Queenie's alienation from her own half-Chinese identity. The single hair growing on Mom's eyelid becomes an inescapable marker of her foreignness in Queenie's world. This story was in many ways the basis of my first novel, *Belinda's Rings,* which also features a young half-Chinese protagonist. —*Corinna Chong, 2015*

About the Author

Corinna Chong received her MA in English and creative writing from the University of New Brunswick. Originally from Calgary, she currently teaches English literature at Okanagan College in Kelowna, where she's also the co-editor of *Ryga: A Journal of Provocations.* Her writing has been published in *Echolocation, The Malahat Review, Grain,* and *Ricepaper.* Her first novel, *Belinda's Rings,* was published by NeWest Press in 2013.

No Sleeping on Bench (excerpt from novel *Progress in Process*)

Ricepaper 19, no. 2 (2014)

SKY Lee

It was March 15, 1953. After finishing up the morning's orders, Florida Waters sat down to a sandwich at her tiny desk when the intercom buzzed her again. She had reason to believe that it was another rush order but it turned out to be a phone call from Seymour Defoe Inman.

"Flor, Trixi's been released from the asylum and she already left town. I'm sending Chas down to pick you up in a couple of hours. He'll have your necessaries packed. Then he's coming straight over here to pick me up and then we're all going to find her. Don't be late!"

"But what about my job 'n my boss?" cried Florida, greatly surprised.

"I'm your boss." Click.

Certainly Florida knew better than to question him. First of all, if it hadn't been for him, there was no way in hell Florida would have gotten her job with Los Angeles's biggest movie distribution company. It was a fine privilege for a black woman to sit day after day in her very own claustrophobic cubicle with a pinging ceiling fan over her head. It was where she made a significant contribution to the comings and goings by the cartload of stores of inane Hollywood comedies in weighty metal canisters. As well, her husband, Chas, was one of Seymour's many drivers. And then, as if to seal their fate, after Chas and Flor were forced to sell their house five years ago, they had to make do by moving into a series of apartments indirectly owned by Mr Inman. As patrons went, Seymour was patronizing in his paternalistic way. As a result, Flor and Chas were vulgarized in their subservient way. And that's generally about as far as laundry goes between coloured and white.

So Chas drove in his grey worsted driver's uniform while Florida sat stiffly beside him in stately silence. Behind them, Seymour prowled uncomfortably about in the carriage of the Cadillac until he passed out with the help of a fine-tooled silver flask. He ground his teeth as he slept fitfully. After a while, Florida drove while Chas fiddled with the radio to keep her awake as best he could. Finally, Seymour drove while Chas and Florida sprawled in deep sleep all over the buttery luxury of the leather interior. They arrived at the Salt Lake City bus depot in the late afternoon.

The moment they got there, Seymour sprang out of the car and rushed into the public building. There didn't seem to be a shadow of a doubt in his mind but Florida hung back until curiosity got the better of her. She gathered together her handbag and gloves and asked Chassis, "D'ya suppose ol' Trix is in there, or is he here to meet someone else?"

"I don't know, baby," cautioned Chas, "but when the time comes, try not to get involved, sweet-hon! You know how those two are."

Flor thought about that. After a thirteen-year hiatus, how would Trixi and Seymour behave in each other's presence? Seymour was so obviously in one of his manic moods made ever more inflated by his insane workload and gaudy wealth. If not for the fact that he had become their employer now, Florida would have asked him directly, to his face, like back in the days when she was able to do so, when he wasn't quite the giant that he had become, when she was much younger, with much more egalitarian cheek than she had now that the social and financial gap between them had split wide open.

She took an extra moment or two to pin the beaded and netted hard-shell cap firmly onto her skull. And Chas, in hat, knee-high boots and buttoned-down suit, had already hopped out to open the car door for her. Together, they looked the class act. But even as he helped her out of the Cadillac, a police cruiser pulled up sharply behind them. Suddenly lots of people stopped to stare. Chas and Florida dumbly awaited the advance of two cops.

"Sir, you're parked in a no-parking zone," began the cop.

Chas and Florida breathed an invisible sigh of relief. To be addressed in such a reasonable manner was a very good thing.

"Ma'am, are you the owner of this vehicle?"

"No, sir, she's my wife," replied Chas protectively.

"Our employer went inside that building."

"What is the name of the vehicle's owner?" asked the cop, with notebook in hand, while Florida quietly withdrew and seamlessly merged with the gathering crowd of gawkers. But even as she did, she paused to listen to Chas work his usual routine, "Well, young sirs," began Chas, with his usual scratching of the humble head, "I'm guessing that the owner of this here vehicle might actually be the Star Gate Movie Studios in Hollywood, California, but in fact my employer's name is Mr C. Defoe. He's a Hollywood movie producer."

"You don't say!" The young officer wrote it all down.

Florida grinned at the slight distortion of Seymour's name. It was one of the underhanded ways that she and Chas and Seymour had always slithered around as a team, unnoticed by outsiders in general.

"Yes sir, why just the other day, while I was driving Mr C back to his Bel Air home—are you acquainted with Mr C?"

"Well, ahh … yeah, sure, I am!" said the cop.

"Well sir, Mr C was telling me how it's too bad how folks just get caught up with the stars and don't pay enough mind to the real men behind the movie scenes."

"Hey, I think I've heard of Mr C!" cried the other cop.

"Well sir, I'm glad to hear you keep up with the movie business …"

As Chas rambled on, Florida simply let the irresistible sweep of being human push her through the glass and bronze Art Deco gates of the Salt Lake City Train Station and Bus Terminal. Once she was inside, Flor gazed up at the high ornate ceilings of the grand little edifice. The overhead spaciousness immediately lifted her visceral fatigue. She let her heart be lifted into the air like a dust mote on a sunbeam while making her way through the anxious press and collision of bodies in search of human purpose and fulfillment. As soon as she stopped struggling against the rush-hour crowds, Florida felt it. It was an intimate moment of spiritual fullness that she knew well because she already lived it and dreamed it many times over.

Right away, she noticed a little dark–chocolate girl in a starched yellow dress, winking and smiling at her with such warmth and awareness. And when the girl's gaze wandered off, Florida happily followed it until she spied Seymour, of all people, in his rich garb, hunkered down on a bench full of folk along with all their ragtag baggage and sundry. Florida thought it marvellous that she should have found him in this way. He pretended to be catnapping but, in fact, he was intent on watching the tiny coffee shop seemingly situated like a shining glass display case in the propitious middle of everything.

Inside the brightly lit coffee shop, Trixi Lee sat on her ten-minute break at the very end of the counter and was about to dig into a large bowl of vegetable soup, to which she had added a whole cupful of finely chopped parsley and a big squeeze of fresh lemon when, by finely honed instinct alone, she felt sharp eyes boring into the back of her head. She was about to turn her head for a tentative look-see when she almost brushed noses with Annie, the waitress, who had leaned in very close in order to teasingly say to her, "Aren't you the stranger one, Missy Hu?" Annie called her "Missy Hu" because it was the way Trixi Lee identified herself a few days ago when she first came in to ask for a job in the kitchen.

"I have never in all my bored days seen anyone eat a bowl of soup like that," Annie continued. "Waddya call it? Halfa soupee, halfa saladee? Sure would save on a manure-load of dishes around here if more customers ate like that!" Annie paused to light her hand-rolled cigarette.

"Hey, kiddo, Garfy there thinks you're so cute, he wants to take you home with him. Waddya say, li'l lady? It beats sleeping in the garbage lock-up at night."

Trixi Lee looked over at Gar Foo, the Chinese cook, again. He'd been mooning at her nonstop ever since she arrived. Was it his eyes that she felt? She ducked her head as low as it could go.

"Hey, listen!" Annie again. "I know you shur da heck don't say much, but you're shur a good l'il worker, ya know, 'n' I already ast that cheapskate, Ed, if he wans ta pays ya some decent money, ya know, jes in case you wanna stay mor'n a week that is, 'n' waddya know, he said okay!"

That was when Trixi noticed Ed, the boss, eyeing the both of them from behind the cash register as well. It was altogether too much attention, and she just wanted to disappear from all sight!

"So waddya say? God knows, hon, we all been down 'n' out! We all been there, ya know, sweetie. Done that 'n' all. Ain't nut'in ta be ashamed of. Hell, you kin even come home with me if you just wanna couch for a few nights. I'd jis'asoon kick out that drunken dog of a man of mine ..."

Aiyee, the kindness of strangers, thought Trixi Lee, as she closed her eyes to better feel the warmth of the moment. Annie kept flapping at the mouth. "Hey, I know you're really shy. But that ain't no reason to be scared, honey! We don't bite."

Trixi wanted to thank Annie, Gar Foo, and Ed for their humanity, but she already knew that her time had come. She could feel the tug and pull of forces beyond her control. Already, in her mind's eye, she could see the *No Sleeping on Bench* sign in the cold early morning shadows of the bus depot's waiting area. And the vision of the sleeping man on the bench unfurled into real flesh and life's blood. He rose and ignited the night with his steaming, hazy glow. There was an ill-omened corona around both the moon and the man as he stepped forward to make contact.

Trixi suddenly realized that she could not allow herself be trapped at the end of a coffeeshop counter like this. Annie and Ed and Gar Foo and all her new friends would not in any way, shape, or form, be able to understand or protect her, and she knew she would have to leave the establishment in order to meet the man head on.

It was just the nigh impossible matter of summoning the courage. Yet with a quick intake of air, she did just that—because she had no other choice. She rushed out into the howl of the cataclysmic wind.

At the first sighting of Trixi Lee, Florida's white-gloved hand shot up to stifle her gasp. She too felt the propulsive force of a pent-up fury that was gathering momentum. She herself had harboured it without even realizing. But now, it blew open her floodgates, and an emotional outpouring began with a deluge of heavy tears.

Drenched to the bone, Trixi could barely see through the downpour in her heart. Yet she clearly saw Seymour Defoe Inman as he stood by himself. The tragic solitary force of him could be specifically located even though its cyclonic power spitefully rushed at her from multiple directions. She faltered in confusion, not knowing in which direction to run from him.

It was in this split second of hesitation that Seymour mustered his advantage. He was suddenly upon her with a vise-like grip on both green-stick arms. He dealt her a forceful slap upon her cheek, grabbed both her child-thin shoulders, and shook her until she rattled.

He felt he had to do this in order to keep her under his control. He needed to keep her disoriented or else she could slip away like she was nothing at all. He told himself to throttle her throat, anything to keep her from flying off on her witch's broom! He had this one instant to bear down on her. And pound her with all the physical engagement of ... his need ... to leave her gasping for breath! Damn her all the way to hell!

"Damn you, bitch, for making me feel like this. Don't you ever dare try to get away from me again!" Grunting, he even got on top of her and locked her down with the weight of his portly person as tightly as he could while she squirmed like an electric eel under him. All his exertions overheated him. Breathing hard, he got an erection as hard as he had not had in a very long time. And this was one fuck that should have lasted forever except from the faraway edges of his consciousness and zooming in fast, he began to notice some scattered pedestrian faces hanging in the air, frozen in horror at the beefy sight of him with his diamond-clipped silk tie and ripe air of Los Indios Cuban cigars on top of a greasy little Chinese kitchen helper. But there was no epiphany here! Even with his lingering hard-on, he would have climbed off by himself eventually but for the fact that the two cops in their youthful enthusiasm had hauled him off and struggled to keep him off. He still needed to keep his eye on her though.

"She owes me money," he bellowed unconvincingly. He was so wound up he could barely unclench his fist in order to whip back his fallen forelock.

"Sir, do you want to press charges?" asked one of the rookies without skipping a seal-trained bark before a man of means.

Seymour's heart skipped a couple of beats when he realized what he had done. He stopped short and slumped back in abject defeat while Chas pushed through the crowds and stepped up to the plate by loudly declaring, "Oh no! Mr C, you done made a mistake! You got the wrong person. D'ya heah, sir? That's not him. You must not be feelin' good agin. You be havin' an episode."

Under his breath, Chas hastily warned Seymour of the inevitability of trouble. Already, there was a small-town, camera-ready newspaperman rushing in for a story. "Mistah Seymour, take a look, five o'clock, newsman, fast, we go now!"

"Oh fuckin' hell!" ejaculated Seymour with all his blistering might. He looked all wide-eyed and red-faced around for Trixi Lee, but true to magical form, she had already disappeared into thin air.

Meanwhile Chas begged the constables, "Officers, please help my boss-man back to his automobile. He has to sit down and take his heart attack pills. He's not well. All this fuss'll kill 'im. And all you gent'min kin talk better in the Cadillac. Please, this way, sirs!"

"Where'd she go?" persisted Seymour, even as he was carted off by three burly uniforms. "Where'd she go?"

"Ain't nobody there for yew, Mr C !" cried Chas. "Y'all jes scarin' the bejesus outta folk. We's need to get back into the caddy ta git u heart pills. Everything gonna be fine, Mr C!"

Florida watched them leave, and in their flamboyant wake, she simply whispered the words, "Miz Trixi?"

To which Trixi answered, "Miss Florida Waters, how nice! You haven't changed. I like your hat. Come with me, will ya!"

And just like that, as if the thirteen-year hiatus was nothing at all, Florida fell into easy step with Trixi Lee. She marvelled at how Trixi had not changed one iota under lock and key. If anything, Trixi looked younger, smaller, and more innocent than ever before—as if that made any sense, as if she had not lost thirteen years to incarceration but gained time instead!

Trixi instructed, "Help me say goodbye to these nice coffee shop folk that took me in. I can see that they're pretty shaken up. And then you and I should leave as soon as we are able. I don't have anything to pack except a cardboard satchel with my life story inside."

Florida said, "Okay! Oh, and life story! Okay to that too! We'll get to it eventually, I guess!"

In reality, after the cops got a little something and went away happy, Chas drove Seymour's caddy around to the back door of the coffee shop in the alley and turned off the engine. Both their reunion with Trixi Lee and her goodbyes to Annie, Gar Foo, and Ed lasted just under two hours. It turned into quite a friendly little party without one word said about the curious incident between Seymour and Trixi. It looked entirely too personal, so people dismissed it as a mistake that perhaps never should have even happened.

Annie the waitress came out to the car and took everybody's orders a few times over. They ate with relish Gar Foo's grilled pork chops with applesauce, as well as two peach cobblers and a blueberry pie. Trixi shared her vegetable soup with Florida. Ed and Gar Foo were kept busy in the kitchen but they came out, peered into, and hovered over the car multiple times. Annie was the only one with the temerity to actually get into the Cadillac and get a load off her feet. Seymour offered to buy a round of beer for everyone, so Ed had a big wooden crate of bottles delivered. Everyone used the public restrooms in the terminal. Seymour used the phone booth a few times over before leaving in his Cadillac with his uniformed driver and motley female passengers.

Author Commentary

In my attempt to describe colonialism in "No Sleeping on the Bench," I chose a perspective derived from the radical feminist adage, "the personal is political." In this excerpt, there is a key meeting between a black woman and Chinese woman, although this point is easily missed in the often violent swirl of historical forces around them. There are two strong elements in my story. One is social placement as often defined by labour, and the other is the shifting of social placement. For instance, after witnessing an inexplicable event, a group of strangers undertake to share a meal. In terms of labour, there is a carefully considered delineation of who sits who stands who cooks who eats who serves who pays. In contrast, there is the strong element of travel or, if you will, the shifting of social placement: Each pilgrim converges upon a place as prosaic as the bus depot in Salt Lake City, Utah. The Chinese woman as a fragile outsider sits up on the bench in the waiting area and remains vigilant, while the white man, ostensibly a veteran of World War II, lays his weary head down whenever and wherever he feels like it. To me it is a Dorothea Lange record of a moment in time, imbued with the transcendent power of being human. *—SKY Lee, 2015*

About the Author

SKY Lee is an author and illustrator with a BFA from the University of British Columbia and a diploma in nursing from Douglas College. She is the author of *Disappearing Moon Cafe* (1990) and *Bellydancer* (1991).

Túshūguăn

Ricepaper 19, no. 3 (2014)

Eric Choi

Fénshū carefully studied the boy with the book.

The youth looked to be in his early teens, but it was difficult to tell. Contemporary Běiměizhōu children always looked much older than their years. This one resembled a skeleton, more bone than flesh, with grimy bug-bitten skin, laddered ribs, twig-thin arms and legs, and bloodied, swollen feet. His face was gaunt, topped by a tangled, greasy mess of long black hair. He also stank, reeking like an oily, salty fish.

Fénshū looked into the boy's green eyes, and while it was impossible to get a sense of the boy's soul, she could discern a certain fire—perhaps of intelligence, certainly of strength.

"Nĭ jiào shén ma míng zì?" she asked. The boy was silent.

"Nĭ míngbái ma?"

Still no response.

"What is your name?" she said at last in English.

"Wu," the boy said. His yellowish-brown teeth were chipped and twisted.

"Hello Wu, I am Dr Fénshū Zhèng", she continued. "I am ... an historical archaeologist. Do you know what that is?"

The boy fell silent again.

"How are you, Wu?"

The boy did not answer, looking instead at his inquisitor and returning the question: "How are *you*?"

Definitely intelligence. The boy's verbal language skills, at least in

English, were excellent. Fénshū was quite impressed.

"I am sixty years old!" Fénshū cackled in a high-pitched voice, trying to smile.

Wu simply stared.

"Do you have something for me?"

Wu nodded, his calloused hands reverently handing over the book.

"Thank you, Wu." Fénshū gestured to the floor of the tent. "Please, sit down. My colleague will be back for you shortly."

Wu hesitated for a moment, then sat on the ground as instructed.

Fénshū pushed her spectacles up the bridge of her nose and examined the book. It was a brownish-black hardcover, about sixteen by twenty-four centimetres and perhaps three centimetres thick, enclosed within a clear sealable plastic bag of the type that had once been a common means of storing food in pre-Fall Běiměizhōu civilization. The book was in fairly good condition, except for a serrated gash that penetrated the pages from cover to cover. Also inside the plastic bag, collected mostly along the spine, were clumps of a white powdery residue. She held the book up to her nose and sniffed. Through the punctured plastic, it smelled faintly of camphor and another odd odour she could not immediately identify.

"Where did this come from?" Fénshū asked. "Where did you find this?"

The boy looked up.

"Where did you find this?" she repeated.

"In the old shit and piss!"

Over and over again, Wu's mother would ask him the same thing.

"What do you do if you see a Jiangshi?"

"Run," Wu would answer.

"Why?"

Sometimes Wu would hesitate, and his mother would insist.

"Come on. Why?" she would repeat.

"Because a Jiangshi will hurt you, kill you, eat you."

The road upon which Wu walked was wrinkled and cracked like the skin of an old man. Weeds and wild flowers sprouted from every fissure, heaving apart the decaying asphalt. With slow certainty over the long years since the Fall, the pavement was being reduced to the constituent stone, gravel, and bitumen from which it had been formed.

For much of this day, Wu had been fortunate in his solitude. It was not to last.

Wu stopped in his tracks and squinted. In the far distance, a Jiangshi came into view. He recognized the brainfrizzed monster immediately, a stained and filthy figure slowly shambling in his direction with that distinctive jerky, unsteady gait.

He didn't think he had been spotted, but he wasn't about to stick around to find out.

Wu ran off the road, through the tall grasses, into the trees. Twigs and branches lashed his body and stones cut his bare feet, but neither slowed his flight. Deeper and deeper into the woods he ran, until his lungs heaved, and his heart felt like it would burst from his chest.

Finally, he stopped ... and stared.

Before him was a ruin of the old world. A house had once stood here, but it had long ago collapsed and been assimilated by the living woods. Only the chimney remained standing, but Wu could see that its bricks were dropping and breaking, little by little, as the mortar crumbled and powdered. Some kind of vine grew everywhere, climbing through the broken windows and up the bars and grillwork.

Wu circled about the stone tower, fascinated.

There was a shallow hill across from the remnants of the foundation. He walked to the hill and climbed. Suddenly, he stopped and looked down.

He had run over something.

Tracing back a few steps, he spotted a patch of dead leaves and twigs collected within a rough square. Resting on his knees, Wu swept away the detritus with his hands. A grey slab with a square metal handle imbedded on top appeared before him.

Wu stared in wonder, uncertain of what to do next. Finally, he reached down and grasped the handle with his small, bony hands.

Nothing happened.

He extended his legs and dug in his feet for leverage, pulling harder with all his strength, but still it did not budge. Exhausted, he released the handle and fell backwards, his legs splayed.

Something moved in the bushes.

Wu turned in the direction of the rustling noise, his eyes wide. He pulled a slingshot out of his pouch, his other hand frantically sweeping the ground for a suitable projectile. Grasping a stone, he loaded the pocket and pulled back the bands with trembling hands.

The leaves rustled again.

Wu drew back the bands a little further, then released.

The happiest times were when his mother told him stories about the things from before, the old world prior to the Fall.

"People flew?"

"Yes. In flying machines. Anywhere in the world, without fear."

And she would tell him about the music that came from a box smaller than your hand, and the heat and light and clean water that came with a touch, and the pictures that moved, and the buildings as high as mountains, and the places with piles of fresh food, and the artificial stars that let people talk to one another across the world, and most wonderful of all, the bound volumes upon whose pages were recorded the knowledge and beauty of Běiměizhōu civilization at its height.

"Books."

"Books," Wu repeated.

The boy emerged from the bushes a split second after Wu launched the projectile. Eyes wide, he instinctively ducked. The stone whizzed over his head, striking the trunk of a tree just behind him.

"What are you doing?" shouted the boy indignantly.

Wu grabbed another stone and reloaded his slingshot, drawing back the band and keeping it trained on the stranger.

The pale, skinny boy looked to be about Wu's age. With the exception of his short curly brown hair, Wu could have been looking at a reflection.

"What are *you* doing?" Wu challenged. He studied the stranger. The boy, though as emaciated as he was, did not slur his words, and he stood firm without the jerky twitches that were the stigmata of those who consumed the flesh of others.

"Are you a Jiangshi?" Wu asked rhetorically.

"Are *you* a Jiangshi?" the boy echoed in retort.

Slowly, Wu lowered his slingshot. "I am Wu."

"I'm Vancott," the boy said. He pointed at the crumbling chimney. "What's that ruin?"

Vancott walked up the shallow hill to join Wu, and the boys found themselves looking at the slab and handle in the ground. They took hold of the handle together and managed to lift the grey slab.

Putting the lid aside, they went to the opening and peered down into the darkness.

Wu squinted. "Something's in there!"

A very faint odour wafted out of the opening. Vancott sniffed.

Recognition came to both of them at the same time.

"Stupid!" Vancott shoved Wu, sending him sprawling to the ground. "This is—"

"Old shit and piss," Wu said. He remembered his mother's words. "Skeptic tank."

The two boys sat silently, pondering their next move.

Suddenly, a flock of dark birds took flight from the trees, swirling noisily into the sky. Wu and Vancott turned.

There was a rustling in the bushes.

Vancott grabbed Wu's arm. "I saw a Jiangshi today!"

Wu shot Vancott a fearful glance. "I saw a Jiangshi too," he hissed. "On the road."

The boys looked about, knowing they were badly exposed atop the shallow hill. At once, the same desperate idea occurred to both. They got up quickly.

Vancott slid the concrete lid partially over the opening, while Wu gathered up some dead leaves and twigs and piled them on top. It wasn't much in the way of camouflage, but it was better than nothing. Vancott squeezed inside first, followed by Wu. With great effort, they managed to get the lid almost closed except for a thin sliver.

Wu peered through the narrow slit, and before long saw the monster stumble out of the woods. The gangly, twitching figure, no longer really human, was the same one Wu had seen on the road.

Quietly, the boys drew the lid fully closed, and darkness enveloped them.

Wu and Vancott waited silently in the musty dark for a sound, a voice, a sign ... something.

They were sitting on a pile of flat rectangular objects. Wu felt around with his hands. The objects were all roughly the same shape but in different sizes. He remembered seeing something when they first opened the lid, but without light he could do nothing to identify the objects even while sitting among them.

Breathing was difficult, and the boys were getting sleepy. The stale air would not sustain them much longer.

Cautiously, they pushed the lid and opened up a small crack to look around. The brief inrush of fresh air hit their lungs with an almost icy sharpness, and it took all of Wu's willpower to not dash out right away.

Finally, they pushed the lid all the way open and climbed out. Wu moved to follow, but on sudden impulse grabbed one of the rectangular objects on his way up. Outside, the boys collapsed onto the sweet long grass of the shallow hill, lying on their backs, lungs heaving as they gulped fresh air, their mouths open and trembling like those of fish out of water.

After a long moment of rest, Wu rolled onto his side and saw the flat rectangular object lying on the grass. He sat up and took it with both hands, bringing it up to his eyes.

Wu stared at the object for a moment before recognizing it. "A book!"

"What?" Vancott asked.

Wu turned the book about, examining it from all sides.

It was brownish-black in colour and sealed in a transparent pouch, probably made of the material that Wu's mother had called plastic. A hard seam ran along one side. Wu examined the seam and eventually figured out how to pull the pouch open. There was a faint medicinal smell, and clumps of a white powder fell out.

With deliberate care, Wu reverently extracted the book from the plastic pouch. There were symbols on the cover that he recognized as words, but like all contemporary teenagers he didn't read. He slowly flipped through the yellowish pages, each dense with indecipherable text.

"What is it?" Vancott asked again.

"A book," Wu repeated. "From the old world, before the Fall."

Vancott's eyes widened.

Wu was illiterate, not stupid. He had the sense to know, on an instinctive level, the importance of what he and Vancott had found. Somebody had done this on purpose, creating an improvised library—a túshūguǎn—either before or shortly after the Fall, in the hope that someone like Wu might find the treasure.

Wu put the book back into the pouch and resealed it. The boys covered up the hatch again with leaves and twigs before setting off. They would need to find a person who could read.

Wu and Vancott wandered aimlessly for days. Sometimes, they would walk for hours in one direction when Vancott would suddenly change his mind, and then they would turn about and retrace their steps. On other occasions, they seemed to be walking in circles. Wu began to doubt whether Vancott had any idea where they were going.

Beside him, Wu heard Vancott's stomach growl. His companion always seemed to be hungry. For such a thin little guy, he ate an awful lot. Not for the first time, Wu wondered how Vancott had managed to survive on his own for this long.

A feral rakunk bounded out of some shrubbery a short distance ahead. Vancott had seen the black-masked, fluffy-tailed animal first, putting out his hand to stop Wu and signalling for silence. If nothing else, Wu was grateful for Vancott's sharp eyes. His companion might eat too much food, but at least he was good at spotting it.

Wu slowly knelt to pick up a rock, quietly pulling out his slingshot at the same time. He steadied himself, drew back the band, took aim, and fired.

Killing the game turned out to be the easy part. Starting the fire to cook it proved much more difficult. It had rained earlier in the day, and the boys had trouble finding dry grass and leaves for tinder. More than once, Wu saw Vancott eyeing the book. He pulled it closer.

Night had fallen by the time they got the fire going and cooked the rakunk. In the chilly dark, Wu and Vancott managed to find some comfort in the warming flames and meat. When they had finished eating, they lay on their backs and gazed up at the twinkling tapestry of stars above. Wu thought about his mother's stories of people in flying machines, soaring amongst the clouds and even out to the dark heavens beyond.

Wu closed his eyes, and as sleep came, the book slipped quietly from his arms and fell to the ground.

He dreamed.

It was a strange dream, the kind Wu knew was only a dream even while he was dreaming it, because he was seeing things that he could not possibly have known or remembered. He was in a vast cavern, within which were rows upon rows of shelves, each packed end-to-end with books. The volumes were all of different sizes, thicknesses, and colours, with incomprehensible words along the spines. There must have been hundreds, if not thousands, of books stretching further into the depths of the cavern than Wu could see.

He reached out to a book at random and tried to take it off the shelf. The book came out about two-thirds of the way and then abruptly jammed.

Wu pulled harder, to no effect. He grabbed the book with both hands and yanked with all his strength.

The entire bookshelf began to fall towards him.

Wu let go of the book and stepped back. The bookshelf was still falling.

Walking backwards, he tried to quicken his pace. He looked up and saw that the bookshelf appeared to be of infinite height, stretching upwards without end. There was nothing he could do to avoid getting crushed.

The bookshelf came down.

There was a scream.

Wu woke with a start. The scream had not been his.

Beside the smouldering remnants of the fire, Vancott was locked in a desperate struggle with a monster. His attacker had pinned him to the ground. Vancott squirmed, kicked, and punched, frantically trying to free himself. The Jiangshi was as emaciated as the boys, but he was taller and armed with two lethal weapons—madness and a knife.

Wu was frozen in momentary fear. He tried to yell, but no words came.

The Jiangshi brought the knife down—once, twice—

Before there was a third stroke, Wu sprang forth and launched himself at the monster. He ran into the Jiangshi's back and pounded the smelly, sore-ridden flesh with both fists. The Jiangshi grunted and took a swing, sending Wu sprawling to the ground.

Lying on his back, Wu looked up at the looming monster's gnarled, weathered face with its long, filthy tangled hair, twitching unfocused eyes, and rotting yellow-brown teeth. Wu backed away on his elbows like a crab.

He hit something on the ground.

The Jiangshi raised his knife to strike.

Wu grabbed the rectangular object and brought it up with both hands. The knife plunged into the book, piercing it from cover to cover, its point protruding out the back.

Grunting, the Jiangshi twisted and pulled on the knife, finally extracting it from the book but stumbling backwards a few steps.

Wu threw the damaged book at the Jiangshi, hitting the monster on the side of the head. Already off balance, the Jiangshi fell onto his haunches. It didn't take long for the monster to get up again, but the delay gave Wu just enough time to load his slingshot and fire.

The mote scored a direct hit into the Jiangshi's left eye.

Screaming and clutching the bleeding eye with both hands, the Jiangshi dropped to the ground. The monster rolled side to side, shrieking and twitching uncontrollably as blood and vitreous fluid oozed between his fingers.

Wu got up and walked over to where Vancott's lifeless body lay in a pool of his own blood. Vancott was on his back, mouth and eyes still wide open. In silence, Wu simply stared at his dead companion with a lack of emotion that would have shocked his pre-Fall ancestors. He left Vancott where he lay, picked up the book, and simply walked away.

Behind him, the Jiangshi's screams went on and on, the cries of a wounded animal. Wu kept walking, book in hand, until he could not hear the inhuman noises anymore.

"I am sorry about your friend," Fénshū said when Wu finished his story.

Wu said nothing more.

"You are a brave young man," she continued, "and extremely lucky as well. We are the first expedition to work in the Vancouver ruins for years, and it is only possible because we were able to afford the armed guards to protect us from the Jiangshis." She put the book on the ground. "Did you see anything else down in that ... um, 'skeptic' tank?"

The boy fell unhelpfully silent, once again.

A young woman entered the tent, carrying a small bundle of clothes.

Fénshū pointed. "Wu, please go with my colleague. She will give you some food. You need to rest, and when you are better, we will need you to take us back to this place you found. Do you understand?"

Wu nodded.

"Gēn wǒ lái," the young woman said, taking Wu's hand and leading him out of the tent.

Fénshū waited a moment, then picked up the book and took it outside. Near the centre of the expedition encampment, a small fire burned. She walked towards the campfire, and without a second thought, casually tossed the book into the flames.

The plastic wrap melted quickly, evaporating like water on a hot-plate. Then the flames attacked the book itself, consuming it from the outside edges in. The words on the cover—A Novel, *Oryx and Crake*, Margaret Atwood—were legible for a few moments until the dust jacket blackened and crumbled away. Acrid smoke billowed briefly when the white residue ignited, causing Fénshū to cough and blink. The spine was the last to endure, but eventually it, too, yielded to the flames.

When the book had been reduced to ash, Fénshū returned to the tent and settled back in her chair. Pre-Fall Běiměizhōu texts were of academic interest and had some nominal value on the antiquities market, but her backers in Běijīng and Clavius had little interest in them. Excavating the Vancouver II site was a costly and very risky venture. Her expedition would need to find something of much greater value, and soon. The boy would take them back to the other site. For her sake—and to some degree, the boy's—she truly hoped that artifacts of real value were still out there, somewhere in the ruins of the old shit and piss.

Author Commentary

The central idea in "Túshūguǎn," of someone trying to preserve books before the fall of civilization by storing them in an underground septic tank, was taken from *Lucifer's Hammer*, a post-apocalyptic novel by Larry Niven and Jerry Pournelle, in which someone in the Los Angeles area does exactly that just before a comet hits the Earth. I moved the action two thousand kilometres north and introduced the Chinese archaeological team excavating the ruins of Vancouver as a parable of Western fears about the re-emergence of China. My main character was named for Louis Wu, the protagonist in the *Ringworld* series of books, also written by Larry Niven (whose middle name is van Cott). Some of the imagery of the post-apocalyptic world was inspired by the nonfiction book *The World Without Us*, by Alan Weisman. As part of my research, I tried to burn an old book and was relieved to discover that it is actually more difficult than one might think. For the record, I thoroughly enjoyed *Oryx and Crake* by Margaret Atwood and, in fact, my story has a few homages to the novel which I challenge readers to find. —*Eric Choi, 2015*

About the Author

Eric Choi is a Hong Kong-born writer, editor, and aerospace engineer living in Toronto. His Asimov Award-winning novelette "Dedication" appeared in Japanese translation in *The Astronaut from Wyoming and Other Stories* (Hayakawa, 2010), edited by Toru Nakamura. With Derwin Mak, he co-edited the Aurora Award-winning anthology *The Dragon and the Stars* (DAW Books, 2010), the first collection of speculative fiction by authors of the Chinese diaspora. He is also the co-editor, with Ben Bova, of the new science fiction anthology *Carbide Tipped Pens* (Tor Books, 2014).

Poetry

Souvankham Thammavongsa

Ricepaper 8, no. 2 (2003)

A FIREFLY

A firefly

casts its body

into the night

arguing

against darkness and its taking

It is a small argument

lending itself to silence,

a small argument

the sun would never come to hear

Darkness, unable to hold itself

against such tiny

elegant speeches,

opens its palm

to set free a fire

its body could not put down

Reprinted with permission from Small Arguments
by Souvankham Thammavongsa (Pedlar Press, 2003).

About the Poet

Souvankham Thammavongsa is the author of three poetry collections: *Small Arguments* (2003), *Found* (2007), and *Light* (2013), which won a Trillium Book Award for Poetry.

Fred Wah

Ricepaper 18, no. 4 (2014)

SITKUM

By-and-by
but behind
now awake
I was younger

Before noon
I was younger
but a small half

a mind brown
In the afternoon
by dinnertime
I would dream

of other ways
Day was a hurdle
seemed elliptical
fifty cents
through the air

Half as much
time became a bit
an outlet of use

future fractional
Mid sentence
stop at the spades
think aging
these roots, rapids.

"Sitkum" is Chinook jargon for "half" or "half-way." For more on Chinook, including a full lexicon of words, see the *Ricepaper* 17.3–4 article on the subject.

JAN 1/2013

clouds of my mind
hybrid, increase
as I reach for the choices

grain or reptile
between standing
or moving

government platform
I want in house
no dumb science that

is that their power
those clouds that come
from secrecy only

abhorrent cover story
another radio contest
the architecture

of office buildings
I will remember this
this, in the year of water

LIGHTNING

Are we in the air yet?
Is this the bridge, this tree

no deeper than dirt
our obligations to symmetry

burnt through
an underground sky

synapse to heaven ahead
thunder and shrapnel

just memory.
Home

no neutral land
the target confident

-headlamps flicker
and the pulaskis are dull-

this carpet of one to another
settles into moving night

and flickers back at us
in a dance through the smoke

we are in the middle of our ladder
going up.

About the Poet

Fred Wah has published and edited a wide range of poetry and poetics since the early 1960s. His biofiction, *Diamond Grill,* is a well-known text on hybridity, echoed in an online poem at *highmuckamuck.ca.* Recent books include *Sentenced to Light, is a door,* and *The False Laws of Narrative.* He has recently co-edited (with Amy De'Ath) *Toward.Some.Air.*, a collection of statements on poetics. In 2013, Wah was appointed an Officer of the Order of Canada and completed his term as Canada's fifth Parliamentary Poet Laureate. *Scree: The Collected Earlier Poems, 1962–1991* will be published in the fall of 2015.

Kathryn Gwun-Yeen Lennon

Ricepaper 18, no. 4 (2014)

SOMEDAY I WILL

dim sum

siu sum

hoi sum

choi sum

yong sum

zhong sum

dan sum

心

stop worrying that

some
of me is not like the others
learn that I am more than the
sum
of these parts,

that
some
of this heart lubdubs along in
some
place I can't get into

that if these walls were thicker the

sound of words
sumdumbumbling
wouldn't keep me up at night

About the Poet

Kathryn Gwun-Yeen Lennon 姚君妍 is a poet and urban planner. Of Cantonese and Irish ancestry, she was born and raised in Edmonton on weekend dim sum, river valley bike rides, and Chinatown haircuts. She was a member of Edmonton's 2012 Slam Poetry Team and the Victoria Spoken Word Festival's all-star ensemble. Her work has appeared in *Ricepaper, Alternatives Journal,* and the Toronto Reel Asian International Film Festival. She was a contributing artist to the exhibition *M'Goi/Do Jeh: Sites, Rites and Gratitude* at Centre A (the Vancouver International Centre for Contemporary Asian Art).

Michael Prior

Ricepaper 19, no. 2 (2014)

ANY OTHER PHOTO I

Awake or not? He can't quite tell. He walks
upon a dream's meniscus, looks beneath
at the stars sieved through cloudbank, the island's
endless silhouette bleeding into night.
Overheard through oceanic static:
accidents on the freeway, a TV's
foreign whisper in his ear. Dim voices
unravel his fears in small attritions:
a coat's lost buttons, a misplaced handful
of change. Perhaps they're always awaiting
rediscovery. A pallid photo
in the attic, a younger man within.
And when he brushes back the dust, he hopes
to meet the boy who offered him this skin.

ANY OTHER PHOTO II

So, he's awake. The pact he made with age
clipped and shuffled neatly into a drawer.
His other quiet covenant remains
engrained in imagined frames of cedar,
wasting skeletal. Stalks of crabgrass, bruised
sky of thistle: a dim communion.
Perhaps it's there, where he buried four years,
that he could map memory onto place.
A lost lure stirs up the silt in his brain,
while names he can't recall drift pellucid;
their spines and fins are slim tines of shadow.
The bed sheets crease between his knees, sculpting
valleys, fences, cedar shacks: a country
he had to forget in order to know.

About the Poet

Michael Prior's poems have appeared in numerous journals across Canada, America, and the UK. Michael was the winner of *Magma Poetry*'s 2013 Editors' Prize, *Grain*'s 2014 Short Grain Contest, and *The Walrus*'s 2014 Poetry Prize. His first chapbook, *Swan Dive*, was published by Frog Hollow Press in 2014. His first full-length collection, focusing on inter-generational memory and his grandparents' internment as Japanese Canadians, is forthcoming from Véhicule Press in spring 2016. In fall 2015, Michael will be starting an MFA in poetry at Cornell University.

Crecien Bencio

Ricepaper 19, no. 2 (2014)

FAMILY OF THIEVES

We are a family of thieves. We take your things from the
lost and found: the single wool mitt, the water bottles, the
abandoned umbrellas. We bring our own Tupperware to
buffet restaurants and sit in a booth against a wall, the
perfect formation to transfer food to our laps. The hats
you left at the park after dark, the plastic toys strewn
on the beach become rightfully ours. The novellas you
have yet to read on your bedside table slip into purses
unbeknownst. Your medicine cabinets pilfered at your
housewarming party. Our pockets overflow with packets
of sugar, brown on the left, Splenda on the right, with
stir sticks hidden, like a hair pin beneath our bangs. But
look closely at our hands, for our faces will always be hidden,
in the back of restaurants, in the corners of crowded
rooms, alone, beneath a wall of darkness and trees you
will never see, you will never know, but our hands, flickering
like moths, quick, like paper burnt to ash.

About the Poet

Crecien Bencio's poetry has previously been published in *Ricepaper* magazine. His work revolves around the dynamics of his family and the bridging of Filipino and Canadian cultures. He lives in the Renfrew-Collingwood neighbourhood of Vancouver.

Rita Wong

Ricepaper 19, no. 4 (2014)

JOURNEY TO THE WEST

canoe journeyers are
coast protecting itself
where ocean meets rock is home
when ocean meets oil is poison
one container crash turns
fresh sea urchin breakfast
to wretched carcinogen
if nothing ever spills, leaks or collides
(implausible & impossible)
the burn itself still bankrupts children's lives
forecloses futures

earth monkey, girl spirit, one of millions
whose parents migrated to turtle island
on this journey to the west
modestly does what the coast calls us to do
to protect future monkeys
even a future for corporations
depends on guardians
protecting the coastal home
that we are part of
home in the big sense
ancient as basic stone

mischievous monkeys don't always want to be seen
they want to be together-doing
with Mission monks, Musqueam mothers
Tsleil-Waututh stewards, urban res relations,
Penticton peach trees, Peace River pigs,
Squamish sisters, Hope horses,
Nanaimo nannies, Chilliwack children
Tofino teachers, Clayoquot crows
this could be a new story
in an old world
thousands of Coast Salish years
of advanced forest coexistence
to be respected, together

BODY BURDEN: A MOVING TARGET

bone, tendon, muscle, joint inflamed
knuckle, wrinkle, nail, ten half moons
a seven-pound skin, well distributed
so light i don't feel what i carry
rashes, scars, bruises, faint scratches
eczema reminds
fragile barrier, easily broken
inner oozes out, itchy lymph
fluids that came from
swallowed water
that came from
a river that came from a lake
that came from a glacier
receding from industrial glare
pulse quickens
shoulder tenses
sorrow deepens
send signals down spine
fourteen facial bones adapt
mandible stretches, maw yawns

iron, carbon, nitrogen flow
oscillate, oxidize, optimize
cellular symphony
perennially sheds, regenerates
walking mineral body
a watery deposit
chemical composition
shared with the pacific
kuroshio current within
dark salt, sunlit
benthic bowels
a family forest of microfauna
digesting come what may
but thyroid's receptors confused
by polycylic pollution
getting mixed signals
hyper or hypo
as plasticizers slide into
sulfur, magnesium, phosphates
calcium carbonate

eyes float in moist sockets
while body sweats
& sweats, porous
ongoing experiment
rich in nurdles
poor in ecological literacy
atrazine in your armpits?

an orchestra of nutrients
infiltrated by capital's loud shout
consumed while consuming
disoriented in propioceptive profusion
seepage from decomposing bottle not just
plastic but democracy degrading
inner monster muscles up

PCBs in your pelvic core?
furans in your feet?
dioxins in your diaphragm?
cells burst a chorus
a need for

as daily toxins come & go
a revolving door
heads & shoulders
knees & toes
reprieve nose & mouth

About the Poet

Rita Wong is the author of four books of poetry: *undercurrent* (Nightwood, 2015), *sybil unrest* (co-written with Larissa Lai, Line Books, 2008), *forage* (Nightwood, 2007), and *monkeypuzzle* (Press Gang, 1998). *forage* won Canada Reads Poetry 2011. Wong received the Asian Canadian Writers' Workshop Emerging Writer Award in 1997 and the Dorothy Livesay Poetry Prize in 2008. Building from her doctoral dissertation, which examined labour in Asian-North American literature, her work investigates the poetics of water and the relationships between social justice, ecology, and decolonization.

Evelyn Lau

Ricepaper 20, no. 1 (2015)

JANUARY

These are the days of not writing.
January, the month of no words.

Wine tastes watered down, food
so flavourless I gnaw a hole

in the side of my mouth.
mining the salt crystal of blood.

its candy tang. The fog again,
shrink-wrapping trees and buildings,

erasing the bay. The opposite shore
a leaf etching under wax paper,

milk glass, the faint sketch
of a fossil in stone. It's not

the light, or lack of it. Small birds
rustle in the bare trees,

searching for winter berries.
Nothing's missing. What's not here?

VISITATION

A mosquito in cold October!

The season's gone haywire.
I wake to the insect's furtive buzz,
a miniature chainsaw zipping past.
The welt rising on my cheek
like a port-wine stain.
The dream torn open into consciousness—

The superstitious might say
you're a restless spirit hovering
between two spheres, message-laden,
unavenged. We are again by the sea
—a place we never were—
white boats tilting on rough water.
For whole blind minutes after waking

I can't recall how you died, then remember
you drowned, in a way (the sea),
aspirating your own vomit after days
of drinking. The black dogs again.
That loneliness Renee said *no one person,*

no crowd, could assuage.
Outside, the generator hum of the city.
Roars of agony, revelry. Sirens speeding past,
slashing through the downtown arteries.

Laughter in the distance, first light.

MID-AUTUMN FESTIVAL

In August you bought a box of moon cakes
and ate every last one by yourself.
Even kept the beribboned gift bag
for yourself. You refused to remember

the traditions, to honor the ritual
of sharing these symbols of family unity
and togetherness. The cakes sat
in your belly like cakes of soap

or packed mud, so dense and heavy they hurt—
the salted egg yolk crumbling between
your teeth, the grit of seeds and nuts
and chunks of sugared melon, the furrowed

pastry stamped with calligraphy
you never learned to read. Maybe this
was compensation for something that drifted
out of reach your entire childhood ...

But even if love was never said,
even if they called fat little pig,
they kept nothing for themselves.
Drank mug after mug of hot water

to trick their stomachs into fullness
while feeding you mounds of rice
piled with pork and pickled vegetables,
bowls of congee studded with century egg,

pastries swollen with red bean and lotus seed.
You were a monster: hungry all the time
and furious, squeezing slices of Wonderbread
and gobs of margarine into raw yellow balls

you shoved into your mouth, sobbing.
It was worse than hunger, said the Japanese monks
in training, worse than the beatings—
those weeks when they trekked into the cities

to beg and were forced to eat every morsel
heaped into their copper bowls. The pain
of satiation worse than the windy emptiness
howling through their bellies the rest of the year.

About the Poet

Evelyn Lau is a Vancouver writer who has published eleven books, including six volumes of poetry. Her first book, *Runaway: Diary of a Street Kid* (HarperCollins, 1989) was made into a CBC movie starring Sandra Oh in her first major role. Evelyn's prose works have been translated into a dozen languages; her poetry has received the Milton Acorn Award, the Pat Lowther Award, a National Magazine Award, and a Governor-General's nomination. Evelyn served as Vancouver's Poet Laureate from 2011 to 2014; her most recent collection, *A Grain of Rice* (Oolichan, 2012), was short-listed for the Dorothy Livesay Award and the Pat Lowther Award.

Carolyn Nakagawa

Ricepaper 20, no. 2 (2015)

RESEARCH UPDATE

Went to the library, ran my fingers up rows of "Jewish Canadian" until it switched to "Japanese." Built an FC106 stack longer than my arm: the best representatives. Found my cousin's eyes in a photo history, a trace. Someone's brother, names I recognize, maybe own a piece of. Tried to read the text, get a sense; made my choices. Upstairs, saw my poetry professor. *Did you get the good ones?* Stammered—my heritage was showing. Tucked them in my bag, forgot to laugh. I've got a list. I don't think I'm in it. Is this what you had in mind?

THE GOOD ONES

touch everyone's heart. Can be held close
like a pocket mirror. Draw their borders
gracefully, within
what can be done.

have clean (white) pages. Won't look you
in the eye. The good ones will know. Recommended
by doctors, teachers, mothers. Well
executed.

submit to their place on the shelf, demure,
waiting to be known. Piles of them around my head, all
the good ones, better and better.
The good ones will get chosen.
The good ones will tell you who you are.

About the Poet

Carolyn Nakagawa is a fourth-generation Japanese Canadian poet and playwright. She holds a BA Honours from UBC in English Literature with a minor in Asian Canadian and Asian Migration Studies. Other poems of hers have been published by *QWERTY, The Maynard, Echolocation*, and *The Puritan*; play production highlights include UBC Players Club, Brave New Play Rites, and staged readings with Ruby Slippers Theatre and Vancouver Asian Canadian Theatre. She was born, raised, and, after a year studying in Japan, continues to live and write in the Greater Vancouver area, on the unceded territories of the Musqueam, Squamish, and Tsleil-Waututh nations.

ABOUT THE EDITORS

Julia Lin is a graduate of the Humber Creative Writing Program and a protégé of M.G. Vassanji. She is the author of *Miah*, the first book-length work of Taiwanese-Canadian literary fiction ever published. *julialinbooks.com*

Allan Cho is an academic librarian at the University of British Columbia where he has written on topics about community, culture, and publishing. His writing has appeared in *Ricepaper*, *The Georgia Straight*, and *Diverse*.

Jim Wong-Chu is a writer, historian, and editor. He is a founding member of the Asian Canadian Writers' Workshop, the publisher of *Ricepaper* magazine and co-editor (with Bennett Lee) of *Many Mouthed Birds: Contemporary Writing by Chinese Canadians* (Douglas & McIntyre, 1992) and (with Andy Quan) *Swallowing Clouds: An Anthology of Chinese-Canadian Poetry* (Arsenal Pulp Press, 1999). He is the winner of two Queen's Jubilee Awards for Canadian heritage.